Equality Island

Equality Island

A *vivid story of a* worker's dream

Ethel Carnie Holdsworth

with an Introduction by Michael Crowley

Kennedy & Boyd
an imprint of
Zeticula Ltd
Unit 13,
196 Rose Street,
Edinburgh,
EH2 4AT.

http://www.kennedyandboyd.co.uk
admin@kennedyandboyd.co.uk

First published by *The Daily Herald* in 1924-25

This edition © Zeticula Ltd 2024

Ethel Carnie Holdsworth published under her maiden name (Ethel Carnie) and with various versions of her married name.

Front cover image: Ethel Carnie Holdsworth.
Reproduced with kind permission from Helen Brown.

ISBN 978-1-84921-244-7

Publisher's Note on the Text

'Equality Island' was published as a serial, subtitled 'A vivid story of a worker's dream' appearing in the *Daily Herald* newspaper, six episodes every week, from Monday to Saturday from 27 November 1924 to 26 February 1925. The episodes were typeset daily, by hand, in London or Manchester. Holdsworth would have had no opportunity to read or correct proofs of the text she had submitted.

The finished book extends to about 80,000 words, suggesting a contract of 80 1,000-word episodes. It is unlikely that the newspaper staff consulted Holdsworth about the text, so any conventional editing, as done with a book publisher, will not have taken place. This may then be taken as a first draft, rather than a polished finished version.

The text printed here corrects only obvious typographical errors and standardises the punctuation. Street names, printed variably, are standardised to the most commonly-used format, e.g. 'Binkers Court'.

Chapters, which are not usually named, extended over one or more episodes.

Occasionally, breaks were inserted into the original newspaper episodes. These are represented by a short row of asterisks.

Contents

Possible Futures

An Introduction to Equality Island

Michael Crowley

It is not enough to say that Ethel Carnie Holdsworth was a radical, and her novels express that. There is a broader narrative to her writing that relates to the development of her politics, her reaction to domestic and world events, and contemporary political thinking in socialist circles. Equality Island is a case in point. It was serialised in *The Daily Herald* at a time when Ethel was concerned about fascism gaining traction in Britain and the erosion of political rights in communist Russia. These were new causes for her, more than twenty years into a writing career and a life of political campaigning which were intimately intertwined. That she found a way to conduct these two life-long quests is remarkable. It flew in the face of what was expected of someone from her class, her sex, indeed of someone from East Lancashire. But that can be said to be the essence of Ethel. She was a confirmed pacifist, yet from a young age declared war on society's expectations of her.

Ethel Carnie Holdsworth was born on January 1st, 1886, in Oswaldtwistle, a weaving town near Blackburn. Her mother started work in a textile mill when she was nine years old, her grandmother when she was six, and Ethel started as a half-timer when she was eleven. She had around five years of full-time formal education, typical of girls from her class. What could lie ahead was weaving sheds, damaged hearing, child rearing, the production of cloth, and the supply of labour. Nearby Burnley was the cotton capital of the world. In the year she was born, 50,000 looms produced more cloth than any other town. With the creation of overwhelmingly working-class communities came the establishment of labour movement organisations. Political radicalism was the centre ground, and Ethel was a member of several political parties and organisations.

Though perhaps not a member, as a teenager she attended meetings of the Burnley branch of the Social Democratic Federation. The SDF was formed in 1884 as Britain's first Marxist political party. Marxism, we can take to mean seeking the socialisation of the means of production, distribution, and exchange, as well as the prosecution of a class war by revolution. Although the SDF was relatively small, it did engage in local politics and exercised a disproportionately large influence in relation to its size.

Many future Labour Party luminaries, including Ramsay MacDonald and George Lansbury, were introduced to socialism through the party. The Burnley branch was amongst the most successful in England, with 600 members and two town councillors in 1893. From the SDF, she would have received a grounding in Marxist theory and developed an associated vocabulary. Crucially, the theory was combined with an experience of the factory system, and she concluded at an early age that capitalism should be abolished. Burnley SDF was keen on socialist unity, a cause championed by Ethel throughout her whole political career.

In 1908, Ethel left the SDF to join the Independent Labour Party — a socialist party, initially seeking independent labour representation in parliament and affiliated to the Labour Party until 1932. Being in the ILP brought Ethel into contact with socialist public speakers and would have helped make her effective in public, although she never stood for office.

Although her full-time education ended at age eleven, Ethel attended a technical school in the evenings after she had started work. Crucially, she also joined the Co-operative Society Library at Great Harwood. It was well-stocked with literature, philosophy and politics. She had access to the works of William Morris, H.G. Wells, Jack London, Rebecca West and the Romantics. There is evidence that she read as a writer, for there are direct references to some of her favourite writers in her journalism and their footprints in her fiction and poetry.

Ethel would have brought books to work, tucked down her apron. It was intrinsic to a shared culture of self-improvement. She would have also composed lines of poetry. She was published by the time she was 20, with her first collection, *Rhymes from the Factory*, which came out in 1907. In the same year, her first short story, "A White Geranium", which concerned a mill girl who is seduced and then ostracised, was published.

In 1909, journalist and founder of the Clarion movement, Robert Blatchford, invited Ethel to work on his weekly, *The Women Worker*. Though it should be said that Blatchford was a fellow member of the ILP, this was a considerable achievement. She had written her way out of the factory.

Ethel moved to London. She was 23. She was given responsibility for a column, entitled "The Editor's Column" though she was not editor of *The Woman Worker*, Blatchford was. It was nonetheless a significant expansion of her writing. The paper campaigned to secure political rights and social equality for women and better living standards for the working class on Blatchford's terms. Ethel put forward her pacifist ideals, attacked society's profit motive, and campaigned for child welfare. She defined socialism as, 'working for pleasure instead of for money, serving for the sake of service and not for personal gain, loving for loving's sake and not for a house in Hanover Square, giving oneself as the leaves give their shade to shelter the swallow's nest.'

Within a year, there was a serious disagreement between Ethel and Blatchford over German militarism, and she was replaced on the paper. Ethel returned to East Lancashire and the mill; however, she had become a journalist, a trade she would practice for the remainder of her career. She had also proven to herself and to her editor that she would not compromise her politics in print.

The environment of the mill produced through her a second poetry collection — *Songs of a Factory Girl* — some children's stories and her first novel, *Miss Nobody*, published in 1913, about a young woman in Manchester who advances from working in a scullery to owning an oyster shop. She would publish a further ten novels, most of which campaigned for social causes, particularly women's rights. They attempted to change her reader's politics and spur them into action. From the outset, politics and writing didn't meld in Ethel; they were one and the same thing.

Ethel responded to the outbreak of the First World War with political and literary activity. She opposed the war, and more specifically, she actively opposed conscription. Casualties were such that Britain faced a shortage of combatants, and conscription was perceived as inevitable. The British Citizen Party was formed in 1915 as a pressure group to oppose conscription, and Ethel chaired a number of their meetings, in particular a meeting in Nelson, at which the attendance was over a thousand. This took a degree of physical courage as men in uniform attempted to break up the assembly. Ethel managed to restore order, and eventually a vote was taken that opposed the introduction of conscription.

She married in 1915. Two years later, her husband, Alfred, was conscripted, leaving her to manage alone with their first child. Ethel was industrious and resilient. In 1917, her second novel, *Helen of Four Gates*, was published, just before she received news that her husband was missing, presumed killed. *Helen of Four Gates* was to be her most successful novel, providing her with some temporary financial security and a publishing deal.

Alfred unexpectedly returned, having been in a prisoner of war camp. He was traumatised, and their relationship failed. Subsequent novels often dealt with the plight of unhappy marriages and struggling mothers. In *The House That Jill Built*, the protagonist inherits enough money to build a home for tired mothers. *General Belinda* might be a military pun, but it describes the life of a general servant who organises the lives of others. In *This Slavery*, two sisters make romantic and political choices that will place them on opposite sides of the class divide, and marriage is no less a form of slavery than life in a weaving shed. *The Taming of Nan* places workplace injury and domestic violence in the same narrative.

Ethel Carnie Holdsworth might be described as an idealist, but a tough one. In an age when working-class women couldn't vote, she placed them at the centre of the worlds she created whilst striving to shape and unite the socialist movement in Britain. Today, this seems a peculiar preoccupation for a novelist until one appreciates the context of her formative years. There was a series of strikes by weavers in Lancashire in 1912, the Nelson Weavers Association being a founding member of the Labour Representation Committee that went on to form the Labour Party. The following year, the Dublin Lockout saw trade unionists arm themselves. The First World War sparked the Easter Rising in Ireland and the Russian Revolution of 1917, which in turn inspired the German Revolution a year later. The Communist Party of Great Britain was formed in 1920, the same year that the film *Helen of Four Gates* was released. She lived and wrote under a turbulent sky.

Equality Island is a later novel, first serialised in *The Daily Herald*. Stylistically, it is a departure from the social realism of previous books, perhaps more influenced by her reading than experience. The days of working in a mill were long behind her. Around the same time as *Equality Island*, Ethel had embarked on a political publication, *The Clear Light*, an anti-fascist journal. The most striking thing about *The Clear Light* is its overtly allegorical style.

Equality Island, constructed in a dream world, is a socialist novel, arguably even anarchist in nature. It is a post-revolutionary utopian world in which property does not enter into human relationships. The utopia is social rather than technological, but people are only required to work an hour a day. Social change is managed without violence, and morality has evolved. Citizens are defined as either evolved or unevolved, prophesying contemporary progressivism.

In 1925, in *The Clear Light*, Ethel describes herself as a 'pure communist.' In light of the Russian experiment, she had undoubtedly spent time thinking of alternative outcomes. In the same year that the novel was published, Ethel had joined a campaign to free the Solovetsky prisoners, Russian dissidents from the Kronstadt naval base who had rebelled against Lenin's authoritarianism.

While *This Slavery* was published in the Soviet Union in 1926 and read widely, one suspects Lenin would have described *Equality Island* as utopian socialist in nature. Utopian socialists, he maintained, mistakenly believed that people would adopt socialism without the need for a class struggle.

Holdsworth's novels paint an authentic picture of life in Lancashire manufacturing towns in the early twentieth century. That is now acknowledged. She also attempted to express a range of political ideas through fiction and poetry, to take those ideas out of the pamphlet and make them accessible to working people. Her work can be included in the genre of the socialist novel, but is not confined to that. Her stories are about love, family, struggle, and imagined futures. She is interested in what humanity is capable of and dreamed of how hopes might be realised.

Equality Island

"Understand me well; it is provided in the essence of things that, from any fruition of success, no matter what, shall come forth something to make a greater struggle necessary." - Weitman

"This is the generalisation of all history." - Ingersoll

Chapter 1

I sat by the window in the dusk which veiled the ugliness of the street I knew so well. The films of shadow could not, however, blot out sounds and odours rising from the court below.

The Jones' baby was crying. Doubtless Mrs. Jones was waiting for Tom to return from his day's adventure after work. Dull rain trickled down the windows. It grew darker. Dejection fell on my spirits. I believe I am not alone in the mood that sometimes grips me, usually beginning with a tired kind of wonder that so many human beings can go on day after day in surroundings which they must know are hideous. Such mood gripped me now. I knew its subtle turnings along to its logical conclusion—a stone wall, whereupon was written the futile question, "Why do we exist?"

The melancholy whining of the Jones' infant was a comment on the absurdity of being born in a place like this. It seemed to sob, "Why, why, why?" I heard Mrs. Jones' voice grow sharper. Then my heart leaped to hear her singing in Welsh. I forgot my dejection and my surroundings, and wandered away down a laughing valley of beech and birch, each leaf a-dance to the pipes of spring.

My eyes filled with sudden tears, for I am as quick to be moved as a woman; a fact which is, I think, partly due to an accident which befell me in early childhood, leaving me a cripple, sensitive to a degree which sometimes compels me to do the most ridiculous things in order to avoid the ordinary conflicts about ordinary things which I observe most of my fellow men find pleasurable excitement in.

The Jones' infant must have been lulled to sleep. The court itself grew less noisome. I cannot tell how long I sat there. During this period of unemployment, I often found myself sinking into a state of torpor, lasting for hours at a time. Two cats on a roof opposite must have roused me. I endured their noises for some time, but at length hurled one of my worn shoes at them—to realise with horror that my other pair were held up at the cobblers' until I drew my next dole. Still, I had peace.

The moon was rising. Elbows on the window-sill, I tried to while away the time by thinking of scenes this moon would shine on. Mostly the pictures were created from re-imagination of scenes of which I had read. I thought of deserts under this same moon; of palms motionless in the windless heat.

Old temples passed before me, and old gods, half-buried in the drifts of sand—old gods to which humanity, now dust with moth-eaten arras and spear, had prayed, with throbbing hearts of faith, though their gods were deaf and dumb. Lagoons I saw, porpoises spouting spray, Devon lanes, leaf-gloomed; Keats' nightingale, harvest fields with their ripened stacks for the feeding of those who could afford to buy bread. Fortunately for the poor, thought is not two-dimensional, and sometimes by thus dreaming we get glimpses, through prison bars though it be, of beauty that is yet unmarred. Presently, I found myself sinking back into the old torpor.

Quite suddenly, out of the Nothingness into which I was gazing, I realised that I was watching a panoramic scene. Miles and miles of houses were skidding before my view at a great speed. Swiftly as they passed, I had acute sensations of knowing quite well the types of people who lived in them. They were poor houses, ugly, huddled and mean, and of all countries.

Great masses of palaces next went by. I distinctly recognised Buckingham Palace. A rolling line of prisons rushed by—out of their dark shapes, as thunder rises from clouds, the sighs of those within them sounding like a dirge. Law Courts, Stock Exchanges, Divorce Courts, Parliamentary Houses, also rushed by, with discordant and hysterical voices mingling in a sordid and hideous jargon.

Slaughter-houses and fields of battle came next, with scenes of such horror that I refuse to chronicle what I saw. Murder I saw, and suicide, and melées of half-famished strikers.

Processions of women passed me, faces marked with care and sorrow—so long the procession that I placed my hands before my eyes, hoping to blot out the sight. I realised at once that my physical sight had nothing to do with what I was witnessing. Seeing that it was to be endured, I endeavoured to bear it until one scene of supreme horror brought me to my feet, and I found myself shouting, "Why should I, already wretched enough, have to witness such a sight as this?" Far away I fancied I heard a voice answer me with, "Brother, you have been chosen. Flinch not. You will soon leave this hell on earth."

After that voice, real or imagined, I felt more able, for some little time, to endure the increasing horrors of scenes which gripped me the more in that I knew that I was actually looking on things that were occurring. The limit was reached at length. The fortitude which had come to me so suddenly deserted me. I leaped up, and discovered that I was calling, "Stop! It is too much."

5

"Stop!" I called again, in a passion of revolt. "I have seen enough of Now. Show me To-morrow. Show me the world which will surely rise on the ruins of this. Let me feel its sun and wind on my face. Let me taste its joy, its beauty, its justice. Show me its life, art, drama. Let me study it in detail and yet not miss the whole. Show me its best and its worst. Let me see the forms its struggle would take, economic chains no longer fettering humanity. Show me its wars and its weapons. Let me see its religion, if any, when doctrines are no longer exploited as the mouthpieces of economic dominance. Like any other, greater than I, let me see but a day of it."

I must have walking about the room. Mrs. Biers, standing in the doorway, looked rather afraid of coming in until I had lit my only candle. Somewhat slowly she advanced into the dim room, gradually, however, regaining the confidence she has had in me since the occasion when I told her she need worry no longer about fivepence she had borrowed. Outwardly not unhandsome, she is rather blotchy and purple of colour, and for all her bulk flabby and unhealthy.

"I just slipped in to warn you, Mr. Sniggins. The landlord's below," she said, in an asthmatic whisper.

An acute sickness came over me. Mr. Sparkins is an individual whom I can never meet on his own lines.

"Well, tell him I'm engaged," I beseeched of her.

"I told him that afore," she reminded me.

"Tell him I'm dead," I asked. "Surely that will stave him off."

"Wouldn't," asserted Mrs. Biers. "He'd want to examine the corpse."

I realised the sound reasoning of this.

"Best face him out," advised Mrs. Biers.

She was backing out of the room.

"Here," I called to her. "Come back. I positively refuse to see Mr. Sparkins. Under the present system Mr. Sparkins has a right to his rent. I have not got it. Bring your flour-bag up, Mrs. Biers, and make me look as nearly like a corpse as possible. Let my demise be due to something highly infectious, and by the next time he calls I'll have the rent."

"But—!" protested Mrs. Biers.

I observed that Mrs. Biers did grasp the *summum bonum* of my remarks.

"The flour-bag," I insisted.

Mrs. Biers said she didn't think we ought to pretend to be dead before our time—but seeing it was me she'd stretch a point. I heard her slip-shod feet descending the jungle of the stairs.

I could hear the echoes of the sordid conflict going on two floors below. I crept between the sheets, pulled the top one over my face, and suddenly lost all nervous dread that Mr. Sparkins would not be deceived. A delicious sense of drifting out on a healing tide followed this sense of possession of myself. The voices below grew less disturbing. I could hear Mr. Sparkins ascending the next floor, and wondered jocularly if Mrs. Biers would beat him in the handicap to lay me out. I realised that something had happened to me—something unusual. Mrs. Biers came in and rubbed my face with flour. She spoke. I could not answer.

"My god! Mr. Sniggins," she breathed. "Don't give me a turn. Say something. You ain't dead, are you?"

I no longer felt the slightest desire to answer. She snatched up the candle and held it closely to my eyes.

Then her shriek started the air.

"Oh—Mr. Sparkins! Mr. Sparkins!" she exclaimed.

"Come, come—what's this?" I heard my late landlord reprove her.

I realised that he was in the room—loud-checked suit and all, in which he looked like a hippo clad in draught-boards.

"Mr. Sniggins is dead," I heard Mrs. Biers snuffling.

"Ah!"

There was suspicion in Mr. Sparkins' ejaculation. I realised that Providence, having foreseen that Mr. Sparkins would not be deceived, had flung its weight on my side—for once.

"Tut, tut!" continued Mr. Sparkins. "Was he alive when I was arguing the point with the persons below?"

"Yes—no—that is—"

"If this is imposition," threatened Mr. Sparkins, "I shall take legal proceedings. Hold the candle, and don't shake."

I distinctly received the impression that hot candle wax was dropped upon me. It conveyed no physical pain. Mr. Sparkins took the liberty of lifting my eyelid, whereupon I realised that I had been seeing him through it. Placing his rather heavy hand upon the organ that had been my heart, he gave a start—and retreated from me.

"I'm afraid—er—something has happened," he stammered. He tried to gain courage, and, greatly daring, moved towards me once more.

"My God! His eyes 'ave opened," screamed Mrs. Biers. "He's dead, and his eyes have opened."

"Tut, tut. Automatic action," corrected Mr. Sparkins.

He backed hurriedly to the door.

"I'll get the police. You stay here," he told Mrs. Biers.

"You stay. I'll get the blue-bottle," answered Mrs. Biers.

The tide on which I felt to be gently floating all this while grew stronger. I knew that soon it would lift me out, on strong, victorious waves, from the frail anchorage which connected me with this wretched room. A whimsical thought flashed through my mind that I would like to take Mrs. Biers and Mr. Sparkins with me. No sooner had the desire expressed itself in my mind than I heard Mrs. Biers gasping out directions as to how her washing had to be completed, and Mr. Sparkins, so suddenly relieved of this wicked world in which he had been tortured by obdurate tenants, was frantically shouting directions to his trustees. A policeman's whistle blew, and scores of feet appeared to be rushing up the tenement stairs. Such was my comic and dramatic exit from this world.

Chapter 2 - We Arrive

I have only an indefinite recollection of the transition stage for me from the old to the new world. Possibly a frog feels the same sensations in its stage from water to being able to breathe air as those I felt during these last uncomfortable pangs. The rest was a delicious, mounting sensation, as though, without any effort on my part, I was floating upwards. This was followed by a great drowsiness, to which I succumbed. Afterwards, when I tried to remember anything of these memories, they eluded me, as dreams elude one on awakening.

The voices of my companions roused me to the consciousness. I am one of those people (unfortunate when born poor) whom, in our unclassic, working-class language, are spoken of as having been "born tired". Hence, I had slept longer than either Mr. Sparkins or Mrs. Biers.

The pop of a cork being withdrawn, no doubt, startled me into complete wakefulness. I found my two companions sitting on the grass of rich pasture lands running down, half a mile broad, to a deep river. In the golden, hazy distance of the evening, far as the eye could see, I noticed a bridge, hung like a gossamer thread tossed by magic over the foaming waters. To the left of the bridge, on the crest of a hill, stood a tower, like a pillar of sunset cloud, reared in the exquisite blue-green of evening sky. The moon was rising, with "her pale attendant star". Corncrakes were calling. Breath of clover, heavy-headed with dew, was born to me on a soft wind. A bee droned homewards, past my ear, as I scrambled up from the long grass. Already, quite complete. The hills which rose on each side the valley were purpling. I enjoyed it, vaguely. But I was very hungry. I made my way to my companions.

"That's an observatory," I announced to Mr. Sparkins, pointing at the tower. "Science and agriculture do not appear to have left the earth."

"Damn Utopias!" ejaculated Mr. Sparkins. "You've brought me here by brute force, Sniggins. I have still a free will. I won't see your Utopia. I'll make them pitch me off it. It will be vile. I'll write up to the House of Lords! I'll—I'll be hanged! I'll be shot! Labour's no damned good. Never was. Never is. Never will be. I'm a rebel."

"Mr. Sparkins! You are spilling my share," Mrs. Biers told him reproachfully.

"What's that you've got?" I asked him.

His brow cleared.

"Wine, by the smell of it. Perhaps—poison. Can't read the inscription. Here! Read it. See that we aren't poisoned."

"Where did you find it?" I asked, peering at the label.

"In the grass. Strong stuff, by the smell of it. Evidently—a luxurious crowd! Can you read it, Sniggins?"

I could not.

But I took courage to say that I could, and that I believed it was wine. Shakespeare's English had evidently passed with Kings, counts, and diplomats.

"Alright. You drink the first lot. Excuse it being a cup made from the pages of a ready reckoner."

I swallowed the sarcasm and the wine—the first wine I had ever tasted. Mr. Sparkins allowed me several minutes to drop dead in, then held out his cup for some more. Mrs. Biers, one hand on her hip, held the bottle in the other. I noticed that she had a black eye—no doubt a souvenir from her past life in the Binkers Court. The ill-humour of Mr. Sparkins faded as by magic. I suddenly felt very vital and capable of great feats myself. Mrs. Biers ceased to wonder what Joshua would do to her, on return from furlough without leave. We all sat down and admired the landscape. Mrs. Biers is found a daisy, and wept over it. Mr. Sparkins was staring dreamily before him.

"State of monogamous society, I suppose—still," he hazarded, incautiously.

Mrs. Biers looked askance at us.

"Monogamous, Mrs. Biers," I explained, "is that highly civilised state where one man lives with one woman—a state requiring, as even you may know, an auxiliary force of divorce courts, conjugal rights classes, and a large and increasing number of female unmentionables. Understand me?"

"Have another, Mr. Sparkins. And never mind him!" said Mrs. Biers disgustedly.

I laughed. Mrs. Biers was startled, laughter being unusual with me.

"Gone to your head," she remarked to me, winking at Mr. Sparkins.

Mr. Sparkins had another. So had Mrs. Biers. So had I. Our social vanities began to vanish. We realise that we were brothers, long-lost. I was, I admit, very much muddled. Even more muddled than I was after a week at Oxford, in which I tried to fill my system with the oxygen or hydrogen of culture. More muddled than when I read middle-class economics to explain the puzzling facts of working-class exploitation by the very wise and learned, but unproductive, gentlemen who tried to enlighten my gross darkness.

But one thing the wine achieved. It broke down the English caste system. Need I say more? After emptying the bottle we fell on each other's necks, and vowed that we had from time immemorial misunderstood each other. The moon rose.

We took our way along a valley which ever grew more dim and reeling to my sight. I stopped once, believing I saw a titanic piece of sculpture rising from a rock—a great plough with the figures of godlike men, standing against the stars. Mrs. Biers dragged me on. We became vocal.

Suddenly, after what space of time I cannot tell, a mass of lights shone on us. We were approaching a civilisation which dared imperil its serenity with green wine which would have made revolution in Bow or Poplar. Either the wine lost its effects sooner than with us, or we were sobered by the spectacle before us. I suddenly became quite normal. So did we all. We found ourselves walking on a road.

"Footpath!" gasped Mr. Sparkins.

He rushed us to another road, almost as broad as the one we were on. Something flew past us, like a great luminous albatross, silently and without odour.

"Speed's up," said Mr. Sparkins. "They may well have rewards for pedestrians."

We went to sit under spreading chestnuts on rustic seats.

Another car, like a great white bird, flew through the night.

"I suppose there's no buses left," said Mrs. Biers, mournfully.

Mr. Sparkins answered not.

He was staring, with a look of frozen horror, across the three roads.

I followed the direction of his gaze.

"There's somebody walking over there," whispered

Mr. Sparkins. "Jupiter! He looks 6 feet. More. He's looking this way. I'm off."

Sarband

"Oh, no. You don't hop it," Mrs. Biers told Mr. Sparkins. "I'll take charge of him, Mr. Sniggins. You call and interuse the 'enemy'." Mrs. Biers was progressing. She had tried a three syllable word. But I did not move. Although they are in the shadows of the trees, stood the Unknown, with who knew what vital powers pent within him.

I realised that approaching him created a situation similar to primitive man creeping up to me and claiming kinship. I realised that we should kill primitive man if he appeared in our midst—that he would be a menace. The situation was the same. Mrs. Biers nagged me until I had to move off. My responsibility for bringing the pair of them here became crushing. Forgetting that the central road was for traffic, I walked slowly upon it, pondering home to address the shadowy figure walking under the trees.

Midway in the road a piercing note, like the cry of a wounded eagle dropping into the sea, brought me to a standstill—paralysed. I realised that I was in the path of one of the advancing albatross-machines. A groan escaped my lips. Then—I was flung out of the way as by invisible hands, my whole body experiencing a galvanic shock. I had a lightning-swift impression of Youth, clear headed and glorious, standing on the outstretched wings of the albatross, with something like a frail rod in its hands, which it waved at me. The motions of those hands said, "Fool!" So. The world had moved on, without human nature changing at all, essentially. What a blow that would be to startle opponents with on my return.

The current applied to fling me to safety had actually tossed me up and gently set me down on the path near the trees.

The moon had come out from a cloud. I saw my skimpy shadow on the silvered grass. I grew conscious of my deficiencies. Then I thought of Israel, singing among the stars—and those scrambling all their lives for of bread, like myself. A certain fierce pride shot me through. What I was I had been made. What they were with all their excellences, they had been linked to us. *Nay, where they are not us—developed?* Still, he would be shocked. I did not wish to startle him. He was not watching us. Sparkins had been wrong. He had not even seen my narrow escape from death. He was standing quite motionless now. I wondered whether any inhabitant of a bread-free world could think so deeply about, as to be quite oblivious of anything passing around him.

Slow step by slow step I advanced. I took stock of the build of this, the first denizen of the new world I had seen. Well—the first male. The individual standing on the full board between the wings of the albatross-machine had only been a woman, and women had never thrilled me, perhaps because a scrounger after work can't afford to let himself be thrilled. We have to tutor ourselves to be cold and thoughtful in our passions, and fierce and impulsive in General Elections. The man standing under the trees was certainly over six feet, but looked less startling as he was so perfectly proportioned. In our world, I recalled, people often looked as though they have got jumbled up together, in puzzle fashion, and set together by chance.

He wore a cloak, tossed back from the shoulders. The moonlight touched a clasp which held it, and it became molten silver. He wore knee-breeches, once worn in our world by duelling cavaliers, court flunkies, and servitors on affluence. He was hatless, moustacheless, too. His hair was close cropped, without giving that criminal look a close cut invariably gave us, the difference due, I think, to the fine shape and poise of the head. I realised somehow, how, I cannot tell, that this was no ordinary dress but one worn to celebrate some joyous or solemn occasion. He moved slightly. I held my breath. Had he seen me? But no. He turned to the shadow again. But, better that I should take him off his guard than that he should startle me by speaking first. There was something hauntingly familiar in his figure. Yes. I had best speak first.

"Friend," I heard a voice saying. (Was it my own?) "We are people of the world on which yours is built. We cannot break the laws of birth too early. We shall have to return. Vile as we must seem unto you, we were becoming aware before I left that we yet contained in ourselves forces liberated in your kind. Unheroic and ugly as we are, we have fought battles you cannot dream of, just as we cannot know what struggles men fought to break away from beastdom. In the names of our best, martyred up the ages, we claim the right to travel through your country."

He stood still, after one forward step, until I finished.

Then he strode towards me with outstretched hand as my voice died into silence. The moon came out in all her brilliance, and the radiance touched his features as he came over nearer.

Some primal ancestor, coming face to face with myself, might have felt the awe, the fear, the wonder, he excited in me. Our hands met. I winced and almost cried out. When he loosed his grip I could feel tingling to my shoulders. Abomination of feeble vitality that I was, his expression registered only warm friendliness, touched perchance with dim stirrings of pity, which I at once resented.

Then, as he came still nearer to me, as the magnificent physical and mental magnetism of his personality flowed round me, a living thing, as living as electricity, upon the warm air of the still summer's night, as he looked into my eyes, and I into his, I reeled backwards. The face I was looking into was the face that might have been mine—had—had I not been born till the battle-smoke had rolled, till the war trumpets were decayed, till the last fight between the excluded class and their excluders was fought—to a finish.

I try in vain to set down in words the emotions which rushed at me. Fresh and imperishable, they haunt and thrill me still. Tears such as I had never known sprang to my eyes. Even now my eyes grow dim— remembering those sensations, and the first glorious word he spake, with its meaning beyond our feeble sense of it, even when it denoted the tie of blood.

"Brother."

That was the first word of greeting I heard in the new world. Impossible to describe all the voice speaking it conveyed. All the organised Brotherhoods we had in our world, with all their sentiment, became poor things, woven of moonshine and folly, beside the strong sunlight of that vigorous kinship expressed for me by this man, who embodied ages of progression between himself and me. I forgot my insignificance, the pivot of all my shame. For, truly, is it not a shame that any human being should be insignificant, seeing that he embodies in himself all evolution?

The blood beat rapturously in my veins as again I held his hand. Even I, Edmund Sniggins, of Binkers Court, holding his hand, forgot that I had only been one in a great mass of individuals called 'citizens' in election times, and 'the lower order' at other times—a large mass so muddled that it had been equally susceptible to be a pawn for all kind of intriguers, some on the side of progress, some against it.

"Brother. My name is Sarband. I justify my existence—as an animal who must eat—by making shoes. You have been expected. For some time we have desired that explorers from your primitive world would have the audacity to travel this way, and the greater audacity to return, and tell their fellows what they learned during their sojourn with us. Perhaps I had hoped you would not come this night. Nevertheless, you are welcome, you and your friends. Where are they?"

I pointed across the way. I noticed the generosity with which he accepted our intrusion, and my friends as his own.

Whether he quite knew what he was accepting rather embarrassed me. Then, I recalled that Mr. Sparkins and Mrs. Biers were, after all, more akin to me than this man—that we were all, indeed, very poor specimens, and that even my pitiful attempts to culture myself had, after all, ended in my own confusion, and might have led me away from working-class struggle had I not happened to become unemployed.

I surveyed the superb figure. So like myself. So unlike myself. That was the bitterness of it. Would that I had been Sarband. Would that Sarband had been Edmund. Even so, from all inequalities are sown the seeds of struggle, and it is by the path of struggle man has moved at all, ever climbing to something beyond him.

This the idealists call 'Self-interest', shrieking out that human nature will have a change, and pointing out that it never has changed, terribly illogical, since we probably have two hundred thousand years of cannibalism behind us, and that cannibalism was solved, not by human nature changing, but by the discovery of how to grow food-crops.

Thinking thus I followed Sarband. We crossed the road by a subway whose entrance was like a grotto. We were walking through a garden, not between those chilly, tiled walls which made us feel to have inadvertently strayed into a bathroom, minus path but brightened by revue posters.

No one was in attendance on this garden, a fact at which I marvelled, neither were there any notices warning people not to take the flowers. Two squirrels were leaping from bough to bough of a tree unknown to me. As we passed them two bronze figures of small size tapped their rods against discs, which they held, and a cooling spray was diffused over a wide circle of the flowers and shrubs.

Death-rays having been disposed of, Science had evidently focussed itself on how to remove the curse of toil from Adam. In the diffusion of light which streamed over us from an unknown source, I limped after my companion, with the humiliating feeling that we must look not unlike Pan, the half-beast, and Apollo, the sun-god.

I was even glad to step out into the kindly and large security of the night, which veiled my imperfections, and to be approaching the common-place figures I had left behind—an age since, so it seemed. The moon shone mildly down on Mr. Sparkins and Mrs. Biers. They looked so pathetic in their super-ugliness, (I had always thought Mrs. Biers not bad-looking till now); their weariness, their unscientific way of breathing, that I almost felt for one wild moment that death-rays had been good enough for the lot of us.

They were humanly grotesque—the kind of thing we in our world loved to see on music-hall boards, and which the papers reviewed as 'the human touch'. They were asleep. Mrs. Biers' head had sagged upon Mr. Sparkins' shoulder. I felt myself smiling and looked at Sarband. He was not smiling. I wondered if even our sense of humour had been a development to save us from the too tragic appreciation of our shortcomings.

"You awaken them, brother. I might startle them," said Sarband, much as though he were speaking of two hysterical children. He went into the shadows of the chestnut.

I tapped Mrs. Biers on the arm.

"I'm getting up, Josiah," she grunted.

Finally, I awoke her. She soon awakened Mr. Sparkins, who stared fearfully around him.

"Oh! Did you speak to him?" he asked. "You told him, of course, that we were amenable to—er—reason? And that I, at least, am associated with various public bodies, who, in case of any injury to myself, would, in short, publish it to the great British Press."

"He is here," I said, shortly.

Despite myself, I moved away from the vicinity of Mr. Sparkins.

Sarband advanced.

"There is no need to fear us," he remarked. "You are the dangerous ingredients in our society now."

Mr. Sparkins revived.

"Sir, I was always on the side of law and order," he observed, sententiously.

Sarband laughed.

"That," he said, "is always safest."

There was light and genial irony in his tone.

Mrs. Biers was staring up at Sarband, and endeavouring to make her hair respectable.

"My name is Amelia Biers. Married. Respectable. Hard-working. Husband's name, Josiah, followin' occupation of sand-hawker. An'—I'm as good as the next man, and takes off my hat—where is it, they have—to nobody. That's me. 'Ave you got it?"

I experienced a violent shock.

Was this Mrs. Biers?

Sarband was looking at her in a thrilled way.

"Madam," he said gravely, "you have without knowing it, expressed the greatest democratic emotion in the universe. People take off their hats to nobody do get somewhere. Is this the article you are in search of?"

For Mrs. Biers had arisen, and was hunting about like a retriever. She took the 'article' from Sarband's hand, planted it on her head, and we involuntarily look to him for guidance as to our next movements.

"We will go the quickest way," he said, speaking half to himself. "I have to meet my comrade, and— yes, we will risk a call. The machines are busy just now. This way."

He steered us towards an obelisk, radiant in the light of two great side-lamps, whose light was of the same nature as the light in the garden under the road had been. As nearly as I can describe it, it was like a burst of natural sunlight, and everywhere it fell the objects shone out as in the glow of a perfect morning. The obelisk was inlaid with tiny squares of variously-coloured stones, in the centre of each square being a button.

"Districts," Sarband explained to me.

He pressed a button. Two minutes later one of the great bird-like machines came skating along.

Sarband stood beside the machine as it stopped with the silent grace of a bird. Upon the space between the yet swaying white wings stood the first woman of the New Word I had seen. Standing there, erect, fearless, and no taller than the tallest of our women (giantesses excepted), she looked like a spirit woven out of the night and the stars. I thought of Beatrice,

Portia and Rosalind—combined. Even then they did not foot the bill. At the moment I did not notice what she wore. I could only stare, like an idiot, at her face, over which a light which the car gave off flickered, like dancing Starshine, making the air quiver.

"You, Messeia!"

Such was Sarband's greeting.

She stood, perplexed no doubt by his use of a dead language. Then her gaze dwelt on us.

"Yes. These are the pilgrims. You must polish up your English," Sarband told her.

I realised that he was warning her not to speak in any other tongue than ours—lest we should imagine ourselves deceived. I blushed, realising our utter corruption.

"I had difficulty in getting them to let me bring it," she told him, taking her gaze from us and nodding at the car. "Even for you, they said, they could not spare it. However, I won."

I judged her age at about eighteen.

She was dressed in some warm, rich material, and wore a little cap with two silver wings attached to it.

"You made them, of course," Sarband told her. looking at her with strange sadness. "You are still very unprogressive, Messeia!"

She laughed, rare melody of delight in her 'unprogression,' whatever it was. I withdrew my gaze from her face and looked at Mrs. Biers. The contrast gave me an inward shudder. It was not likely that Mrs. Biers would be able to get into a Divorce Court on account of her journeyings.

"How goes the fight?" asked Sarband, eagerly.

Fight! I could scarcely believe my ears. Was humanity struggling yet? Was there no rest, no peace, no standing still, but eternal struggle? *"And Eternal Progress,"* a voice within me whispered. But I felt discouraged. One dream had vanished.

"Magnificently—for us," answered Messeia.

I realised that they were antagonists. Yet he accepted her word, without question, as to how the battle went. They did not lie, even to their *"enemies"*. I stared up at Sarband's divine apostle of the opposition. But she was looking at him. I saw, written indelibly upon her face, so wonderful and beautiful in its mingled Intelligence, joy, and charm, an expression of almost terribly intense affection. I think in our feeble tongue we should have called it *love*. It became a word quite inadequate, through our mud-stained associations with it, to express that feeling which was on her face for a lightning second only.

Mrs. Biers' raucous voice aroused me.

"Well, are we gettin' in?" she asked.

We "got in".

Messeia touched some mechanism which half covered us 'in', the great wings vibrated. She touched something else, urged us to sit tightly, and to Mrs. Biers' shriek of "My God!" we were rising in the air. Sarband sat next to me. We could see Messeia's head and shoulders outlined against the starry spaces. She performed a few 'stunts', purely, I believe, to see how cowardly we death-dealers were when threatened with doom—the machine almost turning over once.

"Messeia!" called Sarband, in reproof.

I saw him sit staring at her outline, like a man confronting some sphinx that has got to be answered or will swallow him.

"My God! They'd never have given a girl like that a licence on our planet," said Mrs. Biers.

"Without actual determination on the part of Messeia to bring us down," said Sarband, "we are quite safe. And Messeia, having no claim over our destinies, dare not bring us down."

Messeia's laughter trickled to our ears.

"She doesn't seem to care," moaned Mrs. Biers.

"They're like rabbits, Sarband," called Messeia, suddenly.

I blushed, and for a moment detested her cordially.

"Only—rabbits *are* harmless! They don't kill other rabbits, except in mating season," continued Messeia.

Then silence fell about us.

We were now at a goodly height from the earth. Far below us squares of soft gloom, streams of quivering lights, solitary lights of which I could not understand the size, seeing we were so far from them, shone out like planets. Sometimes these lights were veiled, shining luminously, as through mists.

"What are those?" I asked Sarband, touching his sleeve.

"Observatories," he explained.

"But—the light they give out?"

"Yes. They stand as the pillars of science. It is the material they are made of. They flash signals to each other on making discoveries. The children like to go on the hills at night to see them. It appeals to their imagination. Not that *that* needs much appealing to. Your great difficulty was in stamping it out in them, wasn't' it?"

We left the lights. Gloom lay below as. The air was cold and intense and—

"Yes, the sea," Sarband told us.

"Might I arsk?" began Mrs. Biers.

"Anything," Sarband told her. "You want to know where we are going?"

Mrs. Biers gasped at his accuracy.

"I have read that our predecessors always wanted to know what the end was, before they had well-nigh set out—anywhere; even reading the ends of their romances first," said Sarband, gaily. "Madam, we are going to Oxford. The place you arrived at was once known as London, but as its inhabitants had been exterminated by gases ten years after your war to end war, when we rediscovered it we blew it up by atomic pressure and built it again."

"But—" I protested.

"You did it yourselves," Sarband told me.

"But—there were hills when we arrived," I said.

"Certainly. We decided it lacked hills. Atomic pressure did the rest."

Fear began to fall from me. I began to experience the exhilaration a bird must know as it goes through the air.

"Oxford," I said, "will still have kept its traditions as an education centre."

I felt Sarband's smile.

"Oxford makes shoes," he said.

"Shoes!"

"Yes. Minerva was outed by St. Crispin. They made a bad job of heads. We reversed all that. We started on feet. Oxford is known the world over—for *shoes*. Other things, of course. It is still the home of lost causes. That is why *I* live there."

He began to pour out vivid descriptions of the places we were now passing over. Then silence fell on him. He was staring ahead at Messeia, steering her way fearlessly through space.

I saw his hands move once, restlessly, noting that humanity had not lost that token of its disturbance. I recalled his frank speech that perhaps he had rather we had not come tonight. Was tonight in some way momentous to him? Certainly, this was not the cut-and-dried world enemies of Progress had threatened us with under Socialism—if it was Socialism. Had *that* been left behind?

High in the air as we now were, stray radiances told us that we were passing over inhabited places, some large, some small. I reverted to the shock I had received on hearing that Oxford's chief concern was the moulding, not of souls, but soles, and 'uppers' that were not of prunella but for the world-roads of life. I was about to ask Sarband something more of this revolution, but again I saw that he was gazing before him, deeply preoccupied, He seemed to feel the gaze I had fastened upon him, and came out of his ruminations.

"You seem to be interested in Oxford," he said. "Therefore, it will perhaps rejoice you that you are, *if you choose,* going to stay in my home, which is built from the ruins of Balliol, a college famous in your day and generation. Ugly as what remains of it is, it has that peculiar fascination for me which death-yards had for some of your strenuous livers. An engraving of these corruption-memorials is in our Museum. We found it when we discovered London."

Death-yards! The strange phrase fell oddly on my ears. I stared at Sarband.

"Death-yards!" I repeated. "Do you mean the peaceful acres where we buried our beloved dead? Surely—"

"I mean those corruption beds where you took little children to learn the fear of death, and often stood mortifying yourselves with the thoughts of what you had done and said to those bones below when they were padded with flesh and the light could yet flash in the eyes. We call them death-yards. Some day, if you stay here long enough, you shall see how we pass and how our friends give us good-bye."

He was silent.

I sat speechless.

"Poor Edmund!" said Sarband lightly. "Birth with you did not prepare you for life, nor life for death. As some of your ancient litanies had it, there was no health in you."

His voice was without scorn. But I winced under it.

"Messeia!" called Sarband.

I noticed that Messeia's voice came to me, clear above the air currents, through a small eyelet in a brass plate in front of Sarband, and guessed that Sarband's voice was carried to her by the same means.

"Yes?" she asked.

"Alight by the statues of Shallon." The machine took a dive downwards, gradually slackening speed. Statues! They still had hero-worship then, if not death-yards. But we were descending. The lights of a landing-stage flashed upon us. I saw quivering streams of light in waterways and the greenery of willows and grasses bending over them, realising that this was that same Isis whereon I had sailed, in my past ignoble existence, trying to attain culture in a week out of the year.

"Thank God!" said Mrs. Biers.

Mr. Sparkins was no less relieved to be set on common earth. They got out. I sat on in the machine, whose swaying white wings made patches of light in the water. That sense of inferiority in myself, which Sarband's hand-grip had scared away, returned to me. People were passing to and fro. A quick and furtive glance revealed to me that their dress varied in style as that of the people of our world: but there were no marked distinctions arising from skimpy shabbiness, sham finery, or entré distinction. There was a simple and joyous note in their choice of light colours.

Dazed from my memories of Binkers Court, I felt like a grey moth strayed amongst beautiful butterflies. But what oppressed me most was not the beauty of colourings which had suddenly flashed opalescent out of space, but the superb figures themselves. They looked as individuals who had come into the world by choice—not by chance—who had come to conquer life, not be conquered by it. Had they been dumped down in Bethnal Green, and dressed in the coverings of a thousand rag carts, nothing could have hidden their symmetry, grace, and vigour. I cowered in the back in the machine, wishing, like Thoreau, that I had never been born. I observed, ironically, Mr. Sparkins, strutting about in his checked suit, and envied him his sang froid. Perhaps I have not spelled it right. (My French dictionary was eaten by the mice.) Mrs. Biers, arms akimbo, was surveying the scene, and I heard her say, disgustedly, "We've got amongst the nobs." In my keen sense of demoralisation, I turned instinctively to Sarband, and and touched his cloak timidly. But he was not looking at me. There was upon his face the same intensity of expression I had seen for a lightning moment on Messeia's, though he was calm, too. His gaze was seeking someone in that delightful throng.

I heard a laugh on the other side of the machine. Sarband leaned across in front of me.

"Arlene!" He said. I saw her. No wonder he had forgotten me. One of the strange lamps threw its radiance on her face, her utterly joyous, utterly fearless face, with the wide-spaced dark eyes staring straight into the eyes of Sarband. Her fair hair was scattered with rose-petals. I looked away, dazed. It was scarcely the femininity we had known. Sarband was getting out, without haste, I noted. They spoke together, by the side of the machine, and I saw her gaze travel to my puny figure, and cringed.

"English," said Sarband, just as he had said it to Messeia.

"You know how I love to keep you waiting," said Arlene, in rather stiff 'English'. "But tonight I had to take Jacqueline home. So I left the dance quite early."

Again I felt her gaze staring towards myself. I saw Messeia standing on the wings of the machine, preparatory to taking it back.

"I could not have got here without Messeia's aid," Sarband told her.

"Messeia! I had not noticed that it was you, Messeia," said Arlene, warmly.

Messeia came down and joined them. Sunlight and Starshine, side by aide, expresses them as well as I am able. In one the joyous beauty of morning and all cheerful things; in the other I realised what Shelley had meant by 'blood that ran like lightning through the veins'. Messeia's head barely reached Arlene's shoulder. Arlene and Sarband were of the team stature. But what Messeia lacked in height was compensated for—stumbling for a word, I can only think of electricity.

"Yes, I brought him," said Messeia, simply. "You love to keep him waiting. I bring him."

Arlene laughed. A women's laughter in our world could mean anything, and has sometimes driven crude men crazy in its cruelty. Arlene's was the laughter of an appreciative, light-hearted child.

"That was good of you, Messeia," she said.

I saw that Messeia was eager to take back the machine—eager, somehow, to escape.

One minute later she departed. I watched the wings of the machine beating their way through the night, from whose beauty she might have been created.

"Arlene," said Sarband, "this is one of our visitants." As she came towards me, I solved the physiognomy that gave them their calmer, larger expression. In Arlene it was particularly noticeable. The space between their eyes was many degrees wider than with us. But this placidity of look was contradicted in the eyes themselves, wider open than our eyes were, and with a curious magnetism in them which I afterwards attributed to the entire lack of timidity in them.

Yet, as Arlene approached me, quite without fear, or repulsion, evidently having expected something terrible from what Sarband had told her of our laws, customs, and conditions generally, as she held out her hand, I saw the smile of greeting on her face fade. She was close to me, now. We were staring into each other's eyes. A faint vestige of uncontrollable repugnance swept her features. The next moment she had controlled it. She took my hand. The same magnetic, tingling warmth rushed through my arm as when Sarband had held it. With sickening clearness I was realising that between my insignificant and ugly self—undeveloped self, rather—and this divine creature, radiant and gentle as a summer morning, with the birds singing in her voice, was some dark and fearful bond of recollection. A fire, a filthy hat, a being matted and beastlike, with a brass band round his neck, and shadowed against the fire-glow, a woman, singing a rebel song, without rhyme, plaintive as the wind amongst the river reeds. Why should this picture drift into my mind. I did not know.

"Welcome to Equality lsland," said Arlene.

I realised to the full the unconscious irony of her greeting. Equality became something attached not to things, but to human attributes, now that classes were swept away. I turned, half-bitterly, away, another illusion gone, and met Sarband's understanding gaze. Always, from the first to the last, he understood. But he did not know that at that moment—I shudder to set it down—I almost *hated* him.

Looking around, I found that Mr. Sparkins and Mrs. Biers, in Mrs. Biers' own 'patois' of Binkers Court, had 'done a bunk'. Arlene said that as everyone in Oxford knew that the pilgrims were under Sarband's wing, anyone would safely convey them to the house.

Arlene said we would walk, if I wasn't too tired. Decidedly a 'turn of the tables' from a world in which we insulted womanhood by imploring it to take our seats, as though it was egg-shell china, though, occasionally, we treated it as though we still ran about in the stage before Julius Caesar landed in Great Britain! Nothing could more utterly have convinced me of the historic reputation for physical degeneracy both the men and the women of our world had created through our annals, of the selves we had thought worth praying for.

I mumbled something, hot with shame. Arlene walked with her hand in Sarband's. Yes. Through the throngs, quite openly, they held each other's hands, like children. Sometimes they so far forgot themselves as to stop, despite my embarrassed presence, looking at each other with silent Joy.

"You see," explained Sarband, turning to me once, "we have not seen each other for three days."

If he had said three years I could have understood it. But, three days! Most men and women of our world were exceedingly glad to escape from each other for three days, three weeks, months—or as long as finance would allow.

Though a bachelor, my amateur knowledge of married people had convinced me this was true. I could only think that they must be an ideal couple, though in our world I recalled even ideal couples were often, justly or unjustly, suspected of not being quite so ideal in private life. However, perhaps they had not been married long.

After our two-mile walk, during which I felt as comfortable as a herring on cobbles, we arrived in Oxford. I had thought its architecture would appeal to me. But the buildings (I vaguely realised that my first visit to it, in my past life, had exaggerated my ideas of its beauty, by comparison) went past me like a dream. Arlene had been right. I was tired. I was suffering from shock, envy, and—let me confess it—jealousy. It seemed unjust that a hairbreadth's chance had left me undeveloped in Binkers Court and had given Sarband all this.

She suddenly snatched her hand from Sarband's, and ran—ran with so infectious a joy to her home, that I felt overcome, recalling poor Mrs. Jones, in Binkers Court, weeping over her croupy infant while I burned the cupboard-door off Mr. Sparkins' property—recalled Mrs. Jones saying, in a choked voice, "I think I'd gladly die, Mr. Sniggins, to get away from Binkers Court for ever!—if it wasn't for Tom and the baby."

Arlene flung open the door, set in the grey walls of the college. A lamp hung over the door, lit with the strange radiance which had no flame. The lamp was in the shape of a shoe. and the letters upon it merely said 'Sarband'. The radiance fell on Arlene's hair, the colour of golden smoke. It fell on her perfect, happy face. Joy became Beauty as I looked at her. Sorrow became ugliness, saving when it was courage, and Courage is never quite Sorrow.

I realised that their house door was never locked, and smiled inwardly, recalling people in Binkers Court locking up their rooms, lest leaden spoons should be pinched.

I followed them in, mean, shadowy, weak creature that I was—I followed their sunshine like the inevitable shadow. Wretchedness dimmed my observation of all save that a fire blazed in a room beyond. To this room I followed them. The glow suffused their faces, staring again at each other—in passionate delight. Perhaps Sarband read some of my feelings in my face. His hand fell on my shoulder.

"I have not justified my existence—to-day," he said, gaily. "Arlene will give us supper. Whilst she gets it ready—I will work. This way, Edmund. I will show you something as vital to my existence as Arlene—my work. I've been running away from it to-day—because there was other work beyond justifying one's animal existence. Mind the steps. This way. There. Now we have light."

He had blazed the passage into the broad radiance of noon. I was glad—glad that he had not left me to talk to his "Wife", "Comrade", or whatever name these people chose for their mates. Supposing that her repulsion for me was caused by that same dim memory I had had! I almost groaned, hoping this was not so, hoping that only the mediocrity of myself as a type of the mediocre of our world, had been the cause of it.

My cowardice stirred in me. I perceived that Sarband would not have me in the house if I caused Arlene any cloud. I realised that it would be dangerous for my continuance in his home if Sarband discovered that in any way I menaced the perfect joy which was the key-note of Arlene's character.

Chapter 3

With these foolish fears in my mind I stood in Sarband's workshop, once a refectory. The dull, ceremonial look it had last worn when I had seen it (curious as a child in a peep-show) was quite gone. Only its lofty space remained. I, who had seen pale and weary apostles of St. Crispin crouching over little benches in various kinds of dark holes, was amazed at the type of room in which Sarband worked. There was no clock. I noticed that at once. The long windows were unblinded to the night now throbbing with stars. Yet within was the glow of broad noon, which lent to the scene outside, wind-swaying dark trees, netting the stars, almost an uncanny contrast. He took off his cloak, hanging it on a peg, which I rightly conjectured was more than a peg and had some other utility. I flinched at the broad and deep-chested glory of him cloakless. He went to another peg and took down a loose linen robe, and over this he placed the immortal leather apron. He looked, indeed, a god of a cobbler—whistling cheerfully, and eyeing his bench with evident welcome. He turned to me with a smile.

"How many shoes would a cobbler make in an hour in your world?" he asked.

I stammered that he might make a pair, but I was not sure. Then he saw me staring at the light.

"Radium—attached to atomic conservation forces," he explained.

Upon the wall, which would meet Sarband's sight whenever he lifted his head, was a picture which filled one side of the room. I looked at it now, overawed by it, yet scarcely understanding its message.

"Yes. That is a wonderful picture," said Sarband.

He stood with his back to the window, with the brown, obscure, lawn outside, the swaying trees, like leafy nets, catching stars. On each side of him the beauty of the straight lines of the long walls, and before him the picture.

From the roof, cunningly hidden, the light was diffused into the room, natural as daylight in its effect on the night. A shadow, soft as a twilight mist, momentarily swept his face, then passed, leaving it calm as before.

"Shallon, the painter of that picture, passed last year. A mystical genius, perhaps not to be fully understood by our race until it is liberated from what is now checking it. Why do you frown when I use the word mystical? Cast from your mind the idea that mysticism can any longer be used against the race. Yes. Shallon left us last year. Too dangerous to the existing order to be popular, even where he was understood. Fortunately he was born in our age, not yours, and so could not be starved, boycotted, or penalised by statute. As he justified his existence by production—he was a loom-maker—and as he was passionately devoted to his art, he wore himself out, forsaking all pleasures for the one pleasure of challenge. You can say of Shallon that he painted with his life-blood, until the last drop of his energy was gone."

"Then," I said, thickly, "the martyrdom of man is not ended."

Sarband slightly shrugged his shoulders.

"Your philosophy of life was to follow the line of least resistance," he asserted. "Your martyrdoms comprised the epochs you broke down, with the great masses as pawns involved in the struggle between dual forces, both dominant. Here we have no passive masses. The martyrdom comes about by the leaders who represent them getting jammed between the two active forces. To be a leader is to be the servant of the masses, often passing prematurely in their service. Shallon was one. He served. He passed. Who can say he passed before his time, since he achieved as much in his lifetime as any ten of us?"

"But do you mean to say that you are in a revolutionary crisis?' I gasped. "I thought, oh, brother, I did think—"

"You thought evolutionary struggle would cease when you had won the bread battle," Sarband said. "You thought you were going to win to a calm heaven. Well, you were mistaken. It was the beginning of a higher, keener, nobler struggle, which is even now culminating towards crisis. Oh, do not shudder. Ours are purely evolutionary struggles. It was, after all, only the organised iron force of your oppositions which made your evolutions into revolutions. Here, it is organised intellectual forces, wrestling all the time. Bloodless, but terrible enough. We fight like men, not beasts, fighting for more than food.

"The worst thing that can be said against you was that, by ever delaying your conflicts to end the material struggle, you hindered the beginning of this greater one. So long as you saw no blood, you thought all was well, even with all your shameful records of destitution, prostitution, millions of lives cast away, nonentities when they ended as when they began. You could only understand blood-letting as force. And *always* it was *your* blood. By Evolution, Edmund! You could not help it; but Messeia was right in this: hares had as much courage, and of the same quality. You always ran away, and, running away, ran into the trap you feared.

"Well, if things go as rapidly as they have done this past few months, you will be an evolutionary upheaval. There will be no blood-letting, but I warn you it will be a terrific thing, and, if the Unprogressives win, it is on the cards that I follow Shallon!"

"You—you will not die!" I exclaimed.

I ran to him, staring horrified into his calm face.

He was silent.

"They do not kill their leaders who lose battles, do they?" I asked.

He smiled, a little wryly, then.

"How fearfully melodramatic you were," he said, sorrowfully. "Death was to you the one terror. You would endure all things—dishonour, want, treachery of friend—giving up your bodies and souls to all things, rather than 'die', as you call It. No. They do not kill us for failure. We kill ourselves."

"You mean—"

Involuntarily, I shrank backwards.

"I mean that we never surrender, we are never mastered by Unprogression; we go on till we kill ourselves, pouring out our energies till there is no more to pour. Then, realising that our work is done, our life completed, we pass. What else is there to do?"

"You—commit suicide?" I asked.

He looked at me a little impatiently.

"How difficult it is to make you understand," he exclaimed. "Listen! *Having nothing more to give to our fellows,* we die. We will to die. So we die. Would you have us live to grow reactionary, having spent ourselves? Surely, you would not have us live to be renegades?"

There was so vibrant a contempt in his voice, I saw what he meant at last. They preferred, in this country, death before dishonour. How strange, how startling, such a society would be, I vaguely understood, standing dazed before its unwritten laws.

"Of course," said Sarband, "we also are following the line of least resistance. We have that same basis of human nature. But as we have developed will and intellects, forces with demands as powerful as your bread-needs were, it becomes difficult to flinch when they demand Progress. Bread is free. Shelters are free. Prisons do not exist, save where they are preserved as relics of the dawn of civilisation. Therefore—with these new necessities to supply—you will see we are just the same human nature as yourselves.

"Just as you sometimes fought for bread, with weapons turned against you, scrambling like beasts for food and shelters, we fight like men, having left bread-struggle behind, and irresistibly driven on to satisfy our other hungers.

"With you, kept close to the bread-struggle, death seems to appear as the supreme tragedy. The gift of what laughter was in you was used to help you to endure life. To live—that is, merely to continue your existence is, however mean—you would do anything. Even though it meant living half-dead amongst half-dead people, you preferred the living death in which honour went down as the swine to the husks.

"You perished, trying vainly to live at any price. You slaughtered each other by millions to avoid being killed. If men and women of courage and intellect arrived, you feared them more than if they were wild beasts or iron guns. Invariably you killed them, in one way or another, then, a century later, you raised monuments to them, and crawled before their effigies.

"You accepted negation of life, full life, but you gave thanks for mouldy crusts and the rags of existence, thankful if you could just continue to exist. The world's billions were nonentities, governed by a handful of legalised robbers on the one hand, and pitied and wept over and harangued by a small handful of enlightened people on the other, who occasionally were martyrs for them, but sometimes turned renegade, overwhelmed with the spectacle of their passivity.

"Your great thinkers, altogether, could have the sum total of their greatness piled together in a few hundred volumes.

"Well, you perished trying to live, children of chance. We perish widening the way for the race, children of choice from birth to death. If there is an afterwards, assuredly we shall still be children of choice. Life is a great incident, taken seriously."

I heaved a deep sigh.

"I did think struggle would cease."

"That is, you thought Progress would come?" said Sarband, smiling.

I realised the truth of his deduction. Struggle ceasing meant a standstill. Unprogressives in our world often had said it would be a dead-level world if the bread-struggles ceased. How far away from the truth they had been, I dimly realised. But the titanic thought of the continuance of struggle from the low to higher forms became obsessive.

"Can you tell me the end of it?" I asked.

He smiled gently, and I realised that Sarband's smile was sweeter than that of any woman's I had ever seen in our world—even my mother's, who, enduring like a Spartan the indignities of our world, had kept the sweetness of affection for her children to the last.

"*Who knows?*" he asked, lightly, yet tenderly. "From mud to the dawn of civilisation, and from the dawn you knew to this noontide of ours? Who knows what lies beyond? Is there any end? I know not; but instinctively, cannot think there is an end. Finally, maybe, to each individual being so in sympathy with his fellow that to do any deal by intellectual force would be as impossible as it would be to us now to shoot each other down, as you once did."

I walked up to him.

"Then," I cried swiftly, "struggle would cease."

"Then—intellectual dominance would cease," he agreed. "Some other form of society would arise, with developments on lines of sympathy rather than lines of antagonisms, and the struggle might be a struggle to solve the Universe and conquer the secrets that throb through it to the remotest star. Discovery is boundless, brother. Our fight at the present moment is to break down the bureaucracy of intellectual dominance—that is the *tyranny of personality*.

"The number of your historic personality forces could be counted on the fingers of two hands. Consider our problems! After the beast bread-struggle ended, the millions became personalities. Think of the diversity of variation, even though you were most of you only elementary in your variation, and its developments, and you have the struggle of our world outlined."

Despite myself, I shuddered.

Sarband laughed.

"And you think the final struggle for the overthrow of Intellectual Dominance will take place while I am here?" I asked, in terror.

"Poor Edmund! You can only think of force in terms of blood-letting," he said, sorrowfully. "What a bloodthirsty crew you must have been! All that will happen will be a terrible conflict of liberated intellects. Minds and will clash. Bodies too! We should scorn to hurl our bodies against each other.

"Mind-forces could never be stamped out in that way. Even in your world you only intensified their appeal by breaking the bodies that held them. Terrible enough it will be. More terrible possibly than you can conceive; but, bloodless. Well, I must work.

Poor Shallon! The last conflict, small to what this will be, killed him—the last straw. Some of us, I suppose, will go down in this."

I could only wonder, and seeing that he had become absorbed in his work—the task of making shoes—more absorbed than I have ever seen any waged worker become, after staring in bewilderment to see the noiseless accuracy of the machine he dominated. I advanced towards the picture painted by Shallon—with his life-blood. As I approached it, its unified power and beauty rushed at me.

I saw a divided host of figures standing on the heights of a mountain, the glories of noonday light streaming over their faces.

Peaks, as yet inaccessible, towered above them, melting into clouds which doubtless hid peaks beyond them. The artist had suggested grim electrical conflict between the two hosts by a symbol of lightning shattering of rock between them. One figure in each host stood out distinctly from the rest—evidently their chosen spokesman.

Shallon had conveyed subtly in each figure a vital battler whom the hosts he represented would not allow to flinch. Each figure stood there as the intellectual gladiator representing were swarming hosts—to protect them from the necessity of the conflict of two great hosts.

Between the two hosts and their chosen fighters was only the narrow strip of sunlight and the great rock, split by the dual lightning bolts. Yet in so subtle a way were the few inches of canvas used for this strip, it suggested the progress of an age.

The glory of a shaft of light from a storm-cloud shone full on the face of one of the leaders of the hosts, whose hand was pointing upwards to the climbing of the next mountain-peak.

Dimly seen, spirit vague, amidst the highest of the seen peaks, was a misty shape, shot through as with sun-fire. I recognized it for the beckoning figure of—Evolution! Then, something in the figure of the man beckoning on to the next peak made me study it more intently. I looked at it and then at Sarband. He was standing, propelling a lever to bring a knife down on a great pile of leather. His head was flung backwards, his face glowed, his strength was exerted. He looked like a young classic god.

"Sarband!" I exclaimed. "*You*—you are the leader of the progressives."

My enthusiasm, my hero-worship, fell coldly upon him, disregarded.

"Just at the present moment, I am making shoes," he said, calmly. "See, Edmund! Isn't it wonderful? But this machine is getting out of date."

I allowed him to complete the wonderful stroke, whose mastery he rejoiced in.

"Sarband!" I cried. "Is it possible that you will follow Shallon?"

Emotion shook me. It was like contemplating my own death in a nobler form than nature had granted to me.

"Who knows?" said Sarband, nonchalantly.

And I recalled the heart-ache of some of those in our world, who had only lost their seats in our House of Legislation, but were left, life-force and intellect intact, to go on with their work, breaking down Unprogression in themselves and those they represented.

When Sarband had completed his work, the long bench nobly testifying to his skill and art—every shoe perfectly shaped, and only that hand work left to be done which enriched them into individuality—he asked me if I felt hungry. I did, but I had forgotten it until now. He apologised for their having only two meals a day, saying that as most of our meals had been so innutritious that we had to be fed every two or three hours, he had completely forgotten my body in giving me knowledge which would make it easier for me to understand what I saw and heard. Whistling light-heartedly, he led me back to the room where I had seen him and Arlene stand looking at each other, with such fresh delight, in the glow of the fire. The fireplace was now filled with foliage, and the room radiant under the same light as was diffused in the workshop. I stared at the fireplace. Sarband's eyes twinkled.

"The women of your world had so much dirt and trouble with fires," he said, gaily, "that your fairy-tales for children often gave the girl-princess a broom, and sackcloth and cinders."

I realised that he was referring to Cinderella.

"But how—?" I asked, wonderingly.

"We kept the beauty of the old iridescent flames and glow," he said. "We abolished the dirt. You had a try at it once, by asbestos, but the effect was that of a heap of bones, burning for ever without vanishing— no doubt a concrete symbol of your religious idea of eternal bells."

"They were certainly not so nice as the old fire-glow," I admitted, feebly.

We passed through the room into another. It was like passing into a shell, all warm colour and beauty. The table had tiny lamps with soft, diffused lights. The rest was shadowy, fire-glow and starlight within and without. There was just that degree of soft light necessary to light the table, without those high lights on our faces which in our world caused the ladies of the commercial tyrant-class such torture of mind and of body that they had to have specially devised tool-bags to carry rouge and lip-sticks about. I glanced curiously at the food. We had to be so suspicious of food in our world.

"Fish?" asked Sarband.

He sat next to me, and served me himself.

Then he turned to Arlene.

"Would you believe it, Arlene," he asked, malicious glee in his eyes, "in Edmund's world the women were so engaged in food-disguising, they often had scarcely time to eat at all themselves, and sat down in corners and gobbled when all the rest had been served?"

Arlene laughed like a child told a funny, childish joke.

I glanced down at my plate.

It was certainly fish, with a pinky kind of sauce poured over it.

"You seem to do some disguising yourselves," I told him, a trifle nettled.

"Do you suppose Arlene capable of cooking all this?" asked Sarband.

I started.

"Arlene is a miller. One man one job, so far as getting a living is concerned," explained Sarband. "She runs the house as a *hobby*. But one could scarcely expect her to cook as well. This has come from one of our common kitchens, with a staff of experts, which include, all of them, an expert on food values. Consequently, we have abolished all the terrible stomach ailments which amateur cooks inflicted on you."

"Then woman has left the home!" I gasped, with despair.

I saw Arlene regarding me with wonder.

Sarband looked from me to Arlene, threw back his head and laughed.

"Sarband!" she reproached him.

"Excuse me," he murmured to her. "Edmund is really too funny."

"We had," I stammered, "a—a traditional, beautiful enough regarded in the proper light—"

Sarband laughed again heartily.

"Arlene, I'll try not to laugh, but when I hear Edmund speaking of their regarding women's servitude *in the proper light,* I—indeed, Arlene, I cannot help it. I must laugh."

He did. Suddenly they were both laughing. After a hesitant second the infection of their gaiety caught me. I laughed too, but less heartily.

"For a vivisection, for exploitation, for all unprogression, *you* could find excuses," said Sarband, "looking at them in their proper light. Now, Edmund, you explain to Arlene why you kept your women locked up."

I realised that he was leading me on to oppose Arlene, like a very schoolboy.

"Did you keep your women locked in the houses?" asked Arlene, wide-eyed. The shadows trembled softly about her. She wore a bronze-green dress, exquisite arms bare, and the wonderful throat supporting a head which brought to my mind the lines, 'tipped with gold for awful kings'.

"We—mostly they *chose* to stay in them, or thought they choose," I apologised. "That is, where they *could.*"

She leaned forward—superb, questioning beauty.

"Then you sometimes drove them out of them?" she interrogated.

"They sometimes had to go out to get food," I tried to explain.

"You mean both the man and the woman had to go out to get food?" she asked.

"Yes, and the children, too. You see, it took them all."

She stared at me.

"What dreadfully large appetites you must have had," she said, in an anxious voice. "Sarband! Do you think I've got enough?"

That was too much for me.

She was afraid I was going to demolish all the food on the table.

"No," I said quickly, "you misunderstand. In fact all the lot of them *going out, driven out*, as you call it would not give them as much in three days as there is on this table. It was not that they ate enormously. You see, we had to struggle so to get a very little, and when, sometimes they were not wanted as workers, many of them, they fared very badly indeed. Legislation was beginning before I left which recognised the right not to die of starvation when we were not wanted. A child could claim two shillings a week, or perhaps less— not being a family man, I do not know exactly—so that it did not die. They realised we could not be left to die, absolutely. That was an advance, wasn't it?"

Arlene was studying me in puzzled fashion.

"I suppose two shillings would be money (I know dimly what money means) to buy *all* a child required in your world in a week?" she asked, simply.

I stared at her. A strange cruelty leapt up and me. Suddenly before I knew what I was doing, I was giving her a little picture of one single day of life in the tenements of Binkers Court. I did not elaborate it. I gave it as out of a Blue Book, just the bare outline of the human folk that one lot of tenement houses held, sparing her nothing.

I told her of little Jimmy, sitting on the stairs all day, staring at the half-starved cats which sometimes rubbed against him. Of the girl of eighteen who hawked herself on the streets. Of Bill, the painter, whose wife had had to stop him twice when he threatened to drown his two little girls in the wash-tub, rather than let them come to '*that*'—that being the girl of eighteen.

I told her of the chap left a widower, with three youngsters, who looked after themselves, save when an aunt ran in for half an hour when she could—the night baker, a consumptive man, who could not read any save child books. She grew ever paler.

Sarband put out his hand once. But I went on. I told her a bit about our wars, and brothels, and prisons, and mines and factories, and the men of the fields, striving with clod and stone, and getting no more than the oxen in the stalls, and of our diseases, and murders, and suicides, and superstitions.

"And you called yourselves men, and let the women and children suffer so?" she asked, in a sudden sobbing breath. "You told your women you loved them, and were content to let your lives drag out without daring to challenge such a state of things?"

She had risen.

"Madam," I told her "we proved our valour in going by the million to have the souls blown out of our bodies! We believed we went to save the women and children—at least, we were only just beginning to see we had not done so. Cowards as we were in your eyes, apparently, there were men who would have given the last drop of the blood in their bodies to aid a sick wife, and women also, who bore all things, uncomplaining in a hell of poverty, misery, and horror, speaking cheerily till their brave hearts ceased beating. You do not understand us if you think millions of people bore such conditions because they were cowards."

Arlene was looking at me with troubled eyes.

Then she said slowly this remarkable thing:

"Supposing these millions had gone out in the streets all at once, all over the world, with banners,

47

saying 'We refuse to live such lives. Kill us if you dare! We have no arms. Drop your bombs and your gas us. We prefer *that* to this which we have.' What would have happened?"

I stared at her.

"Madam," I stammered, "that would have been hailed as the proposition of a madman. Besides, they would have made it illegal. If that did not act, they would have—yes, I believe they'd have swept us off the face of the earth."

But I did not feel sure.

Arlene realised this from my tone.

"They did shoot down people who gathered as you suggest, time and again, in different places." I said.

"But, all at once," she said. "At a given signal."

"Madam," I told her, "we were divided, divided by many things—different tongues, lying Presses, terrors of force being need against us, fear of death, fear of religious superstitions, fear of losing the crusts we had, fear of going too quickly."

"But were not the forces of destruction travelling quickly?" she asked, swiftly. "Didn't you see if you did not unite and educate the whole of the people, these forces would bring death to the whole of your society?

"Surely your fight against force had to be as swift as the pace of force.

"You were cowards. What courage you had was passive courage. Weren't there thousands of you who knew why the people were robbed and who saw a change must come? Why did not these thousands tell the peoples what was coming?"

"Madam," I protested, "some of them hoped to stave it off."

"Stave it off, with destruction gaining on you all the time?" she asked. "Didn't they realise only the people could bring that change without bloodshed and horror? You make me *sick*." She flashed past me, out of the room.

"Try some wine, Edmund," said Sarband, calmly. "Arlene has gone on the roof to think under the clean stars. You shocked her. I detest her to be shocked. A full glass?"

"Full to the brim," I said, desperately.

"Brother, do you think you ought to take more than half a glass?" asked Sarband, affectionately. "You were so full of reflexes in your world. Here, at least, each man is a unity, not a contradiction."

"Will she come back?" I asked.

"Who? Arlene. Why, of course. Even now—yes, that is her step."

"Then take it away," I told him, shortly, and pushed it from me.

I had no sooner done so than Arlene entered the room. She sat down besides me, like a child eager to be friends.

"I am sorry I hurt you," she said, without effort. "But I do hate to hear of the lives your women had to lead. Several times I've stopped Sarband reading your old records to me. After all, I don't see what the past has to do with us. Only the future matters."

She held out her hand. Her smile fell on my wounded feelings, like balm on a canker of some sort.

"To prove you are really and truly sorry, Arlene, you must take Edmund down to your mill," said Sarband.

She nodded.

I enjoyed the food, delightful and varied. We lingered over it in the soft light and shadows, and sat as men do, whilst Arlene wheeled the crockery and remains away on a small wagon. She left us together, obviously to get through our detestable task of 'washing up'. I heard the rustle of a geyser of water—a long sizzling sound like the wind whistling in the keyhole on a winter's night—and in five minutes, I am sure it was not more, she was back. Then she sat down, exquisitely idle, not languidly weary, and Sarband turned a stream of music into the room. I cannot describe it. Whilst in this music of the new world there were few minor chords, and its harmonies on the whole were sweeter and higher, there was mingled with its melody sonorous under-currents of thunderous grandeur which vaguely reminded me of Beethoven and the surge of the sea. I leaned back— entranced. I wondered, after a while, what o'clock it was. Sarband noticed my wandering gaze.

"There! Place your ear to that little disc," he told me. "Yes. There. In the wall. Now, listen."

I listened.

Far away, yet distinctly, I heard eleven mellow strokes.

"Centrifugal," explained Sarband. "All your clocks used to contradict each other."

Then he said, "Edmund, drink your wine. I will drink with you, brother. See!"

He lifted it up.

"To—Arlene!" He said, simply.

He handed it to me.

I raised it to my lips.

"To—Arlene," I repeated.

Gazing across at her, I saw the strange distress leap into her face which had come there when we met. I cannot tell how it happened. The glass fell from my hand and shattered. Superstition, the poison in our blood, washed at me. I felt it was an omen. Could an under-developed being such as I mingle with these people without bringing them some sorrow?

"Another glass, Arlene?" asked Sarband.

He took up the shattered vial. She brought another, and filled it with her own fair hands. Yet I saw in her, as in Sarband, that unmoved calmness which took toasts or fame with a kind of gentle laughter at such folly.

"To Arlene, then," I said. "To Progress, to Joy!"

I drank it.

Then I heard someone coming in. It was Messeia. She stood in the doorway, looking in on us; no longer in her working dress. She floated in like a star veiled in cloud. She was apparently about to speak in their own tongue, but, seeing me, recollected that I might think they discussed myself. I blushed at this tenderness for our evidently well-known characteristics.

"Sarband!" I said shortly, angrily, "unless you sometimes speak as you most desire to do—in your own tongue—I shall feel too vile to stay with you."

His face seemed to fade from me for a second or two, then I saw him clearly again.

"As you choose, brother."

I realised that, for the first time in my life, I, Edmund Sniggins, had trampled my super-sensitiveness underfoot. I realised that to live in the space was not to change into some other kind of human nature, but to realise that which was ours—*at our best*.

Messeia spoke rapidly, musically, in the strange tongue, in which I yet detected familiar roots of words. She looked at Arlene, as for some favour, and Sarband looked a little perturbed. Then he also looked at Arlene.

"Very well," said Sarband. "I will go with Messeia. I half-expected this. This battle I told you of begins, Edmund. They are gathering in the great hall for battle. Arlene will make the time interesting to you until your friends return."

I realised with surprise that I had completely forgotten Mr. Sparkins and Mrs. Biers. I realised suddenly that I did not wish to be left with Arlene.

Sarband's magnanimity in leaving a half-developed creature from a world like our alone with so fair a woman overwhelmed me.

"Can I not accompany you?" I asked, eagerly.

"No. These things are titanic. Already you are spent. I hate to say so, Edmund. We may be there all night. We may be there all day, and all the next night. And this is only the beginning. That was why I wished you had not come tonight."

He was putting on his cloak, which Arlene had run to bring to him. She handed to him from a carved wooden box a roll of papers. As she gave them to him, her attitude, her look, was as if she had handed him a sword. She kissed him on the cheek and pushed him away from her, as though she thrust him into the fray, whatever it was, a light in her eyes, a laugh on her perfect mouth.

Consternation seized me. If Sparkins and Mrs. Biers did not turn up, I was to stay in this house, with Sarband's wife, until this assembly, which might last days, was over! My sense of the fitness of things was outraged. I passed out, and followed Sarband, where he stood in the wide hall.

"If my friends do not turn up, am I to stay here?"

He gazed at me, evidently puzzled.

"But you will not be alone, if that is what you fear. There is Arlene."

I gaped at him.

"Yes. That's it," I stammered, nervously.

"You mean you would like Arlene to go to some other house? You prefer to be alone?"

"No, no. You know people of our world simply hate to be alone, as they are flung back on themselves."

Sarband surveyed me calmly.

"Say exactly what you mean," was his advice.

I recall the effort it always took me to do that.

I laughed foolishly.

"I mean, Sarband. You must know my dilemma. I don't wish to cause a public scandal. You must know that in our world if two people living near each other, a man and woman, missed a train, and had to walk back at midnight, they took separate paths, to avoid scandal. Whilst, if they got lost on a mountain in the mist, they've got to marry each other to explain themselves to a moral world."

Sarband laughed heartily.

"I believe we've a few prehistoric comedies on those lines," he said.

"I refuse to take your outlook," I said fiercely.

Sarband gave me a little push. I found myself standing in front of the one mirror the house possessed.

"You are quite safe," he told me calmly. "You don't suppose any woman of our world could possibly dream of getting mixed up with unevolved man!"

We were standing together, my brother and I. By Evolution! (Excuse the phrase, I heard it so often there it often slips out.) Tears of mortification sprang into my eyes. I realised I was quite safe, and whatever folly I was capable of would be met with the true spirit. Arlene could shake me as a lion shakes a mouse.

"Messeia! I'm waiting," called Sarband, a trifle impatiently.

I observed that femininity still kept its old traits.

Messeia, however, came at once.

She was flushed and excited, whatever attraction she felt for Sarband having been, I saw, blotted out by the glory of battle they were both faring forth to take part in—antagonists.

They left me standing dazed. I heard the door close. I felt to crawl like an intrusive worm into the room that held Arlene. My vanity had received a terrific blow. She pointed me to a chair. The room was light-flooded now. Arlene rose and opened the window, turning her chair from the fire, as one who felt the necessity of the outdoor world and the large quiet of the night. I wheeled my chair round also. A narrow space divided us—yet it was the width of ages.

The moonlight cast a magic circle over a splash of red flowers, gently swaying in the breeze.

"That is my garden," she told me.

I fumbled in my mind for something to say—and found it not.

"Do you ever dream?" she asked, suddenly.

I was startled.

"What kind of dreams that the people of your world dream?" she enquired, curiously intent.

I informed her that we were most commonly afflicted with dreams of finding ourselves starving, naked, or falling from great heights, also journeying to places beyond our power to reach—and finding ourselves arrested for some horrible crime, a dream from which we usually awake before our execution.

"We never dream such barbaric memories ever," she said, simply. "But there is one dream which has often wakened me in terror. Perhaps the conditions of your world would explain it if I understood them better. It is probably a race-memory from the time when many of your women were men's property.

"I have dreamed of sitting on the ground, by a fire, my hair all matted, darkness all around like a black wall, and the song of a slow, mournful river moaning through the silences. There were other figures as vile and wretched as mine. Sometimes they were not near me. But always one figure, one face, was near me—"

I held my breath, waiting, as she paused.

Her face looked pale in the moonlight.

I waited for the blow.

"That face, that figure, was yours," she said, in a disturbed voice. "Can you explain it?"

It would have been easy to laugh, to say nothing of my own recollections of some such picture as that she recalled. But as I looked into her earnest face, still free from any coquetry, so simple and valiant in its expression, the great gulf between our society and this, the impossibility of my ever 'being a day of it' overwhelmed me like a flood. I burst into those tears which have ever been my curse, seeing that they are, traditionally, only allowed to women and children. Arlene jumped up from her chair with a little cry of wonder.

I realise that she was looking at me now with the compassion and tenderness women, even of our world, gave to very small babies. She regarded me hesitantly, then her hand caressed my head, as we caress the heads of dumb animals. The touch at once soothed and maddened me.

I tried to explain, throatily, that in our world tears were a social safety-valve. As I looked upwards into her face I saw that she also was moved, as though each individual here immediately shared, in great part, any suffering, however foolish it might seem, which another endured. What we should have said to each other I cannot tell; what mad, incoherent consternation of dim recollections I should have made, what wisdom and tenderness she would have revealed to sweep the shadow from my past once and for all, I shall never know. Life contains ever and forever the elements of the unexpected which constitutes its eternal romance. We heard the door swung open, a great dog rushed in, and I saw, agile and vivacious, (no other word expresses his personality), standing in the doorway, a very old man, who advanced benignly upon us with little springing steps.

Age had rather narrowed his eyes, but they shone, black and clear-sighted, eagle-strong. His manner conveyed an impression of one who had lived very much alone and aloof from things.

"Where is Sarband?" he asked.

"Gone to the assembly."

"Ah!"

He rubbed his chin with a frail, fine hand, chemical-stained.

"A plague on their rows," he said, without bitterness, and rather in the tone of a man who sees far off a great joke going on. "I wanted to show him Neptune through my new telescope. Its visibility is extraordinary. Quite extraordinary tonight. Never again will he have the chance. It's preposterous that he should be out, trying to upset the Constitution! The world is mad, Arlene. Quite mad."

Arlene laughed.

Then her face grew serious.

"After all, Venensley," she told him, "we can't *all* live in dreams, with the stars for our playthings."

"Quite right," admitted the old man. "So long as I'm left with the stars for my children I won't grumble. So you are one of the Pilgrims."

He turned an eagle gaze upon me.

"Ah!" he said, candidly, "I see you belong to the period we call the Age of Destruction. Arlene, may I take him and show him Neptune?"

I gazed at him with mixed emotions.

"If you had lived in our world," I said, "would you not have felt the impulse to destroy? How can you construct without destruction?"

"Perverse! Perverse!" was his verdict on my argument. "You always did things wrong end up. You destroy an old world, young man, by constructing another, just as you destroyed your slum property by constructing better houses. Of course, your mistake was constructing well in one part and letting old stuff fill up in another as fast as you rebuilt. But we do not call you the Destructionists for attempting to smash either your legal machinery or your industrial machinery. *We call you Destructionists because you destroyed each other. Even the sections of your Progressive Parties looked on one another's fighting battalions as only fit to be destroyed.* A most abnormal period. Thank Evolution we are born in happier days. But, Sarband ought to have seen Neptune instead of being out trying to destroy a wonderful constitution. I am a Conservative."

Chapter 4—A Watch Tower on the hills.

Arlene laughed.

"Sarband says you will join the Progressive Party yet, even at your age," she said, mildly.

I wondered how old he was.

Following the venerable old dreamer out into the midnight streets, I felt more like an 'undesirable alien' than ever. Why should I, 'social wreckage' of our world, be wandering about here?

I realised that, even had I been the greatest intellectual giant of my age, I should still have been only 'social wreckage'. Venensley was almost as shabby as myself, but there was this great difference between us. I had been shabby from compulsion. He was negligent from choice. The glorious vestments of the heavens made him forget his attire.

On the road and in the air above us, there was ample evidence that the 'Progressives' and 'Unprogressives' were rolling up to the strange battle. Strange and thrilling sight to me! The air alive with white-winged machines, ghostly in the moonlight. Throngs of superb people, men and women, pouring along on the roads on each side of the machines conveying other antagonists. Echoes of voices in the unfamiliar speech, as changed from ours as our modern tongue was from Chaucer. Clad in the robes which had caused neither grey lives nor grey death, the spirit of electrical fellowship giving them the atmosphere of it being one great happy family, they passed us by. Their average walking pace was swifter than ours had been.

It was impossible to believe, from what I could see, at least, that they had, in whichever camp they were, any bitterness for each other. Yet I realised that this was purely consequent *on all of them being equal so far as material conditions went. They had solved exploitation by abolishing it.* They were now faring forth to abolish what Sarband had called *the bureaucracy of intellectual dominance.*

I laughed inwardly, repudiating his argument that it would be more terrible to witness than our old crude blood battles. I thought of the carnage of broken bodies I had seen, and chuckled to myself at the bare idea that the clash of intellects could terrify more than such sights—real, and not pictorial. I felt fascinated as, a tiny wave in the surging sea of life, I limped on with the old star-gazer. Impulses to leave him and go on with them seized me. The indecision familiar to me in our world made me irresolute.

"Let us leave the mad crowd," said Venensley, noticing that I was embarrassed by one or two people in the vast concourse looking at me a little wonderingly.

We walked along a path running between two fields, which must have been a mile square. On one side of me lay potato plants, the flowers dim in the moonshine; on the other a field of green barley. There were no fences, and no prosecution notices.

Two young lovers were coming along, and drew aside to let us pass, giving Venensley greeting.

So magnificent they looked, hand clasped in hand, standing to let us pass, as gods let common humanity pass, conscious of their glory, that I turned to look after them.

"There," said the old star-gazer, "walks the wisdom of the ages."

He had taken off his hat. His white hair was ruffled in the soft breeze.

"Someday that spirit of identity shall solve all our problems," he said. "It could not in your world, where possessions were concrete symbols of robbery. But it may in ours."

I stared at him.

"A hundred years ago," he continued, "I also walked down this very path—so! It is a little different now. Only meadow grass grew here. A hundred years ago. Yet it is as fresh as yesterday. Only dolts forget. She died—yes—of one of your barbaric diseases, which we had not conquered even then. It is conquered now."

"And you?" I asked.

He pointed to the glory of the milky way.

"The stars became my children," he said. "My passion turned to calm, surveying the universe, its wonders, its mysteries, its secrets."

We had both stopped on the path.

"How old are you?" I gasped. We walked on.

He laughed.

"I was thirty years old, then," he told me. "There," he said, suddenly, gripping my arm. "There is my dwelling-place."

I saw a hill before us. On its crest was one of the towers, luminous, against the sky. As I stared at it, a sudden vibration, like the roll of thunder, passed through the atmosphere. Venensley stopped again.

"It is the signal," he explained.

"What signal?"

"The battle has begun," he said, testily. "By Evolution! Sarband will never see Neptune as clear as tonight. Sheer waste. Cruel waste of life and energy. Why can't he leave Intellectual Dominance to destroy itself? Not that I agree with its *utter* destruction. It ought to be done gradually. I am an Evolutionist. They call me Conservative. Let them. See! Watch! There in the sky. No, over there. That's right."

Upon the space he had pointed out flashed two greater banners of light. They grew ever more vivid. One was white—white and shining as the dawn not yet come. The other was crimson.

"Fools!" He ejaculated, calmly. "It's not a bad world. Why can't they leave it alone—or reform it gradually?"

I walked on, realising that it was indeed exactly the same human nature. They had outgrown our evils, but there were still people who wish to claim the next peak, and those who flinched. Another quivering vibration went through the air.

"Sarband is opening the battle," said Venensley. "Fool! Neptune will be two hundred years before we see it so near to us again. Fool."

Sitting quietly within the watch-tower on the hill, I realised the quiet beauty of a life apart from the herd. The atmosphere of meditation fell on my spirits like balm. Notwithstanding, I felt irresistibly drawn back to the recollection of the banners of light and sky, the reverberating sounds which had typified struggling hosts.

The tower was a queer place, with scientific instruments on the walls which I have never heard or read of. Maps of the heavens hung about. What I took for a lightning conductor, a long rod, stood in one corner. Venensley told me it held atoms which, when they came in contact with other atoms, flashed signals over a wide circumference. He swung his telescope into place, at a loophole of a window in the tower, and to please him I looked through it. The site was certainly remarkable. Such imagination as I had was fanned by this survey of the heavens. Neptune now appeared as brilliant as the planet Mars and Venus had appeared to our telescopes, and the old man was talking eagerly of a newer telescope which would further propel the human vision into space.

"You appear to wish to travel as fast as possible in science," I told him, drily. "But object to travel quickly in social evolution."

He laughed.

"Ha, ha! You've got me there," he said. "Yes, I suppose, being not quite so young as I once was, I object to the trouble of creating new worlds from old ones, or being in the dust of the conflict. Much better for me to look at the process of worlds in the making than join Sarband's party. He almost convinced me once, but I had the good sense to remember that it would upset all my plans. Wonderful! Look there! The milky way! A path of suns, the star-dust of the Universe. Energy! Heat! Vitality—which we also contain, in a measure—yes, in a little measure."

Perhaps I sat for an hour with him.

I saw that he would talk till the sun came up. He was vitally interesting. The tales of scientific discovery he called me were beyond our wildest fairy tales. But I could not lose my sense that a battle was raging.

"Venensley," I said, suddenly, "I will come again. I wished to go to see the fight."

He looked at me pityingly.

"By Evolution!" He ejaculated. "I have shown you Neptune, and you wish to go and see the fight."

"I am young," I explained.

Quite suddenly, quite absurdly, I felt younger than ever I had done in my life. To sit inactive while struggle was going on became a crime. I realised that I was not sufficiently muddled with the culture I had imbibed to be able not take sides.

"Where is the fight going on?" I asked.

"In the great hall. Anyone will direct you to the Temple of Evolution," he said.

"And—you fight there?" I asked in wonder.

"Why not, since all the fights of mankind are chronicled there? Well, then, you *will* go?"

"I will go," I said. "Will they let me in?"

"Certainly."

I rose to go.

Another quivering vibration which felt to shake the tower in which I stood went through the atmosphere.

"Wait," said Venensley.

He rushed to a round window and looked through.

"See!" He cried.

I ran and looked.

My gaze, following the direction of Venensley's eager-pointing hand, encountered a strange sight. The two banners of light were mingled each with each. The result was a rosy flare like the light of a splendid dawn. The sky which was its background seemed dull and commonplace, beside it, for all the glory of stars and moon. Yet through the blaze of radiance, the challenging fire like the founts of the morning boiling over, I saw one dim, pale star. Eagerly Venensley swung the eye of his telescope upon it. I realised that he was only interested in it for its spectacular glory, through his instrument.

"Good-bye," I called, excitedly.

"Here," shouted Venensley. "Don't miss it."

"Dear friend, I'll see it, but not through a telescope," I told him. He watched me depart like a good, if undeveloped, man, lost. For all my excitement my powers of observation were acute. I found my way along the path between the potatoes and barley.

A clock struck the half-hour between one and two. I had lost all sense of my own puny being. The noble buildings of the city rose around me in the moonlight, beauty and strength one harmony.

Glorious to walk here without fear of encountering some wretched slum, the happy, spare-time hunting grounds of morbid charity-mongers. Glorious to walk along without fear of some wreck of a woman stealing out of the shadows—a painted ghost. Glorious to know one could tumble upon no bags of rags and bones, suffering martyrdoms of hunger, as I had seen them in pictures on the Thames Embankment.

I recalled that it had been suggested that those in our world who wished to see things changed, wished it passionately, wished it done quickly—to stop murder of all kinds—had been called unconstructive. Vennensley himself had said they called our age the Age of Destruction, but was referring only to Militarism. A wild surge of passionate joy swept through my heart.

The wondrous starry skies—the stars that had seen the ape-man struggle, seen the savage, seen the barbarian, seen the civilised, struggling upwards, toiling onwards, with blood and tears, and martyrdoms—and now saw this crown of beauty, this city, typical of other cities, with science yoked to its ear, and brute force of hunger and guns gone for ever—I looked up to them in my ecstasy.

Street after street, fair in the moonlight. Archways and colonnades, magnificent roads, gardens, massive public buildings—wide spaces, moon-dappled—and then along a road, coming towards me, a solitary figure. He was reading. I went towards him and spoke. He did not hear me. I touched him, without fear of rebuff, without apology.

"Brother," I said, "can you tell me the way to your Assembly?"

He looked up.

He was well-grown, a boy of fifteen, perhaps. The light shone on his face, stirred with some intense emotion. His eyes were moist, as though he had endured something beyond the telling.

"What is your sorrow, brother?" I asked.

"*I am reading the history of this island,*" he said, "*before Capitalism was destroyed.* Pilgrim! How could you endure to live there? Pilgrim! How will you dare to return? Pilgrim! I do not wish to influence you—being a Progressive—but, were I in your shoes, I would join the Progressive Party, pitch myself into the work. So frail you are, you would soon be dead, and then you would not need to return."

I stood dazed.

Gallantly he was offering me death, glorious death, rather than ignoble life. And the ecstasy I had felt turned into reaction. Dim and dark behind me lay the life I had left behind. Dare I return there? Could I again endure it, after my desire to see this country had been granted me! My brain felt to reel. I realised for the first time that, whichever way I turned, tragedy would be the price of my coming here. To go, or to stay, either way would be terrible. Bitterness of bitterness, I was what Sarband called 'a child of chance', brought up on chance milk, chance bread, chance culture.

I could not choose.

"Brother, I will think of what you have said," I told him.

"I will take you to the Hall," he said. "Come!"

My young friend, with his book of our dark ages in his pocket, was silent as we went on our way. I asked him if he would not be weary on the morrow, losing his sleep in this manner, reading ancient history by street-lamps when he ought to be sleeping.

"Of course, you would think that," he said, compassionately. "Coming from a world where you turned children like myself out in the bread-markets just when their minds were awakening. They had to sleep, those brothers of mine, when they did not desire to, but must from fatigue, and to awaken when they desired to sleep, but must awaken, because they were really *men,* economically, and yet children, because they had immature minds. No. I shall not be weary. If I am, I shall choose to sleep, till quite refreshed.

"You—you do not work at all then?" I inquired.

He was half a head taller than myself.

"I am learning my trade," he said. "That takes an hour a day. For the rest, I am *growing.* Surely you do not expect me to be producing before I have done growing?"

"But—do you find you can settle down to it later?" I asked, haltingly. "Do not look so horrified! I am simply voicing a very common platitude which our Uprogressives held to be a basic truth."

"Certainly I would never have been able to settle *down* to lives such as you lead—after developing," he admitted. "But it is a great joy here to do what would be claimed from us as soon as we had finished growing, even if we were selfish enough to wish to be reared at the expense of society and put nothing back into it.

"There is a probation period in which, if we like, we can choose to work half an hour. This is after we have done growing. Most of us decide to see the world first, and so generally start working as you call it—living as we call it—in some other country."

I stood transfixed.

"But—you have been reared in your own," I gasped.

He glanced at me with puzzled eyes.

"Oh. I remember. But even in your world you sent citizens out of your country—often when there was no work for them," he said. "Don't you know? We look on the whole world as our country. Really, this island is only a province, as you would have called it. You used to be so proud of your provincialism. You called it nationalism, then."

"Then—"

"Your Empires, as you call them, were nothing more than organised Exchanges for cheap labour," he said. "There is only one country—the world."

I turned eagerly to him.

At last there was some progress I could claim where our world had made a step towards this.

"Irrespective of classes?" I asked. "We began that. We had leaders who said class warfare was no good—"

"You mean these leaders asked the weaponless masses to trust the class that had shot them down in cold blood, starved their most helpless in cold blood, and had compelled them to amalgamate even to keep what crumbs they had—by having unions of workmen against unions of the commercial tyrants?"

"Yes," I said, rather staggered by his sudden warmth. "We thought the spirit of Love—"

His clear boyish laughter pealed out into the night.

"How could you have the spirit of Love when there were classes?" he asked. "Behold! I and my brother are equals. 'I accept nothing he cannot accept on the same terms'. You understand. That is from one of your poets.

"How can the slave love the tyrant? How can the robbed love the robber? How shall the trampled love the foot that tramples it—and not go deeper into the mire? But you did—(history proves it) always begin at the wrong end. Classes had to be abolished before the masses could remove their barricades of defence. And classes were abolished not by the meek and the mystical, but by the *Great Indignant* and the simple, who saw that the foundation of society was wrong."

I paused, plucking his sleeve.

"Then the whole lot was removed?" I asked.

"Do you see any of it *left*?" he asked, gently.

Certainly I did not.

"It was, then, attacked from the foundations?" I asked.

He smiled.

"There were only the foundations left—because you allowed it to destroy itself. The first ponderous roof of it fell off during your war to end war. The storm winds, and the sweeping winter rains, and your struggles within it, did the rest. Finally, when you saw *how little* was left, you decided it was not worth keeping."

"Brother," I asked, "what did they do?"

"They organised the banks, and left the money-grubbers with no more than any other person. They organised the industries, and gave them a task.

"Where the manufacturer was too stupid to do more than get repeat orders—because he could not work out the cost of production for new orders, they got those who could to take his place. *Sometimes the office boy did well enough..* They made statutes against inventors of diabolical machines and gases.

"They abolished the Capitalist Press as unnecessary, since there were no Capitalists to represent. They absorbed the unemployed, the wireless stations became international, for the use of the dominant class, the workers of the earth, who now controlled their destinies. A second Genesis began. Capitalism had fallen.

"It had almost destroyed the workers with itself—by Evolution! It almost had! If the soldiers had all been middle class, it might have done so. But they weren't! They couldn't be used to gas and bomb their own people."

Suddenly I saw the error which had come down in history—an error which had been possible only because they had not quite realised how barbarous we were.

"Boy," I said, triumphantly. "Your history books have one mistake. They *did* gas their own cities! It was to stop what we called Revolutions! But they could not proceed. It was beyond human nature to go on from city to city, when Revolution was seething the world over. The gas-droppers turned 'renegade' reactionary. They swung round to Progress."

He stared at me, bewildered.

"You mean your Governments, before being beaten by mass demands, would employ gas-droppers to drop gas on the whole peoples of their capital cities?" he asked.

"I believe they would," I admitted, sorrowfully.

He drew a long, shuddering breath.

"And that was Private Property!" he said. "And you thought to beat it by loving its agents. See! Let us think of something nobler. This is the Avenue of our greatest."

I had been oblivious of all about me.

But now I saw trees, and amongst the trees a long, double line of statues, men and women, most lifelike in their natural attitudes, all speaking of vigour and action.

"Our dead," said the boy. You would have called them heroes. We know they were only humanity—at its highest—yet."

It was, indeed, a remarkable avenue down which I walked with the boy. The chief thing I noticed in the faces of all these personalities in stone was that whilst each one showed in its expression a strong courage to resist dominance, there was none of that dominating pugnacity which all our battlers against Unprogression get—some quite early, others later, accordingly as their struggles developed it.

The brilliance of the night diffused about these figures enabled me to notice every characteristic, as in broad daylight. Varied as those characteristics were, they had that one likeness in common, a gentleness that still had nothing of wavering compromise in its calm, an aggressive strength.

Some of the faces were grave, some smiling, some appeared dreamy, some quickly observant. They revealed various moods and attributes of mind, but all had that lack of dominance and pugnacity, sign of the love of power.

To walk down that white road, where their shadows fell ghostlike and tender, the tremor of shaking leaf-shadows about them, was almost to expect them to step down, disdainful and shuddering, from the pedestals on which they had been placed.

"Who was he?" I asked of the boy.

We stood before the figure of a man upon whose shoulders a large stone dog appeared to have been arrested in the act of leaping up to lick his cheek. So natural, so startlingly natural, were these two figures of man and dog, one half expected to hear the man say, caressingly, "Quite enough hero-worship, my friend. I am not half you think I am!"

The boy appeared to struggle with some emotion before replying.

"He was my father," he said, simply. "His name was Shallon."

"Then these—" I began, and paused.

His handsome boyish face was working.

"Who carved it?" I asked. "It is wonderful."

"This is the avenue of the Progressives, leader after leader, who have gone down in our age, fighting the Autocracy of Intellectual Dominance," said the boy, suddenly calm and controlled again. "He was rather what your world will have called a humorist. He carved that statue himself, ready to join the rest, and presented it to the Unprogressive party.

"He took a great deal of pains to get the dog true to life. More than he took to do justice to himself. *He had no vanity.*"

"But why do they *die*?" I asked. "They are not imprisoned, shot, or starved—as with us?"

"You will see!" said the boy, mysteriously. "In your world they were the weak—the unfit, often the greatest. In our world they are the strong—who resist till they perish!"

I touched his sleeve.

"Sarband?" I asked, swiftly.

"Sarband is leader now," said the boy.

"Yes, I know. *Will* he die?"

The boy raised a radiant face.

"Before ceasing to resist them—yes," he answered.

"But, who are they—these demons who have killed these god-like people."

"Hush!" said the boy, imperiously. "We do not kneel to our ancestors. At least—the Progressives don't."

"But, who are they?" I beseeched him. "And why don't *they* die? They struggle, too. Why don't they die?"

"Because," said the boy, "they are less sensitive. Was that not the hall-mark of your Unprogressives, too? Did not the greatest of your world all perish most quickly?

"Did they not often go mad? Were not the lives of your greatest teachers and poets tragedies? They do not go mad or commit suicide here. They pour out their vigour to the last ounce, and die, unbroken of mind, but spent of life-force. *That is all.*"

The life-like forms about me seemed to breathe very gently "That is all."

I looked at them, suddenly, my heart oppressed with horrible suffering that they should have passed.

"Let us go!" I breathed.

The boy looked at me, understandingly.

"Yes. That is how all Unprogressives feel when they stand here," he said, compassionately. "Youth walks down here and decides to join them. Those who shrink, thinking of the cost, become philosophers, which is the only way of escape from joining one party or the other."

We walked on.

We had turned into a road nobler than any I had yet seen.

Before us loomed a mighty building, built in no period that I could classify, for all my poring over Ruskin's 'Stones of Venice'. Its style had neither the lumbering heaviness of the Norman, nor the delicate beauty of the Gothic. But it had a great dome, which reminded me vaguely of St. Peter's as I had seen it in engravings. There the likeness ended. It was architecture which might have sprung up out of the liberated genius of a new race, wild with a sense of its own freedom. We passed through a gateway.

"Do I take off my hat?" I asked. "Do I kneel?"

"They would turn you out as a heathen," said the boy, smiling gently. "Have I not told you, we do not worship our ancestors, and this temple is only the memorial of their struggles."

I walked after the boy, and, with much difficulty, refrained from taking off my hat. Then I saw a sight which made me forget that *our* tradition was to crawl into our places of the great like worms born to the dust!

Trooping down the long corridor was a procession of Youth, which might have stepped, life-size, from a frame holding Crane's imagery of the buoyant joy and beauty of adolescence.

I realised that perhaps the artist had heard the voices of these delightful spirits, calling down 'some alley of the wind', 'Draw us, dear Brother! Draw us! That your mean and dingy world may know what Springtime will be—when your Dreams come true'. They walked like young aristocrats who had never had need to ask where what they took from society came from. Their free, gay, noble bodies, unbent by toil before they had done growing, shouted aloud against the lie we had believed—that we are born in corruption.

They were proud with the pride that had never been brow-beaten besides the wheel, in the dark of the pits; or bowed to tear the clods of earth till they grew like them. They had grown, just grown.

They had fulfilled their duty in growing. They had also fulfilled their birth. They had taken all, without fear of the morrow. They would give all, without fear of tomorrow. They were fit to live—and die.

I flattened myself against the wall to let them pass. Young Shallon stood with me.

A girl of fourteen, with raven black hair, eyes wild enough for a young poet's, of the untamed variety, swept me with her robe, upholding a banner of azure and silver, strange words scrolled upon it.

I plucked Shallon's sleeve.

"The words are," said Shallon, "Youth Makes New Worlds."

"These are—?"

"The Progressives," Shallon told me.

"You mean, they follow Sarband?"

He looked at me with puzzled eyes.

"Youth follows no one," he said, "but its dreams."

"Then Sarband?"

"Expresses their clamour for the dawn," he said.

"But these are quite young people," I told him. "You said you were immature."

"So I am," he admitted, candidly. "But these are not. In your world they would have rushed me to work, and I *never* should have grown mature, or I should have become precocious, and forgotten I was even young."

I winced.

I was one of this unhappy type.

Their garments swept by me like white, beating wings. Suddenly—the raven-haired girl started it—they were singing. Their voices eddied through the corridor, the surging song of Youth, which will not be denied.

A youth, whose pale complexion reminded me of Messeia, had come to stand beside us. Perhaps he was watching for someone. I saw his eyes twinkle as a tall girl, fair, with blue eyes, deep eyes like summer lightning, hove into sight—a billow in the sea of Youth. He had something in his hand. A quick movement and it was on her back. Shallon looked at me and smiled.

"What is it?" I asked.

"It says," he said, "'I am Unprogressive'."

Someone most have told the tall girl of her label. She hurriedly pushed the strings of the banner she was holding into other hands, and came upon us.

"Who pinned that on me?" she asked.

Though she spoke in her own tongue, I knew she said that. Her eyes flashed.

"I did," said the youth.

I knew he said that.

"He is an Unprogressive," whispered Shallon to me.

The tall girl took the youth by the shoulders. They stared at each other—antagonists.

"Unprogressive, am I?"

That was what her flashing eyes asked.

"You ought to belong to the Conservative Party," said the youth. "Prove that you are Progressive." I knew he challenged her for proof.

She stared at him, nonplussed for any proof that she could give him. The swift fire perished in her eyes. Then, very gravely, very calmly, with nothing in the action that related it in any way to any such action I had ever seen in our world, swiftly as thought can travel from brain to lips, she kissed him on the cheek, turned triumphantly, waving her hand at him, and ran after her companions.

The youth rubbed his cheek as though he had been struck.

He made a half-angry dart towards her, and then, confused, and perhaps for a moment bitter, turned to go, as though he stood in a place where he had been worsted.

"Brother," said Shallon, playfully, "she has left the label with you."

The youth stared down at himself.

There, right across his broad chest, it was—"I am Unprogressive."

He crumpled it up in his hand, and stood, oblivious of us, as one thinking out some knotty point. She had gone on her way, forgetting that moment, save as a triumph over her own unprogressive bitterness. The rose was hers. She had left him the thorn. And in all this curious, yet wholly human drama, sex had had nothing to do with that lightning bit of action and reaction.

They had not picked up their ideas of sex in gutters and factory alleys.

"Where are they going?" I asked young Shallon.

"Those young ones who passed?" he asked. "To their homes. They will probably sing in the Red Square and startle all the doves into flight. Brother! I wish to hear them, and see the wings of the doves gleam like silver."

Then he turned back.

"You would rather I stayed with you?" he asked.

I looked into his face, where the desire to see the doves fly up, and the desire to stay with a poor Unprogressive struggled.

"I will stay with you," he said.

Quite suddenly I could not accept the sacrifice, though I had never seen doves fly up, wings silver-gleaming, at two in the morning, in my growing days. Instead I had seen only dark winter dawns, huddled ghosts skipping after work, hurrying, worrying, whilst the whistles screamed.

"What is your other name?" I asked, irrelevantly.

"Peter."

"Peter, go and see the doves and hear the singing of your comrades. It would hurt me to think you missed it."

His face was a child's, flashing silent thanks.

"Who knows? You may become a Progressive yet," he said, with optimism. I laughed shortly.

"That would be to die, would it not?" I asked. "I think I still prefer Binkers Court."

He did not understand half my gibberish. I continued my way along the corridor, going alone to see Sarband fight.

Chapter 5

So long as I had had Peter Shallon, child though he was for all his growth, with me, I had not felt my insular loneliness—the curse of my life.

I gazed about me, overwhelmed by the beauty of the corridor along which I walked.

Suddenly a door opened, and a man, who looked about the age of our old-age pensioners, stood facing me.

"Which Party?" he asked.

I saw he was the keeper of the gate. He had no official manner, no pompousness. He was smoking a pipe.

"Hanged if I know," I told him, absurdly confused.

His eyes widened.

Then he said, "Of course, you don't. You're one of the Pilgrims from the Middle Ages, when the world was divided into classes and countries. Take this ticket. They'll pass you along. I made one out, lest you came along."

I stared at the ticket.

Upon it were printed these words:

"No definite opinion as yet. In process of evolving. Sit him amongst the philosophers."

I blundered through the gateway he pointed me out.

A minute later I stood bewildered by a sea of faces, tier upon tier, rising from floor to ceiling of a vast chamber.

A great platform, on which stood two figures, ran across the centre of the chamber.

Through the dome light streamed down on the two figures. Sarband was one. But this was not the Sarband I had seen 'justifying his animal existence' with joy. This was not the Sarband who, like a schoolboy, had encouraged Arlene to cross swords with me.

I think I should have stood staring at him a long time, but someone arose, looked at my card, and led me to sit among the philosophers.

Then a great bell rang. I saw the two figures on the platform stiffen, but no murmur, no shouts of encouragement or hero-worship broke from the vast audience.

I realised that these, the gladiators of Unprogressives and Progressives, were fighting to win each other's adherents, during these conflicts of mind. The audience was an audience of *thinkers*, not cheerers. I realised what Sarband had meant now, when he spoke of mind-forces being greater than brute force.

They were fighting with invisible swords, winning each other's followers—until either intellectual dominance broke down, as Capitalism had broken down, or won a new lease of life.

What they said I only read afterwards, in notes, which one of the philosophers transcribed into our tongue.

The annoyance of not understanding was swept away by the fascination of the strange proceeding. Sarband was the calmer of the two. His adversary had more fire. He was an orator.

Once or twice his gestures reminded me of some of our most electric statesmen, who could play on the emotions of their listeners at will. But at such times he was interrupted. A bell tolled a warning note. A man in a splendid robe, called a marker, slashed two marks against him on a great board, in full view of the audience. Those he represented neither hooted nor hissed. They sat quietly, watching him as though in the silence they were pouring out the whole vitalities of their minds to be his asset. I saw that Sarband had one such mark against him.

They went on until my sitting position, and the sense of being caught in an electrical atmosphere I did not understand, though realising its force, made me feel faint and giddy. The ruddy colour was fading from the cheeks of Sarband's opponent, yet he seemed to wait, as one who said to himself, "I can tire him out."

Sarband was a little paler, too. Every time he struck a blow which went home, as the intenser silence about registered, he seemed to have gained force mentally and lost it physically. Suddenly the truth rushed at me—the amazing truth of what was happening. Sarband was suffering more with every triumph than the man he was trying to defeat. Yet he went on dealing blow after blow (suffering because this new bureaucracy had to be broken down) until he reeled backwards, half collapsing, against the board where his two bad marks were set down, against his opponent's dozen. It appeared to be the signal for something to be done.

"Now," I said to myself, "they will go home."

The audience rose to its feet.

A bugler shivered a silver-clear sound through the silence, followed by a stir of fifty thousand people rising to their feet.

Then, out of the almost equally-divided audience, a movement began without any chaos. I saw at least three thousand people cross the open space between the Parties and join the Progressives. There was no hooting. The Unprogressives sat proudly. They would fight to the last ditch against Change. I saw that. But they did not bloodily litter the fields with their enemies' bodies. Perfect order remained. Only there were three thousand more Progressives. The scales had turned.

"Now they will go home," I thought.

To my consternation the audience sat down.

A tall figure, in a robe, approached Sarband and asked him something. He shook his head. He had refused truce. They began again. I sat till the faintness overcame me again like a flood. One of the philosophers saw my plight. He led me out into the open air.

"Is this place more than a temple?" I asked. "What is it? Why do they fight there? And how long will it last?"

The dawn was breaking over the city. Glory and beauty and nobility of man's conceptions in stone rose around the white-bearded philosopher and myself. We had paused on a bridge.

"You called them Parliaments," said the philosopher. "Then we called them Soviets. What they will be called in time to come, Evolution only knows."

I gripped his arm.

"Do the people leave their work to go and watch these fights?"

He stared at me.

"Certainly. It is their business."

"But, doesn't it dislocate things?"

"Somewhat, just now; but work is not the end of our lives," he said. "With you, it was, because you starved or half-starved if debarred from it. It was food you were after. You even had to pretend to be miserable when you could not work ten hours a day."

I looked at the clear river, the smokeless air.

"One would think people had everything here," I said.

"Did you ever find human nature satisfied?" asked the philosopher.

I was compelled to say "No".

"If it had been," said he, "you and I would have been living in caves now, eating our enemies' carcasses."

"Then—" I gasped.

"Certainly we have travelled from the slime to where we are—*because we were not satisfied, never have been satisfied, and never will be.* Brother, I leave you."

He went without ceremony. I turned, to find my way back to Sarband's house. I passed a great square, and paused. A flight of doves rose in the morning sky, wings agleam. This must be—yes. It was the Red Square.

And in the centre, with a gasp of pleased surprise, I saw two statues—and recognised them. I approached their base and stared upwards at them. The rising sun was at their backs. Their heads stood against the pearly white of a cloud, pouring out 'boiling gold'. They had got him well, the genial, mocking smile, ancient dress, the provocative eyes, half-closed. I looked at the other. It was an earnest face, almost simple in its appeal. There was no smile on it. I approached the base of this. I read, in the ancient tongue which we had murdered in Binkers Court:—

John Galsworthy, of the Age of Destruction.
He opened men's eyes with tears.

I walked round to the other.

Underneath were these words:—

Bernard Shaw, of the Age of Destruction.
He laughed before the mouldy
tapestry of 'Civilisation',
and laughing—paused.
The mad critics called him a cynic.

I stood in the square gazing at the statues, then slowly I turned to the world of unfamiliar faces. A child of eight, in a garden, who recognised me as the much-discussed pilgrim from the Age of Destruction and War, came to my rescue, and hailed one of the winged cars for me.

The car ran along the wide road and set me down at the door of Sarband's house. I knocked on the door, and walked in.

Then I came to the door of the room where we had supped the night before. The door was slightly ajar. I saw the trailing richness of Arlene's dress along a space of polished floor, and, drawn by an irresistible impulse, crept in, and saw that she was asleep.

I slunk back to the doorway, then paused, on another irresistible impulse. After all, she was asleep. She would not know that I stood here, looking at her, so that never, never after my return could I forget what free womanhood looked like. It was too great a temptation. I turned back irresolutely.

Beethoven had looked at some highfalutin' dame, and beaten out the splendid passion of his rejection into sonorous glory, thundering harmonies, and chorus of courage and beauty on the poor shifting sands of time. Some such excuses are made for my lingering.

"Sarband?" murmured Arlene.

Temptation assailed me—dark and unprogressive. The mocking irony of it! Yet—why—on a hairbreadth chance in the evolution of the race should I be a loveless denizen of an earthly hell, waiting outside Labour Exchanges in the rain, 'signing on' and 'signing off', bent of body and bewildered of soul, drifting along to ignominious death, and Sarband, just because he was Sarband, born better, have as his this creature free as the winds and beautiful as the warmth of the sun?

My soul cursed against the injustice of it. Why had two mad mortals, forgetting that they were creating a life to its torment, in some dingy, evil-aired alley of the poverty-stricken, have begotten me? 'Children of chance'. Sarband's words came back to my memory. They burned me. Yet it was true.

Picture our world if the bulk of its denizens suddenly thought "Hang chance. I want to do that, so I'll do it." Picture it, oh, reader of these Chronicles, pitying, condemning, shuddering perhaps at this black temptation which I have the courage to confess. Think, in extenuation, perhaps of the things you would do. What bonds flying away, if you can choose. Remember the those who *did choose* left marks on history, from Napoleon to Thomas More, from Joan of Arc to Lucrezia Borgia.

Perhaps you will tumble upon the revelation that dawned on me, as I stood struggling with myself, desperate and disloyal, and, I must be fair, humble and shrinking from this unexpected revelation of myself. The sweat broke out on me know. I realised what impulses lay buried in me—generations of brute-force, of covetousness, of ignorance, of shame, of slavery, of superstition.

My brain reeled in my effort to choose.

Weak words to convey my torment.

Even yet I can scarcely analyse what guilt was in my heart, what tragic hunger, what pitiful cry to grasp, even by force, something which I knew was not mine. At last, I could bear it no more. Shaking like an aspen, sweat on my brow, I touched the sleeping freewoman on the arm.

"Madam," I told her. "Wake up! Wake up, madam! You are in danger—I know not of what—but certainly in danger."

Arlene sat up, still heavy-lidded with sleep.

"What did you say, pilgrim?" she asked.

I stammered that I had just got back, and that it was a beautiful morning.

With this trite and terrible lie upon my lips, I commenced my first day in this new social order. Let my courage stand equal with my guilt. Yes. My guilt. For I learned enough of simple honesty from the denizens in this strange world to know that murder, in thought, adultery, in thought, theft, in thought, prostitution of all kinds, in thought, is the shadow which eventually becomes concrete reality.

But, having come from a society so corrupt and dual as ours, it did not seem to me, then, on my first morning in the other society, very terrible that, after coveting Sarband's wife, I should be devoutly glad that though my voice had awakened her she did not know how close she had been to tragedy. I was not found out. Therefore I could be calm. With loathing such as you, a child of chance, *drifting* into danger, *drifting* away from it, cannot understand, I write down these base words, the moral and social code of this our world.

Arlene thrust back the curtains, went to the time disc in the wall, and told me, with that delightful stiffness in her way of speaking our ancient tongue, that she would have to leave me to my own devices for some hours.

She opened the windows, and left me. I took up some books from a small table, and enjoyed the engravings, though, like an unlettered child, I could only guess at their meanings. Arlene soon came in again in her working dress—short skirt, short sleeves, in a material strong and rather coarse, but of exquisite blue colour. She went to the time disc several times.

"You will be hungry," said Arlene. She went out, and came back with a great basket of hot food, which she thrust into a cupboard which I rightly suspected to be on the principle of a vacuum flask. She spread the cloth in the little shell-pink room, whilst I found my way to the bath-room. There was a rug of cork, with the old word 'Bath' on it, midway in the room. The air was genially warm.

I pulled up the bath-mat, found a plug sunk in a cavity, pulled it, and found I had lifted the lid from the bath. I propped it against the wall, took off my garments, and descended by steps into water just tepid. Brushes there were. But no signs of soap. I had upon my body the dirt of Binkers Court.

I got a sudden passionate regard for my long-neglected body. Where the devil was the soap? Then I saw streaming down into the water little currents of air, partly at the sides of the bath. I understood. Oxygen! They had dispensed with 'pure' soaps. I felt to come up those steps a new man.

Then we sat down to breakfast and looked about for a newspaper. I explained myself to Arlene.

"The newspaper, madam," I said. "News-sheet, journal, chronicle of yesterday's happenings. Do you understand?"

She was helping me to a plate of curried rice, eggs, and cheese, all piping hot, and appeared to be thinking.

"Oh! You mean the documents you had turned out in your world, to keep you from thinking," she said. "Without which you could form no opinions! I remember."

"But how do you know what happens in the world?" I asked.

"The basic facts are wirelessed," said Arlene. "Just the bare facts. How could you have trained experts to dish up comment with facts, and foist their opinions on you, without losing your thinking capacity?"

"But, when there is a murder?" I asked.

Arlene stared at me.

"When a man kills a man, or a woman, or a child, or whole families, or—all these things, you know," I stammered. "How do people like missing their morning papers then? And the trial, and the incidents. Surely, they won't like missing that.

"In our world they used to stay outside prisons all night, praying on the flags, waiting to read the death notice. If the murderer got off, even on a legal slip, they carried him shoulder high. If he didn't, they were glad he got hanged, though some of them did pray for the poor soul ripped out of his quaking body. Our people would never have tolerated a newspaperless world."

She stared at me with a look of repugnance.

"Are there any murders here?" I asked.

"We had one a quarter of a century ago," she said, suddenly, in a sad voice. "There were two men and one woman. They got in a knot, somehow. Tragedy was the knife that cut the knot. We altered one of our unwritten laws afterwards. But it was too late—for them, at least."

"You hanged him!" I exclaimed.

She shrank from me.

"*Who* would hang him?" she asked.

"But society—"

She looked at me.

"He did not need hanging," she said. "Do you think a man could endure to live in our world with another man's blood on his hands? No! The poor tortured human chose to perish. Some day I will take you to the rock where he willed to die. That was the last murder—we hope the very last."

Just then there came a great knocking on the door. Arlene jumped up. She had turned pale. I realised that knocking on the doors here was a way of hinting at unfortunate news.

"Shall I answer the door?" I asked Arlene.

Her pallor and the darkening of her eyes heralded the human gathering itself together to front some disaster. In our world it usually heralded it by our fronting it, and collapsing under it, as most of even our greatest literature proves.

"Certainly not," she told me.

Whatever terror of apprehension she had felt, and I knew it had been a terror beyond my comprehension, the moment of flinching was passed. Faint colour had flowed back into her cheeks. Perhaps she paused a few seconds to get herself in hand completely Then she walked down the passage. I heard the door open, and the familiar voices of Mr. Sparkins and Mrs. Biers. Not understanding the terror they had accidently caused Arlene, they were blundering through explanations which made me smile.

Mrs. Biers, like Eve, took the precedent in 'moral' courage.

"We've been lorst," said Mrs. Biers. "Then we missed the larst bus, well—one of them thingemjigs with wings."

"They run all night," Arlene told her, "when the Assembly holds."

Her eyes reproached Mrs. Biers, not for staying out all night, but for these idiotic lies.

"Now, Mr. Sparkins," said Mrs. Biers, almost weeping, "you takes your share in this. You're a man. Ain't it your fault we missed that thingemjig an' got ourselves in this undemising perdition?"

"Nothing of the kind. Didn't you say—" began Mr. Sparkins, purple and embarrassed. I paraphrased Madame Roland's famous apostrophe 'O morality, what hypocrisy is spoken in thy name!' I went to the window, overcome with something between laughter and shame. Arlene's eyes gazed at me when I came away, as though asking, "Are all your men and women like this?"

Then she gave them breakfast.

I went back to mine, and finished my meal.

"Please don't worry," I heard Arlene tell Mrs. Biers. "It's nothing to do with me. Your behaviour is your own responsibility."

The words were delicately stressed, but Mrs. Biers did not notice it. I did. Arlene was recognising that whereas their ideas of liberty were based on irresponsibility, these in this world were only justified by responsibility.

Mrs. Biers brightened.

"Live and let live," she said, cheerily.

As Arlene poured out her cup of tea, it was almost impossible to believe that only a few ages of development divided them from each other. Yet I recalled a photograph Mrs. Biers had shown me of herself at fifteen, saying "*Would* you ever think that was *me*, Mr. Sniggins!" It was the same human nature. The circumstances that had carved it were different. Nay, thrust Arlene down into the devil's stew of Binkers Court, bang the lid on, sit Authority on the top, in the name of God and Law and King and how many short years would it take to reduce her to something perhaps worse than Mrs. Biers? Did not Shakespeare say lilies that festered stink worse than weeds? I shuddered to think of what Arlene would have become in Binkers Court. Vaguely, I *knew*.

In the simple blue frock that was her workaday dress (its cut suggested an artist's hand, though), she ministered to Mrs. Biers, who drank her tea noisily, and shot embarrassment through that rogue Sparkins, who was trying to cover up his all-night wandering by saying they had been looking for a church.

"That is a lie, Mr. Sparkins," she told him, simply. "Please do stop."

Mr. Sparkins put his cup down.

"Do you mean to say, madam." he asked, startled out of himself, "that you say here all you mean?"

"Exactly," she told him, smiling.

"But, madam, in our world we—er—ahem! It would have got us into terrible predicaments."

"It would soon have turned your world upside down," Arlene agreed.

"Yes. That's it," Mr. Sparkins said. "And, of course, we couldn't allow that."

"But it would then have been right end up," she teased him.

"Don't spoil this delicious breakfast," said Mr. Sparkins. "I compliment you, madam. You can cook."

Arlene laughed.

"I didn't," she disavowed. "All that has come from a communal kitchen."

"Preposterous!"

"No. Correct," said Arlene. "Well, I shall have to leave you. I must justify my existence. Edmund, if you like to come down to the mill you ask for Arlene Geyper's mill. Anyone will tell you. If Jacqueline Shallon comes, send her down to me, and ask her to bring me *any news*. She will understand.'

I promised, but told her I felt sleepy.

"If she comes, she will be here in one hour." Arlene told me.

I said I could keep awake until then. She left us without any further ceremony. After breakfast Mr. Sparkins went into the garden, sat on a seat, covered his head with his handkerchief, mourned the absence of the 'Daily Mail', and slept. Mrs. Biers went into one of the rooms, played 'God Save the King!' on the piano with one finger, and then I heard her no more. She must have fallen asleep.

Sleep overpowered me, also. But by the time disc I waited almost an hour. Then I sank down upon a great settee, and slept, feeling as I dropped into slumber that gentle lifting of the tide which had been the beginning of all this.

Sleeping tranquilly, happily forgetful that I was to return to my own world, blissfully unconcerned about Sarband and his fight for liberties, I felt, at intervals, or thought I felt, whilst sleeping, the gentle lifting of that same tide which had swept me from that hell-hole of Binkers Court. Suddenly, something soft touched my face. I started up. Why did memories of my old life rush back, like furies, so that I thought I was in Binkers Court, and old Sparkins had called for the rent!

"Damn you!" I shouted. "I haven't got it. How the hell can I give you what I haven't got?"

Then I saw that I was staring into the face of a little girl of seven. She had been bending over me, and her hazel-brown curls has swept the pilgrim's cheek. That would be Jacqueline.

"Pilgrim," she said, in 'English' stiffer than Arlene's, "what does hell mean?"

We surveyed each other in unspeakable curiosity.

"Charming little heathen," I answered her, "your religious education has been gravely neglected. Meanwhile, you are to go to the mill."

She was dancing about the room like a yellow butterfly.

All the time I got ready she was singing and dancing. "I am to go to Arlene's mill, Arlene's mill."

"Now," I said, "we will go."

Joyously, she skipped after me.

I recalled that my mother had gone to a *mill* at eight, and the whimsical thought struck me that if every grown man would avenge such facts, social evolution would soon be speeded up as fast as Militarism. The little creature slipped her hand into mine. A child's hand! I remembered that little Jimmy of the large eyes, who studied life amongst the vegetables and mineral matter on the stairs of Binkers Court, would have missed me. A child's hand! Yet, children's little white hands had broken strikes, sometimes women's hearts and men's brains! Jacqueline stared up into my face, evidently unaccustomed to see such shadows as no doubt clouded mine.

"What is hell?" she asked, imperiously.

"Nothing," I told her.

"Can't be nothing—if it's got a name," she said.

"It is," I told her. "It is Nothing. A conception of fear, Jacqueline, with a federation of tyrants behind it, and generations of slaves under their feet, whipped with a long whip, Jacqueline!"

"Was it something they pretended—to play bogies when children were iresome?"

"'Zackly, Jacqueline," I said. "You've got the whole history of man in a nutshell there."

She ran away from me suddenly, dancing down the path.

"Messeia! Messeia!" She shrilled with delight.

With head flung back, with her lips partly open, as though she would draw all the fresh beauty of morning into her very soul, I saw Messeia. She opened her arms, and Jacqueline ran into them. It was a dream of Beauty and Childhood in a field of barley for the feeding of all men.

"You are going to the mill?" asked Messeia.

She looked a little sleepy, but not jaded.

I nodded.

"Tell Arlene Sarband has won six thousand, all told," said Messeia.

"They are at it yet?" I asked.

Messeia nodded at—like one who did not trust herself to speak.

"But, when will it be over?" I asked.

Messeia's eyebrows raised themselves ever so slightly. She looked perturbed.

"When Sarband can't fight any longer," she says.

I stared.

"You mean—he will go on till he drops?"

"He won't drop in a public assembly," Messeia told me. "He'll walk out, somehow, and crawl home, like a wounded thing, and then Arlene will brood over him, and give him rest, and then the fight will begin again. The call is called by the Opposition. That is, by us. The signal for cessation is always given by the Progressives, and Sarband has no pity on us!"

I stared at her.

"No pity on himself, you mean?"

"It's the same thing—to those who love him," she said, suddenly, wildly. "Pilgrim! Have you ever loved?"

"Several times," I answered, promptly.

She surveyed to me with scorn.

"You did everything in instalments," she scoffed.

I laughed. Then, seeing that she was distressed, I touched her on the arm.

"If you don't want Sarband to die, why not leave the Unprogressives, join his party, and take the same risks?" I asked.

"Because I can't see as he sees. I don't see the need for change. When we study your Middle Ages, we see ample reason for contented and gradual progress. Why should men fight till they die to bring it a day nearer?"

I gripped her suddenly by the arm.

"Messeia," I called her, "you speak another tongue, but your words are exactly those of our hinderers of progress. If all of us had said that, humanity would have extinguished humanity by allowing Militarism, reduced to a science, to wipe the lot off the face of the earth. Messeia! Our Unprogression and yours is one. It killed our best. It is killing your best. Now. What will you do?"

Out of my mouth, even out of the mouth of an insignificant dweller in Binkers Court, I had spoken what I could never recall—Truth. I saw its shaft strike home. I saw her try to ward it off. I realised the force of the idea. She stood like one rooted to the ground, statue-pale, *cornered*.

I knew that in that moment Messeia had found her soul. Dimly, I think I foresaw how this attraction Sarband had for her would work out. Dimly, I believe I foresaw even that hour when, to the flare of torches on the sea-beaten shore, I should see a boat drifting out which carried two—who had never drifted, but had been until that hour the Children of Choice. And, even had I believed otherwise, I should now have known that all the storms in the human heart are all the hells there are, and that even they are the tides on which we climb nearer to peace, to the white shining peace of those who have fought well, leaving the race fresh for a nobler struggle.

"Yet, Freedom, yet, thy banner, torn but flying,
Streams like a thunder-cloud against the wind."—Byron.

As I followed Jacqueline along the field-path the reality of what I had done rushed at me. The possibility that I had flung Messeia to 'go down' in this peculiar battling whose forces I did not fully understand became a probability. I realised that life was a sweet, glorious, precious thing here. Yet, by a chance word or two I had hurled Messeia into a struggling current which might end in her death.

"Stay!" I shouted.

My voice travelled over the fields of barley, echoing through the sunny silences. Messeia paused, turning back to meet me half-way.

"Well?" she asked.

"I take back what I said," I stammered.

She regarded me with smiling eyes.

"How can you do that?" she asked, with staggering simplicity.

"Oh, but—I apologise," I answered. "There! Forget what I said. Forget it! Forgive it!"

"But why should you apologise for speaking the truth?" she asked. "What is spoken, is spoken. What is done, is done. What are you afraid of?"

Quite suddenly this magnificent courage, this electrical beauty of mind and body, which was Messeia, made me whimper inwardly at having been the puny destiny sent to end it even by an hour's time.

"Do you not love life?" I pleaded.

She looked from me at the green, weaving heads of barley, at the blue sky, the sweet-scented earth, at the sun, rising into the broad morning.

"As you could not," she told me.

"Then, why not go on living?" I asked.

"Because living with us includes more than the mere mechanical necessity to go on breathing," she informed me. "Don't worry, Edmund. If you stay here long enough you may see me in the Avenue of the Dead, staring in effigy at Sarband's effigy, till my stone eyes fall into dust."

To a puny individual reared with the fear of death as the greatest tragedy which could befall us, these words, spoken with smiling lips, whilst the eyes of the speaker were earnest and shining, sent a shiver down my spine.

"Well, I suppose your life is your own," I said, lamely. Those tears, ever my curse, had dimmed my eyes.

"It certainly *is*," Messeia told me, laughing. "Good morning!"

Smiling and waving good-bye to me once more, she passed. I also passed, catching up with Jacqueline.

We walked half a mile, farther and farther from the city, which we saw afar, a city of dream-towers, columns, and arches, rising in the blue of the unfolding glory of the morning. Suddenly Jacqueline gave a shout.

"Look!" she cried.

Upon the wide space of blue sky flashed like a banner of sheet lightning, that same banner which I had seen as I walked with Venensley to his tower. It drenched the sky in its vivid glory, fading as a rainbow fades.

"The Progressives have won," said Jacqueline. "Arlene will be glad. I'll run on."

She left me. I halted.

I wanted to return to the city, to see them pouring out of the temple, to see how they took their 'victories' and 'defeats' here. But I wanted also to see Arlene's mill. As I went down to the three-storeyed building looming up before me, from which pulsed a slumberous humming sound, I saw again that banner of light flashed triumphantly upon the sky—watched it fade away. Arlene did not see me approach. She was standing on a gallery which ran alongside the top storey. The white dust was on her cap, her dress. Halfway up, suspended by a chain, was a dangling sack of flour, and almost close up to it was a great box, which was being hauled up as the sack descended. She had one finger upon some object I could not see from my position, and had turned, watching the space in the sky where the banner of light had blazed and faded. I held my breath. One false step and she came down—to death. Then she turned to her work again. She looked down, to gauge the space between box and sack.

"Keep clear, Edmund," she called out.

I sprang back.

The sack was lowered gently into the box. The box did not descend. I realised that I was staring at an invention which could clear a load of hay, remove a hundred ash-heaps, or carry up a ton of bricks, as its dimensions were made. And I recalled in a back room of Binkers Tenements, a genial and human inventor who had shown me something similar, saying, sorrowfully, "But I'm damned if I'll sell it. I'll smash it first. It would only cause more unemployment, and that's hell under this system."

"Go inside," called Arlene.

She was going to swing more sacks down into the box.

Realising that she was afraid I would blunder into the way—we often did—I passed through the open doorway into the mill, where a great box was going round and round, and into which I peeped, through a covered opening, seeing the golden wheat being beaten into flour.

"What are you doing, Jacqueline?" I asked.

"Grinding," she said, lifting a flushed face, and tossing her hair out of her eyes. She was pulling a rod in and out of a cavity into the wall.

Suddenly she stopped, as a youth appeared in the doorway.

"Peter!" said Jacqueline.

He greeted her with the superior calm a boy of fifteen has for his little sister. He patted her cheek.

"Arlene!" called Peter. "Come down. Glorious news. Glorious, Arlene!" He spoke his own tongue, and with surprise I realised I was beginning to understand it.

Arlene came down.

"We are going to see the Change in our day," said the son of the dead Shallon. "And, Arlene, the great news! Messeia has joined the Progressives. Isn't it wonderful? They've flashed it over already. Sarband is half crazy about it. I thought he would have kissed her in the public street. But she acted very strangely. She walked away as though she were angry. Isn't it glorious—eight thousand, all told—and Messeia!"

I saw the light and rapture fade from Arlene's face, saw her start quietly, recover—saw the fear that had flashed into her eyes fade away into quiet calm.

"I won't be long, Peter," she said. She went up the ladder, out of our sight. She had gone to her work.

Was not that the same spirit of heroism even we had? In all sorrows, all griefs, all sudden realisations of approaching storms—mundanely to go to our especial task? What she feared I could not tell. I knew it had something to do with Messeia.

Chapter 6

I was burningly eager for Arlene to have finished the 'production' which justified her consumption of the necessaries of life. But I entertained myself with keeping the grinding-machine going, which I found quite easy. Peter Shallon was sitting in the open doorway, reading. Suddenly, he jumped up, pitched the book through the doorway, and yawned.

"I want something to do," he said.

He held out his strong, supple boy's hand for the rod.

We could hear the swishing of the breaking wheat within the box.

"Peter," I told him, "I like grinding. This is the first bit of 'production' I've done which I was dead certain was not going to lead to another war. I claim a pilgrim's rights to justify my existence. You can come to Arlene's mill and grind any old time, when I've returned to the scramble-hole from which I came."

Peter looked at me, and laughed, but went on with the work.

"Are you hungry, pilgrim?" he asked suddenly.

I blushed.

In our world it was manners to say 'No' whether we were or not.

"You see," I explained, "I've been half-fed ever since I was born. I've arrears to make up."

"I wonder what it feels like," said Peter curiously. Oh, reader of these chronicles, if you can realise what it felt like to hear a boy of this happier world express curiosity as to what it felt like to be hungry—if, fresh from the horrors of the world where you are accustomed to read of necessitous school-children going hungry to read of the glories of the British Empire, you had been flung to a world where a schoolboy of fifteen tried vainly to understand the animal-hunger tortures of the age we live in, I think you would understand my feelings.

Peter took me into another room, leaving the machine to continue its work. Then we went out and sat amidst the barley and ate sweet apples. They tasted of the mellow sweetness of the earth. Suddenly he jumped up.

"Sarband!" He exclaimed.

I lay in the edge of the barley field and watched Sarband coming along. I could see the glad look on his face as his gaze rested on the outlines of the mill.

I lifted my gaze to the gallery on which Arlene stood. Again, I saw them gazing at each other with delight, the sun on their faces, the same look chronicled there which I had seen in the glow of a fire. I thought of that terrible conflict I had passed through, in which my better nature had awakened Arlene. But the thought that Sarband would never know appeased my conscience.

Sarband strode past me, then turned and saw me.

"Well, Brother?" was his greeting.

The word smote me like a thousand swords.

But I managed to echo back "Well, Brother?"

I lay down in the barley and sneaked a glance at the open door of the mill. In the golden gleam and gloom of the depths of it I saw them standing, hands clasped in hand, and I heard Sarband's elated voice.

"Messeia has joined us. Messeia! The tide has turned. I feel sure of it. But I never thought it would flood in with Messeia on its crest! Think of it—Messeia!"

I laughed cruelly in my heart.

Arlene was silent.

Behind that silence—that brief silence—there was, to my reading of it, a world of agony.

"You are glad, Arlene?" He asked, suddenly, as though realising she had said nothing.

"Yes. Very glad," she told him.

Sincerity, almost raw in its feeling, throbbed in her voice.

Then I heard: "Sarband, you have forgotten to kiss me."

In the depths of the gloom and gleam of the humming mill I saw him and hated him.

Sarband and Arlene came out into the sunshine.

They walked together between the barley.

I do not know if Arlene realised what Sarband certainly did not. Events were to tell. But the realisation of it was dawning on me.

Sarband was walking blindly towards a chaos in his domestic life. Perhaps, never again, in glow of the shine, or radiance of the sun were they to stand and look at each other as I had seen them look so, so shadowlessly joyful, as on my arrival.

The conditions hundreds of thousands lived under in our world often made such a crash with us 'a blessing in disguise', to save us from something worse. In this world I did realise that it was *tragedy*. Some faint regret I may have felt. After all, one cannot look on two splendid human beings and see them joining up against odds too big for them without regret.

But it also amused me with exactly that same sense of ironic amusement and entertainment with which you read a really good divorce case, conjugal right appeal, maintenance claim, affiliation order, or that first-class passional murder which sent even a hardened hangman half-crazy at having had to be the scapegoat to carry out *your* demands that cold-blooded murder be done, to wipe out hot-blooded murder.

Part II

Foreword

"I speak the pass-word primeval, I give the sign of democracy,

By God! I will accept nothing which all cannot have their counterpart of on the same terms."   -WHITMAN.

Gentle, (or otherwise) and wholly unsuspecting reader of these remarkable, perhaps, to you, foolish chronicles, following them from day to day, wondering whither they are taking you—wondering what ground they are shaking under your feet, what ground they are placing beneath them, even as sometimes you wondered whither your life led you—do not be afraid. For any ground that I shake beneath your feet I will give you ground more secure.

For any hope which I take from you I will give you one more glorious and more irrefutable. For any of the futile excuses you were given by all kinds and conditions of men as to the security of staying where you were, I will give you the grand and natural truths of Nature herself—telling you that you are only insecure by staying where you are. In short, you shall pass with me through all the stages of evolution, doors closing behind us and doors opening before us. Those that open more easily we will pass through, smiling and grateful. Those that are guarded by the guardian demons of Conservatism we will break through, saying gently, "No. Do not check us. Do not make Chaos. Let us pass peacefully. You are not omnipotent. As you were born of the Desires and Dreams of the Past, we are born of the Desires and Dreams of the Present."

Chapter 7

Three months in the house of Sarband had resulted in a strange transformation of the creature who had entered it. I had confessed to Sarband the fact that I had coveted his wife. Still more wonderful, Sarband had not taken me by the collar and pitched me out, but had actually *smiled*—smiled and sat back, saying gently. "And what on earth would you have done with her?" Accept the fact that, despite myself, when he put that pertinent question, I was overwhelmed by a hundred doubts as to what might have been the results, had I managed to take by brute force what was not my own—what could not be my own except as a gift.

"I tell you candidly, Edmund," Sarband had said, "you would never have taken her *alive!*"

Picture the scene if you can—the long room, the curtains mellowing down the sunlight on the polished floor, the great windows open to the scents of the autumnal earth, Arlene's 'rainbow-coloured garden', seen through it, a flame and a glory.

In the centre of that room, doing some hand-carving, myself, with pale, remorseful face bent over the cradle for Jacqueline's doll, hot needles of shame feeling to prick me through and through, and Sarband, just as he had come up out of his workshop, surveying me with wise, tender eyes, easily informing me that his wife would have preferred death to the enforced touch of a slave.

Imagine me staring up with horrified gaze, to hear his calm voice saying,

"Any woman of this society would prefer death to prostitution. That system has never flourished here. In your world it had encroached and flooded its impurities over your very doorstep. By Evolution! You drove each other mad, in the name of Respectability. You treated woman as a commodity.

"Edmund," he continued, looking at me keenly, with that penetration which could read my very thoughts, "you are progressing. You have guessed it. Woman ceased to be a commodity and property when man ceased to be a commodity and property. Poor fools, chained to antagonism against each other by the antagonisms in society, you reviled and railed against each other, not seeing that you stood and fell, or stood and ascended together, indivisible comrades.

"I do not forget that noblest and most heroic of you, men and women alike, would have taken the last crumb you needed to give it to the other.

"I do not deny that even in your Bread-Fights there were untold tales of heroism which would have made the heroisms on battlefields look pale, for, whilst a half-mad man, crazy with the sight of blood and dead bodies and hellish sounds, may flounder impulsively across shell-fire to rescue a comrade, the heroism that could starve slowly, giving up its last crumb, broke more links with the beasts than the blood-maddened soldier—brave as he was.

"But on the whole, taking your average lives, did you not fight each other more vehemently than you fought the conditions of things which made you both less than you were?"

It was true.

I thought of Binkers Court just as I had left it; Mrs. Jones, sitting with the child in her arms, Tom, baffled and worn and desperate, coming in after an all-day's tramp after work, to meet her mother-desperate eyes, which asked silently, "Nothing yet?" I remembered her voice once, drifting to me from their room, poignant, maddened, speaking the thing she knew in heart was not true. She had said "Tom! I'm sure you could get work if you *wanted*." The frail child with the whooping-cough had driven her crazy.

Her reproach had driven Tom crazy. From that hopeless tramp he had returned, and a maddened mother, crazy because she could get no more food till he got dole, had pitched her maddened motherhood against him—her mate. And Tom, his manhood insulted and doubted, had hurled himself at her, pallid with the insult, crying "I'll murder you if you say that again!"

I sat, shuddering, thinking of it all, wondering for the first time how they were faring. I stood up and laid the work I was doing on the table.

"Sarband," I told him, "I realise that men of my development could do nothing with a woman of Arlene's development. I think, when I go back, I will cease to dream of some unattainable ideal. I think I will perhaps find some little mortal who is my equal. I think I realise that Equality is the first law of Love. How long am I to stay here?"

His face grew dim for a moment.

But, perhaps, it was a shadow which suddenly dimmed the room, but through which I still heard the chaffinch singing "Fare-well", a faint, sweet, sad note to glory passing.

"Perhaps," said Sarband, "you will find Arlene. Perhaps, who knows, you have passed her, without seeing her, even in Binkers Court."

I protested vigorously.

To have seen Arlene in Binkers Court would have been like seeing a goddess. I could never have missed her.

"Perhaps," said Sarband, "you will find Arlene as she would have been in Binkers Court. I give you this pledge. Humanity never sets out to Nothingness. There is no dream but we find it, however besmirched, however broken. Edmund, I pledge you to the Arlene of your own society." He opened a bottle of wine. He filled the cup, and drank, and handed the same cup to me.

"This Arlene is mine," he said, "so long as we both shall love. I drink to your Arlene, Edmund, pledging you to remember this toast, promising you that its full meaning shall then be revealed."

Strange scene. The man to whom I had confessed my desire to dishonour him, to dishonour that other self, dearer to him than himself, was drinking my health, wishing me well, telling me that in my own sordid surroundings, was one who could bring me more true happiness than his mate could, because we should be at least Equals.

I set the cup down.

"That's Messeia!" said Sarband.

I had heard nothing.

She came into the room. She was paler than ever. The sunlight gave a curious transparency to her skin.

"Messeia!" cried Sarband.

He started back at the sight of her.

We had neither of us seen her for six weeks.

"What have you been doing?" Sarband asked her, mournfully.

"Living. Working. Thinking. Planning," she told him.

"But Messeia!"

It was almost an appeal.

"Why should *you* kill yourself? " asked Sarband.

She laughed. I could see that her laughter smote him like a sword.

"Is it anything to do with you?" she asked, quietly.

He had no answer. I can see him still regarding her sadly, like a man facing a new proposition, but still, I am sure, quite unaware that he was drifting towards Chaos. And, though he had calmly passed over my terrible confession of brutedom, of disloyalty, I think that even then—responsive as I was becoming to other influences than those I had known—I think even then I was a little glad to see him drifting, and more than a little curious to see what would happen.

I was curious to see a man more splendid than myself *downed*. Perhaps, if I had only known, I was finding out why an Economic Tyranny had gone down, and an Intellectual Tyranny had arisen.

'The liberties we build live after us, become tyrannies, and fail.'

Sarband and I were working in the workshop. I had got, for the first time in my life, a job I liked doing. Sarband had seen me drawing designs absent-mindedly one day, and had said, "Edmund, if you like doing that, make us some middle-age designs for shoes. The community will go for them. They'll be ugly, of course, and the craze will soon die out. Nevertheless, it will bind you to them in their thoughts."

So here was I, working out designs, with Sarband, like a god, at his machine. The workshop had the light of moon. The narrow, great window showed a night sky. Moon and stars looked in on us. Arlene was spreading the table above stairs.

"How did any inequalities arise?" I asked suddenly. "In a community where profit-making was utterly abolished, how could inequalities creep in?

Sarband laughed. He brought a great knife down on a pile of fragrant leather.

"They were what you left," he said, simply. "By Evolution! Capitalism fell. It left us the unfit of all classes, and a heap of hellish miseries and inferiorities. The end came so suddenly, like a thunderbolt, that there was chaos.

"You had not prepared the people for the contingency of Capitalism's end. Panic-stricken and dazed, they had to rely on men the hour produced. These men became leaders—dictators, if you like. The people had always had dictators—but against them. Capitalism had toppled ignominiously down, with *its* dictators, like a savage god falling in dust and debris. So, when with courage, and the knowledge of what must be done, men sprang up and took control, naturally. they were allowed to use their intellect to build up a new order. You recall the peasants' revolt under Wat Tyler?"

I nodded.

"When Tyler was killed by Walworth, what happened?"

"The peasants were demoralised," I stammered.

"Exactly. That is the worst of leaders, however grand they are. When they're gone, those who have depended on them don't know what to do. Well, that was what happened with you, but not so sweepingly. The best of the insurgents, as we call them, and the best of the Evolutionary Opportunists, had been in the thick of the struggle. Consequently, they were dead."

"The devil they were!" I exclaimed, bitterly.

"They died gloriously," said Sarband. "Being dead—with all their faults and their virtues, they were out of it. Other men, mostly unknown till that battle leaped up and took control. Some of them were men who had imbibed the best ideas of the Insurgents. Some were men who had in themselves the best qualities of the Evolutionists. The leaders of these two great mass movements combined. They had to. They were faced with a work like a new creation. A dazed, half heartbroken people, which had not known and not been prepared for the end of Capitalism, brought about by Capitalism itself, which had been unable to control its Capitalist Civil Wars —"

"Eh? What?" I gasped.

"Which had been unable to control its civil wars, which had prepared for another, as soon as the last was over, in 1925."

I laughed.

"The war to end war did not last until 1925," I told him.

"Which ended with the evacuation of enemy troops from the 'vanquished' country in 1925," he said, stubbornly. "A Capitalism which had to have wars, civil wars, in *which it recruited the proletarians, and swilled the earth with their blood,* began after 1925 to *feverishly prepare for another. It had lifted the roof off its own system by the last.* It prepared to demolish the walls—even whilst the Evolutionists, blind as bats, were yelling out for another roof to be stuck on, and calling it 'construction.'

"The Insurgents, born of the disgust and despair of seeing the approaching end of things as they were, went to the other extreme. 'Arm yourselves,' they called frantically to the people. 'Arm yourselves. The ruin is toppling on us.' They were right. It was.

"But the people did not want to 'arm themselves'. They did not want to blow even the Capitalists' brains out. They had also a great sickening repugnance to have their own blown out. By Evolution! What a period that was! Capitalist Civil War approaching, to sweep European civilisation into the dust. Insurgents shouting out to the people to arm themselves, and scaring them with the very idea!"

I hurled away the designs with which I had been busy.

"For God's sake, hush," I asked him. "Sarband. I can't bear it. This was my damned world. These were my people. I will not listen. It is too terrible."

He stopped his machine.

"That," he said, "was why it wanted facing. That was why the whole of the Peoples should have known. They ought to have been told. They could have beaten down the whole odds against them."

"By arms," I gasped.

"By Evolution!" ejaculated Sarband, sorrowfully. "How could they have done it by arms, when they did not want to arm, and could not have armed if they had wanted, *against* a science *that could drop things on them from above their head*s? Edmund, perhaps—who knows—we allowed you to come here, not only to alter your destiny, but to alter ours."

"Humanity knows the horrors it has suffered," Sarband said. "Those it has missed it never knows. By breaking Capitalism's mad weapon—Militarism; by demanding the destruction of all guns, all scientific death-forces, all air-machines, all military forces—they could have fought Capitalism *then,* as we fight Unprogression *now.*

"It would have meant the rapid and vigorous demands of the united peoples of Europe—racing to defeat Militarism—racing to destroy *force* which could *always* be used against them, and then, when it was destroyed, proclaiming to Capitalism—'Force is Dead. You—who have built a hell for us to live in—are defeated. You have governed us by Force. We shall now CONTROL *your* Destinies.'

"Had this happened, Edmund, there would have been no Intellectual Bureaucracy. You would have saved me and such as me having to fight against a Tyranny which arose out of your chaos. Do you think I am eager to die? By Evolution? If only I could live. If only I could live with honour!"

111

Suddenly—as I stared at him—into the agony of his eyes—the great bell rang, which for a month had challenged the city—the bell swung in the Temple by the Intellectual Autocrats who believed Chaos would follow the disappearance of such Autocracy.

"Sarband," called Arlene. "Messeia is here."

We found her waiting.

"Hurry up," she told Sarband. "They are going to kill us. I'll wager you anything you like that they kill me first. I shall stand waiting in the Avenue of the Dead. Sarband—" She turned swiftly to Arlene. "You won't mind my waiting for Sarband, when I'm dead, will you?" she asked, softly.

"No. You can have him *then*", Arlene told her, simply. I sat dazed. So this was the way triangular positions worked out here.

"What's that?" asked Sarband.

He was looking for his cloak.

"Only nonsense," said Arlene.

"Only nonsense," echoed Messeia.

When they had gone I turned to Arlene.

"Supposing Sarband cares for Messeia—as she cares for him," I said. "Could you stand between them?"

She looked at me, playing with a link of beads on her neck.

"Sarband is not my *property,*" she said. "But if he went, he could not return. You understand. If Messeia was good enough to fool with, *he would have to take the whole of her.* We have not a dual code of morals here. But such things *rarely* happen. They are seen to be *Tragedies*. Besides, Sarband does not care for Messeia. He knows she is only infatuated with his intellect. I tell you, Edmund, all is well—"

Then as I stared, she suddenly flung out her hands. I caught a sobbing breath, and she left the room. I was no longer happy to contemplate this tragedy. I could bear the thought of Sarband's downfall. I could not bear the thought of Arlene's grief. I desired, above all, to return to the place from whence I had come, remembering her happy, if alone, in the thought that Sarband had been hers to death.

* * *

When she came downstairs, and we took supper in the shell-pink room. I asked why should Sarband or Messeia speak of dying! "You people are stronger than we were. You can stand more. Why should they die?"

She pointed out to a star, shining in on us.

"That star is radiating energy, is it not?" she asked. I admitted it.

"If with the intensity of pouring out, pouring out, it poured out all its energy, what would happen?

"It would grow dark—dead," I said.

"If I told you that we could conserve our mind-forces, or pour them out at will, to alter anything we saw wrong, you would say, perhaps, I lied," said Arlene. "After all, you were so concerned to live by bread, you knew little or nothing about minds. I would not blame you. It will seem strange to you."

But I had seen too much of these people to be able to say they lied.

"If I told you that when any mind had done its work the body died," she said, "would you believe that?"

I pondered.

"I can see its possibilities," I admitted.

"It is just like that," she said, calmly.

"Then Sarband—"

"Is spending himself beyond the power of rebuilding quickly enough," she said. "Even in your world your best did so. It is the same law extended. They are breaking down Tyranny with their own energies."

113

"The Tyrants being—?" I asked.

"Themselves," answered Arlene, serenely. "Or, at least, others of themselves who work for *glory.*"

"What!" I said, jumping up.

"Sarband and Messeia are two of the greatest Intellectuals of their age," she said. "They object to receive that hero-worship which makes slaves and up-lookers of other men. They are saying, and proving, that to create for Honour and Glory is Death, and the collapse of Intellectual Life. They have thrust the Intellectual Unprogressives into the position of proving it, with every Progressive Intellectual they kill.

"They are not out to take power. They are out to hurl it from them, as the death of the one who holds it. I think they are glorious, but foolish. I like Sarband to *win*, because I am his mate. I hate to see him die, because I am his mate, and for me there will be a life of unutterable loneliness. But, most of all I *fear* that Messeia will take him from me.

"I am torn into pieces, Edmund. I think that Love is the greatest Tyranny on the face of the earth. And that is the Tyranny they offer in place of Intellect. It will rise as a Freedom. It will become a Tyranny. It will make a man unable to leave a woman, whether he loves her or not, if she loves him. It will make a woman unable to leave a man whether she loves him or not *because he needs her,* whilst he refuses to let her go. And it will create new martyrs, and stand as the greatest Tyranny ever erected. It will be the greatest Tyrant in the history of the world, for it will say. 'If this your comrade needs you, you are not free to depart'. They are stripping even Love of its Intellectual and passional bonds. They are rearing it as a spiritual gift, the least evolved claim from the most evolved, to raise them near their own magnificence. They are *levelling* the Intellectual inferiors Capitalism left behind by saying to man or woman, 'Love the weakest, love the most cowardly, love those who are unequal to you. Love them most. The others, do not need it'."

And I realised that Love here was almost a spiritual passion. But I saw, none the less, an ironic tragedy beyond any I had ever witnessed. Sarband was not only fighting for the claim of the weak and unevolved as most needing Love—.

Destiny, which ever laughed at man, was driving him toward Messeia, the Strong, and away from Arlene, the weak, whom I knew would *never* let him go. He was building a law, which he would be driven against—*its first victim.* And I think, had I had it in my power, I would have saved him, even though I still was wildly jealous of him, with all a dog's miserable, dumb jealousy, whenever I saw him near Arlene.

And so they were gone out to protest against Intellectual Dominance and raise Love as a purified passion, which alone could send the race forward in its immortal path. And in that moment I realised Messeia's nobility and courage. She was helping to found a law which would stand as an insurmountable obstacle between herself and Sarband, a tyranny which would make it impossible for one woman to march triumphantly to love over the body of another woman. Perhaps he foresaw that by so doing she was breaking down Unprogression by letting the unevolved evolve and find that Love liberates; but those who love no more remain as martyrs and *sacrifices.*

But I felt overwhelmed.

"I will go and see Venensley and look at his children, the stars," I told Arlene.

She made the first request she had ever made of me.

"Do not go. I fear my thoughts," she said.

It was as though a woman caressed a dog, and told it she liked its dumb and adoring sympathy.

I was fast losing my once intolerable sensitive pride. I was also losing my cringing humility.

Though I was asked to stay—as a dog—I stayed as the dog, an intelligent, dumb dog, who could not express that even if I was kicked I should still love on. Perhaps, who knows, to be kicked, and love on, that priceless loyalty dogs have, *is* Love. But it was painful to me to think that Sarband was going to be the dog who was to be kicked, and chained, and kennelled, and given the crust of Sacrifice, and be asked to 'love on' when Love had become a chain, on which was engraved 'the name of a heavier freedom'.

* * *

That evening I spent with Arlene stands out against all the memories I have known, as the concentrated essence of all that was best in our world and in theirs. Though the company I could give was only equivalent to that a dumb dog gives to its superior human. I was happy to be able to give even that.

Love is not an intellectual essence. Neither is it a mere sex hunger. Though these things enter into it, it is infinitely more. It runs out in ripples of tender feeling to the birds and beasts we do not understand, to the giants of mind and heart whose names travel to us down the centuries. A little child holding a flower or a bird in its hand, careful not to harm it, knows something about it. A boy or girl who loves a bird, yet opens its cage door, to lose it, gives it its freedom, knows more about it.

I no longer wished to touch a creature so infinitely beyond me. Between us was an impassable gulf. Across this gulf we comforted each ether for tragedies each only half understood in the other. It was not even necessary to understand. The Eternal Human Pities brooded between us, with their healing wings.

Yet all this while we sat, I doing my carving, Arlene embroidering, with a little river of music flooding the room, let into it by her touching a button.

We were hearing music which came through the air from beyond the Himalays, music which had all the mysterious eerie charm of Eastern music. Anon we talked of Sarband. Sometimes of Messeia.

"Would you like to hear some of Messeia's music?" asked Arlene.

Gentle reader, imagine a woman of our world, fearing another woman more than anything on earth, and asking in a flash of enthusiasm for that woman's work. 'Would you like to hear her creations?' In a back street she would have pulled her hair off in handfuls. In the West-end she would have done worse; if short of money for lingerie she might have blackmailed her, had she had the greatness of Messeia, had she known her rival could not tolerate a 'scandal'.

It was not until I heard Messeia's music that I realised how this attraction between Sarband and Messeia had come to pass. For, of the two, Arlene was more beautiful. She was happier in herself than Messeia. The joy of the morning things was in her face, whilst in Messeia was always that vague elusiveness, that essence of mystery and the stars which said, 'No man will ever grasp the whole of me. I shall go down to death alone.' Magic in sound! But no, I can never describe it to you in words. All the thunder of the passionate, crying seas was there. All the splendour of the opposing rocks. Life, and love, and death, the titans of the eternities, struggled there. I leaned my head upon my hands and wept for wonder at it.

Chapter 8

"It is beyond me," said Arlene, frankly.

It was scarcely necessary to say it was beyond me. But I knew it was great, greater than anything our world had known.

"Do you know what she would have been in our world?" I asked.

Arlene shook her head.

"A surplus woman," I told her.

She did not understand me, could not understand me, for she did not understand what a surplus human being meant.

I went to my bed, leaving her listening to Messeia's music, trying to understand it, though I know she never would. Sarband was away over a week. The fight was still raging. I got restive. I missed him. Arlene was quick to perceive this. It was another fellow-feeling between us. But she had her life planned out. The mill, Jacqueline's visits, Peter's visits, the house— and to go and sit and watch Sarband wrestle left her no time for my restlessness.

During this week, too, she was always packing things up and sending them away by the machines. There was something almost mysterious in her way of doing this. In our world I should have suspected that she was intriguing with some other 'man'. At last my restlessness seemed more than she could tolerate, though they were very tolerant of my nerve-racked self.

"Go and stay with Venensley, Edmund," she advised.

So once more I went to see the old man of the tower. I found him enthusiastic about the moons of Jupiter. Invariably I went out in the dusk.

It veiled my disparities. The great night, too, always calms me.

Venensley did not look quite so well as usual. The little black cap he wore to keep his head warm made his face look a little peaked and pale.

"The leaves are falling," he said, when I remarked on it. "That is the reason. Well, we can none of us live for ever. And, by the stars, *I have lived*. By the way, I had your friend, Mrs. Biers, here yesternight. Wonderful woman, for the age she was born in and the things she endured. I read her Reichter's 'Dream of Eternal Space', in your tongue, of course. I told her how long that fossil had been in existence. She turned pale, and was running away, quite bowed down with the weight of years. But she came back, and she recited me 'Twinkle, twinkle, little star,' or, yes, I think that was it, though my memory sometimes plays tricks. Pity she can't stay. But there, we couldn't do with you here. No. Quite impossible. Take three generations to evolve anything worth keeping from you. Yes. But I like her. However—"

We surveyed the heavens.

"Could you tell me when I shall be sent back?" I asked.

"Ha, ha!" he laughed. "You are not to know that. That is the only thing we cannot tell you."

"But why?" I asked, resolutely. "At least, I ought to be prepared for the *shock.*"

Venensley laughed, and swung his telescope round.

"Can't tell you. Don't know. It's true. We don't know. You came here by Desire. You will leave by Desire."

I stared at him.

"Then, I shall stay here for ever, and you can't oust me," I said, triumphantly.

"You will desire to return," said the old star-gazer. We contradicted each other. Then he said, "Edmund, let us go out. I will take you to see one of the 'throw-backs' from your society. No. He is not mad. He is just a throw-back. One of those who look at the past and see only its glories. We'll go and cheer him up. Come along."

As we went out into the night of stars, an owl's mocking 'too-whit, too-whoo' came to us, and a shower of leaves from the copper beech near the tower. Yet I felt triumphant and safe in the thought that I could not be flung back to our world until I desired. Passionately, rebelliously, I thought, "They shall never make me desire to return. I will *never* return."

"Too-whit! Too-whoo" called the bird of night.

And another shower of leaves fell on us.

It was like a menace.

We had to enter the city to get a machine. On both side-roads there were eager throngs. On the middle road ran the great luminous cars. I saw a dog get in the way, to be hurled out of it again, yelping with terror.

Venensley used a stick this evening. I realised that he *was* failing—that it was one of his 'weaker days', and that I had seen him before at his best. He leaned on the stick, but not heavily. He went and rung for a car. He waited. A minute later the call was answered.

"Skeeley's house," said Venensley to the steerer, who seemed astounded to hear the ancient tongue.

Skeeley must certainly be famous.

We went along the road, with the side-roads crowded with people on each side of us.

"Brother," called Venensley to the steerer, "do you not think the end is in sight? English. We want Pilgrim to understand."

"Yes. I should say it's coming fast," replied the steerer.

"Yes. I should say the thing will go before many months are over," said Venensley.

"I should think it won't survive *another death,*" answered the steerer. "The masses are getting excited. They'll finish it quickly, once they start in."

I sat back thoughtfully.

Then I plucked Venensley's sleeve.

"Historically, what period are you passing through?" I asked, feebly.

He smiled.

I can see him yet, his face illuminated by the same dancing star-shine glow which came from the machine, his little cap, his lively eyes. as he said, courteously: "we are in that period of transition known as 'the withering away of the State'."

"But what State?" I asked.

"The State which followed Capitalism," he said. "Socialist-Communist, I suppose you called it."

"But," I said, "if it is withering, does anyone need to do anything?"

The steerer heard me and laughed.

"If it didn't object to withering, they wouldn't need," he said. "It doesn't. But the bureaucrats behind it *do* object. Brother! Here you are. My love to Skeeley. Tell him I'm sorry I knocked his wooden bishop down when I was picking a telegraph-pole up for him last time I saw him. I'm afraid he'll never forgive me."

We went up the steps of a great house more stereotyped in form than any I had seen. It was old-fashioned and hideous in comparison with the rest. We rang an electric bell. We were let in by Skeeley, into a room lit by electric light, whose bluey-white glare hurt my eyes, after the light usual in the other houses. He had the room fitted up as a manufacturer of our world might have fitted it up. It was a cross between a commercial room and the heavy splendour of a 'good house'. The carpets threw up dust as we walked.

"Oh, Pilgrim," he greeted me. "See! You can tell me if I have got things arranged right. See! Is that not like a copy of old English society—at the height of its military and industrial glory?"

I followed the wave of his hand.

I realised as I looked that the man was a genius. He had got models of all our institutions, and formed a city of them. In his madness he had left out the ugly things. It did not look unlike an Empire Exhibition.

"Good old days!" he said. "Good old days! Would I had been living then."

I stretched out my hand to adjust a church which seemed as though it was going to topple over, and down went the wooden bishop. Skeeley burst into tears.

"Now you've done it," said Venensley, grieved. "It will take him days to get over that. Come along. It's no use staying. He won't talk to you now."

"But, does he live here alone, this lunatic!" I asked, as we went out.

"He never hurts anyone," said Venensley. "And, after all, had you not men who saw more glory in the past than in their own present. Edmund, any man who builds for the future must see the tendencies of his own age. You see how impossible it is for us to keep you here. You do not belong to this present. You belong to your own. Come along. We'll go to see Arlene, Edmund."

So Venensley and I went back to Arlene's. And as we sat at supper we heard shouting in the street. Arlene turned pale.

"Do you think *it* has come?" she asked Venensley.

I stared at them both.

"Think what has come?" I asked, rudely.

"The insurrection," said Arlene.

"Insurrection!" I gasped.

"There! There!" said Venensley, a little impatiently, "It only means a rising of the People."

"But," I said, shaking in every limb.

"It only means their voices become the voices of destiny," he said, patiently now. "It only means they assert themselves as intelligent enough to build up a Future on new lines, as they have built up the Present. There is no Force to oppose them. Force went with Capitalism. They only come into the streets and proclaim their wills. Listen!"

A surge of singing, youthful singing, came to us.

Then a hurried knock on the door.

I saw Arlene gather herself together.

She pushed our aid away, and went herself to receive him from them.

He staggered up the steps towards her.

He was as feeble a man as I was.

He had spent all his energies trying to turn the tide.

From outside came a burst of singing. I think he waved his hand to them as they passed. Venensley closed the door. I opened a bottle of wine. I think he was laughing. I also think he was *almost* dying. I splashed the wine into a cup, and handed it to Arlene. He took it from her hand, looking into her face, then held it up, the light shining through it.

"To the least evolved, who shall one day be equal with the best of us," he said, and drank. I left them, and ran up the steps of the tower and stood on the roof, over the street. Banners! Marching feet! Youth! Song! Their voices came up to me.

"Liberty! Equality! Fraternity!" It was the immortal song of the human race, which would ring down the ages as long as any inequalities remained. I realised now that humanity would always struggle towards other horizons. As the old serfs had marched against their wrongs, as wage-workers of our world were marching. Bread gained, 'Peace' wrenched from the bloody hands of Capitalism, the march of Intellectual and Moral Equality would begin—a struggle glorious in its results, and only possible because we had claimed *'all things in common'*.

I watched them stream away, those tides of nobler humanity, beating down their own Autocracy, and I was no longer oppressed by the endless struggles, the achievements of mass following mass. I stood bare-headed under the stars, and, looking at them, felt that humanity was not less, but more than I had thought it—yea, even in Binkers Court. And into my heart crept a great and surpassing love for my brother, Sarband—who had shown me how to fight. It was a love 'passing the love of woman'. To dream vaguely of the future was as mad as Skeeley living in the past. We must all fight, in our own way, in our own time, in our own place. No man, no god, even, could do more. We should have to save ourselves in our world, as they were doing here.

***

For the first time since I had reached Equality Island I saw Sarband resting.

He was lying now on the great couch in that room where I had first seen him and Arlene looking at each other in the fire-glow. Usually, in this room, the curtains were drawn together. Sarband had asked that they should not be drawn. There were only a few dim stars. Old Venensley's 'children' looked tearful. I could see the dark tree-boles, snow-patched outside, the fire-glow dancing on the windows against the snow. That dark sadness of a misted winter's evening, in which the sun had gone down like a flaming cannon ball, was over the outside world.

Three days ago the 'fight' between Sarband and Heldon had ceased. As he lay there motionless, I got that terrible fear Love puts into the heart of women sometimes, as they bend over a cradle. Sleep and Death look strange. I did not shake him as I had once seen Mrs. Jones shake her infant in panic, saying, "God, Mr. Sniggins! I thought he was gone!" But I stared at him and walked towards him. He opened his eyes.

"Oh, it's you, Edmund," he said.

His eyes, opening as I stood there, terrified me. I had looked down into their depths where a new thought, volcanic in its intensity, was burning.

"If you and Heldon could settle it." I whimpered. I wanted to save him. He smiled faintly.

"It isn't as though it were mine and Heldon's to settle," he remarked. "You see, we are down under the feet of a divided mass of riven intelligences. My business is to try to convince Heldon's mass that they are wrong, till Heldon is left free, to be Heldon. Poor Heldon! If only they would decide *quickly*, and set us both free. Edmund, I do not believe Nature has ever produced a man who has not feared extinction. The Eternal Me cries out 'Let me live'. But, after all, it is not fearlessness that makes heroes of men. It is facing fear, and *defying it*."

I, who had never defied a single fear, heard him with shame.

"How is it they don't settle it themselves?" I asked.

"Would you mind reaching my pipe?" he asked.

Never before had I heard Sarband make a demand of any living creature.

I was only too glad to do any small thing. He knew it. At such times, when I hurried to do any service, his eyes mocked me genially, as saying, "You are a most faithful dog, Edmund." But I did not mind.

"You asked why they don't settle it themselves," he said. "Well, they would be pitched up against each other. You would have men and women arguing in gangs all about the public streets. We still have a social machine. It has got reduced to two cogs. I am one. Heldon is the other. We go on, grinding, grinding. When we are done, they get two more. Bureaucracy looks a bit ridiculous, does it not, when it has got reduced to two individuals who are the greatest nonentities in the social scheme. In your world they would have called us great men. In our world they have reduced us to great nonentities."

"Nonentities!" I gasped.

He puffed away and nodded.

"Men who must not express their individuality at all," he explained. "When I express myself, down goes the marker's chalk. Poor Heldon forgets most often. That is why I am beating him. I am a greater nonentity."

I stared at him in astonishment.

There was a note of rebellion in his voice.

He sprang up suddenly.

"When shall I be Sarband?" he asked, mournfully. "When shall I be Sarband? When I am dead, Edmund."

We were facing each other.

"Do you know," I asked, bitterly, "that has been the cry of my soul in Binkers Court: when shall I be Edmund?"

He held out his hand.

"Two nonentities, Edmund," he said. "Just two nonentities. But, after all, you had billions of them. They have reduced their numbers. You had a State which reduced the Masses to nonentities, who could not choose. The Masses have marched on. They have reduced us to nonentities, who cannot choose."

"Children of Choice!" I said, with sudden sarcasm. He smiled.

"Children of Choice, who *do choose*," he answered, gently. "Even our own extinction as Individuals, our own extinction by death, *to serve the whole.*"

I think I saw it then.

"But if only for one single moment I could do something, something which would proclaim me to the liberated Individuals who follow this mad bureaucracy, something to shout down the ages, 'This was a human called Sarband', I think I would die happy."

He sat down again, smoked, and we sat in silence.

"Where's Arlene?" he asked me.

"She was going out to a dance," I said.

It sounded a little callous to me, as I told him. But the fact was accepted by him as nothing extraordinary.

"She loves it," he said, quietly pleased. "I like her to be herself."

Then he said, "Hush! What was that?"

I had heard nothing.

"I thought it was perhaps Messeia!" he said.

I repeated that I had heard nothing.

"Was not that a dog barking?" he asked sitting up alert.

I listened.

The streets were very quiet. The people were in their homes, or in the concert rooms, dance rooms, or roaming the wide galleries where their own sculpture and art mirrored their age, or challenged it, or foreshadowed a new one. Or they were gathered in their debating societies, waiting for something to happen, wrangling genially as to how it would happen, and when, and what spark would be the chance that made choice no longer impossible. It was very quiet here, save for the long, shuddering moaning of the wind in the trees.

"I did hear something," I told him.

Then we heard a knock.

Sarband sat bolt upright. Across his face passed a grieving shadow.

"One of our friends; he's very ill, or dead," he said. "Who can it be?"

He sat down again. I think he felt almost too weak to stand. We heard Messeia's footstep. We heard her call "Slave! Slave!" to her dog.

Slave bounded in on us first. He had been having a most glorious roll in the snow. His tongue was lolling out. His whole attitude was 'Fight on, you mad mortals. I am glad I am only a dog.' Into Sarband's eyes crept a wistful look as though he thought 'these creatures without dreams may be Slaves— unevolving—but they are gloriously happy'. Then we saw Messeia, leaning against the doorway. She had some kind of electric blue cloak on, trimmed with a substitute for fur. She threw the hood of her cloak back. We saw that she had been weeping.

"Who is it?" asked Sarband.

"Venensley," she said, quietly.

"The knock *disturbed* me," Sarband told me. "I thought for one dreadful moment—"

Then he stopped.

"I thought it might be *You*," he said. "So it's Venensley. How?"

She gave a little half-hysterical laugh.

I had not thought it possible she could care so much. I thought the loss of the fear and superstitions connected with death would have made them callous.

"He was leaning too far out of that window, it is supposed, looking at Jupiter, and he overbalanced. They've taken him to the Temple. The atomisation takes place in ten days."

I realised that in our world he would have been an old age pensioner, and have gone to that awful place, the mortuary, and they would have said, "He is out of his *misery*."

"So, he's gone," said Sarbend. "We shall miss him. We must break it gently to Arlene. She will miss him most of all. Queer to think he will come no more. Well, he has lived gloriously, in his own way."

That was all.

Just then the door was flung open.

Mrs. Biers came in.

"I've just seen them a-taking him," she snuffled. "Oh, my God! It was awful. All smashed up. The poor old man! Oh, my god! Shall I ever forget it? Give me something, something strong."

I got the wine.

She was shaking in every limb.

"An' he was such a happy old man," she gulped. "Such a happy, innercent old man. Oh, my god! Why couldn't he be let live for ever? An' only the other night he was yarnin' out about the Definity of Space—"

Sarband helped her to the couch.

"That is how we shall remember him," he said, gently. "Just looking out of his window, dreaming. If you *can* help it, don't please think of him all *smashed* up."

Mrs. Biers gulped.

She took a long pull at the wine.

"Set it down, Mr. Sniggins," she said. "I feel a bit better."

When Arlene returned from the dance, radiant and a joy to behold, I no longer felt that there was anything callous about it. Sarband was fighting. In his heart he liked it. She had been dancing. She liked that. Sarband's face lit up as he looked at her. Arlene saw the table.

"You've set it like a man, Sarband," she said, light-heartedly critical.

Sarband smiled.

"Edmund set it," he told her. "I helped him."

"That's Messeia," said Arlene, suddenly.

From the tower under the stars came the strains of music—wild and wonderful, mysterious and joyful.

"And she's playing the 'Dead March'," said Arlene.

"Who is it! Quick! Not—not Venensley?"

"Yes," said Sarband, grudgingly. "Now—"

She took a couple of blind steps. His arms went round her.

"After all, he was old, Arlene," he said, gently. "Not long ago he told me he was prepared to die. He got very tired—and he hated to feel tired."

I left them and climbed to that room under the stars, where the music was beating out, a threnody of rapture, and mystery, and peace. In that dark tower, by the dim light of 'Venensley's stars', she was playing him his 'Exit'. I sat on the top step and listened. She was singing. I had never heard Messeia sing. Her voice floated out to the organ-strains like a voice over a dark, mysterious sea—unfathomable yet glad.

"To all mysteriously arriving—serenely—"

Whitman's great chant on the Democracy of Death. I crept away. I felt a very worm.

I went down to Sarband and Arlene, and to Mrs. Biers, who was having 'another'. Arlene was resetting the table. Venensley would throw his happy shadow across it no more. The world wagged on. I wondered if any-one had left Binkers Court since I came here. Messeia came down, her normal self.

"Why have you stayed away, Messeia?" asked Sarband. "Isn't it enough for me to be beaten about by the tides of the world without you deserting me?"

Messeia turned to Arlene.

"You see, you are not enough for him," she said.

Sarband laughed.

"Certainly she's not," he admitted. "Don't I want Edmund, with his eternal 'Why, why, why?' and Arlene, with her laughter and dancing, and love, Messeia, and Mrs. Biers with her 'I don't hold with that. That is not my opinion—' and certainly Messeia, Messeia also, with her music and her mystery, and her 'I am sufficient to myself alone' air. And Slave—"

Slave barked and jumped up and licked Sarband's face as he heard his name.

"There's patriotism for you, Edmund," Sarband said, with a twinkle in his eye.

Mrs. Biers bristled.

"An' don't you say nothin' against one's love of one's native land," she challenged.

"Did you love Binkers Court?" asked Sarband.

"Don't mention that place to me," said Mrs. Biers. "Though I catches myself wondering how Joshua is. He gets chilblainds in the winter. It's the wet an' cold an' his old boots."

"That was your native land," Sarband told her.

"Liar!" said Mrs. Biers, fiercely.

Sarband laughed till the tears stood in his eyes.

"Prove me one," said Sarband.

Mrs. Biers sat down to prove it, finger up like a school ma'am, talking the most ridiculous stuff about Union Jacks, and 'Dominions' and 'Conquest', and the good we have been to the 'niggers in India'!

"Come! Describe your native land," said Sarband.

She saw where he was driving her. Mrs. Biers was progressing.

"Oh, I can," she asserted boldly.

He encouraged her.

"The sea is all round it," she said. "It's a tight little island—" Quite suddenly she picked up her skirts and hopped into the middle of the room. I think it must have been the wine. She was dancing to 'Rule, Britannia', humming as she went round.

"As for your dancing," she said. "I've been with Mr. Sparkins. He's common. I shan't go no more with him. He got us turned out. Could you lick this?" She was waltzing to her humming of 'Only a Pansy Blossom', with Slave jumping up. She took his paws, and we watched them go round.

"Now," she said, pausing and freezing, "ain't that a bit of all right? And this is one of our love songs. Excuse me voice. It's me own, and it's *natural*."

They sat and watched her, fascinated. She was teaching them more of the past than all their annals of it had done. She managed to get the pitch at last.

She stood, arms akimbo—this woman from Binkers Court—her gaze on the ceiling, as though she saw visions there—visions of things she had never had. I went a bit thready myself as she sang Chevalier's old song, in her raucous voice, for even that could not utterly spoil it—the song of the faithfulness of the proletarian to his 'Old Dutch'.

I translated the words into English as she went on, and handed them to Sarband. He read them with glowing cheek.

"But that other rubbish, Mrs. Biers," he said, as he thanked her, "about Britannia—you never could believe that."

She winked.

"Bless your heart. I ain't quite green," she said. "Though I always stood up for me King an' me Country. Sorter o' made you feel you did own something. Howsomever, I was washing most of my time. Now, can you beat that little song?"

Sarband shook his head.

"No, that song is always the same," he said, "though we've no Old Dutches. Only these kind of horrors."

He flashed a glance at his 'Old Dutch', then at Messeia, and then we heard another knock at the door.

"It's only old Sparkins," said Mrs. Biers. "An' he's like a sign o' death himself. Where's he been, I wonder?"

Mr. Sparkins came in.

He looked thoughtful, worried.

Later, he told me, in our bedroom, that he had been woman-hunting. The dreadful things he said about Equality Island because he could find no prostitution will not bear repeating.

He raved like a lunatic half the night because he could find no exploited womanhood. I tried to solace myself, and likewise keep out of his atmosphere by memorising Whitman.

Next morning, at breakfast, Mr. Sparkins demanded his passport.

"We don't allow you to leave before you've seen our Revolution," said Sarband.

Mr. Sparkins turned green.

"Revolution!" he gasped. "I demand my passport."

Then I saw *Sarband,* Sarband expressing himself.

"For your property, Sparkins," he said. "You sent millions of men out to be shot down. To defend those filthy holes where Edmund and Mrs. Biers will live, even yet you would see soldiers shoot down Edmund and Mrs. Biers, who have worked *all their life,* when they were allowed.

"You are going to see a Revolution here, and I want you to realise that but for men like you, who would spill the world's blood to save your Interests, Proletarian Revolutions would only be the same. Now, you are just going to stay. We don't hope to convert you. After all, you are *nothing.* You have lived on others.

"You have been here all this time and never offered to produce anything. You have no pride. No independence. No social morality. You are a depravity.

"You stay here. We want to study you. We want to see how you act in a time of Change. Autocratic, of course. And this only applies to you, Sparkins, only to *you,* who will eat and drink and live on your fellows, and pour their blood out to save your interests. You are a mass of corruption, dead matter, parasitical, horrible—horrible—so horrible that it has taken all my will to endure you, humming and strutting about the place, whilst I and Edmund work for you, and Arlene—by Evolution! you have let Arlene produce for you. Mrs. Biers is producing. You are letting her help to feed you. You are the only one who has not changed. You are depraved; socially, you are a cannibal."

Mr. Sparkins backed against the wall.

I can see him yet, with his eyes rolling, his tie awry, where he had clutched it himself, choking with indignation, the big checks of his now shabby suit standing out like prison bars, and his face purple. He stuttered, froth on his lips.

Sarband stood staring at him, Sarband—not the spokesman for a riven mass of intelligences, but Sarband—even the Sarband I might have been, had I had the courage. Remembering Sparkins so, never again, I knew, would I tremble before him when he said "Rent, Sniggins." More likely I should feel like throwing him over the banisters.

"When I return I shall write up to the 'Daily Mail' against my unjust detention," he said.

Sarband laughed.

"Tell them why you wanted to return," he said, shortly.

Mr. Sparkins gasped.

"Sniggins," he said, "you've given me away."

Sarband came between us.

I think he thought we were going to fight.

"Do you think I have not watched you," said Sarband. "You are lower than the beasts of the field, Sparkins. You think you can buy a woman. Perhaps you bought your wife. It would be like you. The proletarians, with nothing, were noble as gods beside you."

And, standing watching them, I realised now what Sarband meant by *the tyranny of personality*. Sarband had not touched Sparkins. Yet he was leaning against the wall, like a man struck with a hundred darts. I trembled to think I might see thousands of personalities hurled each against each if they rose. And yet I now desired to see it. For would not that save me from seeing Sarband's death? It was my personality to desire to see the noblest 'live on'.

Chapter 9

Mr. Sparkins was sitting in the room looking out on the garden. He had acted very strangely, very suspiciously, since that moment when Sarband told him what he thought of him. He had no one to go out with. Mrs. Biers had suddenly found him 'common'. I did not feel inclined to go out with him. We all had our duties to perform, and, though they left us a lot of leisure, there was so much to read, and see, and study, the days seemed all too short.

I felt that the heyday of my life had arrived. I knew I must return. Vague shadows of perplexity and pain sometimes crossed my Joy. But at least I was *living* this *once*.

Mrs. Biers came in one afternoon when I was sitting reading a book, 'The Materialistic Conception of History'. She had been washing. She had done her hour. They were letting her 'go' just when she liked, to 'get her out of her rut'.

She was full of enthusiasm for her revolutionised 'job'. She could talk about nothing but 'them machines' and 'them great drying-rooms' and them 'radio-machines as ironed the clothes'.

"You lazy, skulkin' hound," called Mrs. Biers to Mr. Sparkins. "Are you a-sittin' thinkin' of your sins, yet? Eatin' the bread what I'm a-puttin' in your mouth. You can't say what Edmund *could* say, in our world, that *you* can't get work.

"Work is noble, when you don't get too much of it.

When you do, it makes you a devil. You've got to work your hour a day. I've got you a job. Edmund an' me is a-takin' you to it."

"Ah!" sighed Mr. Sparkins. "What is it?"

He looked at Mrs. Biers, in her well-cut woollen dress, in the thin porous mackintosh overall she had forgotten to take off, through 'watching them grand machines'.

"You've to look after Skeeley, what they would have called a lunatic in our world, for an hour a day. They ain't so rude here. They calls him a 'throw-back'. You've got to keep Skeeley *happy* by agreeing with all he says, and picking his wooden bishop up when he tumbles against the church through Skeeley moving the armies up and down! Now, you come along. It's light work. You can keep your coat on. It'll keep your thoughts a-occupied!"

"I am to look after a lunatic!" gasped Mr. Sparkins. "I refuse, point-blank."

"Blinketty-blank!" said Mrs. Biers, carelessly. "Well, the Progressive Youths is a-comin' to fetch you, if you can't prepare your mind. After all, Skeeley is one of your sort.

"He's making a lot of flags now, and preparing for a battle. You see, if you look after Skeeley, it releases a workman to do *his hour*. Git your things on, Mr. Sparkins."

Mr. Sparkins sat back.

Then a cunning look overspread his face. Suddenly, he beamed on us. I watched him, my finger keeping my page open in the middle of my book.

"I submit to the inevitable," he said, affably. "I go to render my services to the community. I go to prove that even a property-owner has a soul. You know, Mrs. Biers, and you, Edmund, in my heart I have believed in the Brotherhood of Man."

Mrs. Biers laughed.

"You used to look like it, when you used to threaten to turn us out in the streets, poor kids an' all, when we *couldn't stump up*," she said.

"Let bygones be bygones," said Mr. Sparkins. "I go to help this poor man with his ideals of an age that has happily passed. I go to pity the unfortunate one who is in a minority."

And so he went.

We heard him in his 'grand manner' commanding the amused steerer of one of the machines to take him 'to his work', mentioning Skeeley, famous all over the city for wanting to bring a dead Law and Order back in all their pomp and power. Mrs. Biers looked at me.

"Think he's genuine, Mr. Sniggins? "she asked.

"Do I the—" I began.

"Thanks. Neither do I," said Mrs. Biers.

She sat down.

I went on reading.

"Mr. Sniggins," she said.

I looked up.

"Life's worth livin' here, ain't it?" she asked, pathetically.

I nodded, staring at her.

"But there's times when I feel a selfish creature stayin' 'ere an' Joshua trundling his sand-cart up an' down in the rain. Not 'at 'e ever thought much o' me. I ain't much to think much of. Sorter got wild with me when the sand got wet an' his rheumatics was on. Queer 'ow 'e didn't see it wasn't me, but Society, and give me a black eye, wasn't it? When I was a-young, Mr. Sniggins, if anyone had told me I'd take from any man what I've took from Joshua, I'd a-said 'Liar'. Queer 'ow we get *tamed* down to things, ain't it? Queer 'ow you takes blows from your own 'usband, an' knows it wasn't meant for you, but things that

138

was all wrong, Mr. Sniggins?"

I laid the book down, and closed it.

The tears were standing in Mrs. Biers' eyes.

She was speaking with an effort—an illiterate woman, opening the long-closed doors of her crude heart.

"Yes?" I said.

"Don't you think it's the sime love they have here, but more animal-like?" she asked. "For me to be worryin' 'ere because Joshua'll go 'ome, an' no fire."

Gentle reader, a hundred times in Binkers Court I had said to myself, "Mrs. Biers is rather coarse". I stared at her now, as though I had never seen her before. I had said to myself, "She is utterly ignorant. Human nature will have to change before we get anything better". It was startling to find Mrs. Biers pointing the way back to the horrors we had left, thinking a miserable sand-hawker, who mistook her for the cause of his miseries, needed her just to light the miserable fire, and clean the miserable place they called 'an English home' in the Empire journals.

"I suppose it is love," I stammered. "But wouldn't he give you a good hiding on your return?"

Chapter 10

A pained look came into Mrs. Biers eyes. Then she laughed.

"He'll give me more wages to make up for it—afterwards," she said.

"Mrs. Biers, I'm reading," I said, disgustedly.

"A nod's as good as a wink to a blind horse," she said, with dignity. She was leaving me, but turned in the doorway.

"Mr. Sniggins," she said, "I don't trust Mr. Sparkins. I think he's up to something. I believe, in 'is heart, he'd blow us all up to bring private property 'ere, just for the joy of drawing 'is rents."

I saw her later—standing in the garden, talking to the birds, throwing them crumbs. I had seen her throw bits out in the yard of Binkers Court. As I watched her—appreciating humbly the fact that Mrs. Biers had been much better than I had dreamed—Messeia came in.

She was paler and more beautiful than ever.

"Where's Sarband?" she asked me.

I told her that he had told me that in this lull he was going from place to place, trying to unite the riven mass intelligences.

"When he returns," she said, "tell him I called. Tell him that, henceforth, I am working *alone*. Tell him the *storm* is rising. Tell him I am going to be a tyrant, to save him from annulment. Tell him if I go down first, I shall wait for him in the Avenue of the Dead. Tell him I am so sure the moment is at hand, that I have written the music for the Triumphant Overthrow of Intellectual Tyranny."

I stared at her.

"And you are going to be a tyrant?" I asked.

She smiled.

"The Unprogressives will never be beaten till their own weapons are turned against them. It was so in your industrial overthrow. The soldiers became the Children of Choice. They would not have done it had you been armed. I am a Child of Choice. I am also that 'Chance' which will fire the mine.

"Don't you think, Edmund, if there were only two slaves on the face of the earth, going to their deaths without choice, it would be worth pulling an Autocracy down to save them? Nay, if there was only *one*. And think! You had millions, the world over, dying, dying, of disease, hungers, wars, miseries—never sure that a month would not hurl the whole of your civilisation to dust and ashes.

"Well, give Sarband my message. Tell him I go to turn their own weapons against the Unprogressives. I go to make them kill me."

"Messeia!" I called.

But she had gone.

I was sitting dazed, when the door opened. A swift, strong step sounded. I looked up.

"Oh, the Pilgrim!" said a voice.

I stared.

Before me stood a younger Sarband, looking at me with Arlene's eyes.

"Where's mother?" he asked, boyishly. "And, Pilgrim, who was *that* I passed on the steps?"

"That was Messeia!" I told him. "Your mother—"

He grasped my sleeve.

"Messeia! Did you say that was Messeia?" he asked. "Messeia, the musician. *That* Messeia?"

"Yes. The same," I told him.

He stood, in a dream, with that same look on his face I have seen only once—on the pictured face of Dante, as he stands on the bridge watching Beatrice pass by.

Something impelled me to blurt out the fears I had latterly had.

"And your father," I said, desperately, "is falling in love with her."

He started back.

"You lie!" he said.

I felt terror.

"I'm afraid it's *true*," I said pathetically.

"You mean to tell me," he demanded, "that a man whose work in life is almost completed, who is old in struggle, and in sorrows, has dared to lift his gaze to the face of a woman of a younger generation?"

It took my breath.

From a world where we would marry a half-grown girl to any old dotard, or a stripling to a woman old enough to be his maiden aunt, if these ancients had *money*, I had not realised that Youth would regard what I took to be a catastrophe as a crime. They had evolved a Morality beyond anything we had known. And I realised that this was the "man" to whom Arlene had been sending her 'little packages'. He was her son.

I looked at him again.

He was worth looking at.

The face of Sarband's son was the most turbulent-looking face I ever saw.

I shudder to think what he would have been in our world. If, on the side of the ruling classes, like their most famous and 'great men', I think he would have ridden roughshod to 'glory' over the bodies of slaves, without the slightest compunction. If, on the side of the masses, I fear he would have served half his 'life' in prison for scoffing at Authority, which said the world was all right. The flashing scorn which had leaped out from him as he spoke of his father had almost paralysed me. The sentence he had spoken throbbed yet in my brain. "How does he dare lift his gaze to a woman of the younger generation?"

I wondered where he had been that he did not know Messeia, famous for her music throughout the city.

I had thought him very like Sarband when he came in. I thought him most unlike him now. Their personalities were as wide asunder as the poles. His eyes challenged mine.

"Well, pilgrim!" he said, at length, "what do you think of me?"

Embarrassing question.

"I was thinking," I told him, not without some nervousness, "that in our world you would have been either a magnificent tyrant, or a rebel slave, or, I think, you would have been an insurgent."

"Good," he said, "for a pilgrim! I happen to be neither. Fortunately, for your world, I was not on it. I'm an architect. When I'm not planning new buildings, I'm living in the woods. I'm one of the new Progressives."

"Going back to Nature," I suggested.

He laughed heartily.

"Going back to *what*?" he asked. "Do you mean going back to the thing that n*ever* goes back, never looks back, never mourns the dead, always shouting 'Youth! Youth! Youth!'? Now do I look like anyone who would try to solve the problems of life by trying to go back to mud?"

"Then why do you live in the woods?" I asked.

"Because I've loved to live *alone* since I was eighteen. It's a joy, a rapture, to feel that one can stand quite alone, night after night, day after day, dreaming,

dreaming, dreaming, and then bringing one's dreams back and flinging them into reality. Where is my mother? And oh, I do think you must be wrong about my father. If you are *sure*, I must question him on this matter at the first opportunity."

"Oh, but you can't," I stammered.

Fancy a young man of twenty four questioning his father on his infatuation for a young woman in our world. It would not have been discussed saving in boiling rage, when either Sarband might have met a sudden death.

"But he doesn't know," I said.

"What!" exclaimed the younger Sarband.

"I mean—he's drifting that way," I said.

It was an unfortunate word—drifting.

It annoyed the New Progressive.

"Very well, then. I must open his eyes. We make our minds up quickly on those things. We don't *drift*. Now—my mother. Why is she out? She knew I was coming!"

Just then the door opened.

"Sarband!" cried Arlene. She had been to meet him, and had missed him.

The youth who had lived alone in the woods, planning his sky-flung 'dreams', caught her to him. Then he held her a little way from him.

"As beautiful as ever. But what's the shadow?" he asked.

"None—none—none. There is no shadow," asserted Arlene.

She had paled. But she could not lie well enough.

It was the first lie from these people I had heard since I came here. It was a thing we had lied atrociously about, and, therefore, did well indeed.

"The pilgrim has told me," said the younger Sarband, abruptly.

"Edmund!" said Arlene. "But, Sarband, dearest, *he* does not know."

"Very well, then, we'll tell him," said Sarband the younger. "Anyhow, I've seen Messeia. I passed her on the steps. She's for a younger man. Youth belongs to youth. Besides, I've dreamed of her for eternities out in the woods, where I found a torn scrap of her music in a briar. I set out today *to find her.* I passed her on the steps. She did not see me."

Wrapped in her 'dream', Messeia had passed him.

They had not conquered these things. 'Nature' laughed her cruel, terrible, beautiful laughter.

Though the whole of the populace were liberated intelligences, beating out the music of their divided dream, with only two who could not choose their path, and must express the other's till one perished, these were things they could not control.

They will never be controlled, the insignificant things on which the tide of what we called individual destiny swings. They can only be *faced.*

Even Nature's terrible tragedies are never merely wretched, saving where 'human' laws block their way and pervert them, and turn them into horrors.

As mother and son looked at each other, as the younger Sarband's eyes said, "I am Youth, the Conqueror. Nature is on my side," in dreadful panic I heard the door open and Sarband's step.

As he came in through the doorway, I saw his face, calm yet tired, and with that same gentle look which was stamped on the faces of all the Old Progressives.

I would have spilled my blood to have saved him what I feared was coming. His face lit up as he saw his son. Their hands went out. Sarband looked into his son's face wistfully, as a man looks back on his own youth, vibrant and masterful. Their hands gripped each other, father and son, equals, as I had rarely seen them equals in our world, where youth sometimes cringed to maturity or over-maturity to youth, economic needs chaining them together.

"Father," said Sarband, "you have not ceased to love my mother? The pilgrim says you are drifting into loving Messeia, without knowing it. Is that true? If it is, you will, I know, leave the house at once. You will not degrade her by staying here."

The first words my brother Sarband spoke in answer to the thunderbolt his son had dropped at his feet were very human words. He had a very dazed and human look.

"Have you lived in your woods, dreaming your dreams, aloof from your kind, until you have taken leave of your senses?" he asked.

Though there was strong protest and amazement in his tone, it held none of that vigour of parental authority so eminently popular in our society, which held the vulgar belief that children must look on their parents as half-gods merely because they had brought them into the World.

Yet I noticed that Sarband the elder looked like a man stricken with a new and unsuspected agony.

"Then, the pilgrim was wrong?" asked Sarband the younger.

Bitterly I saw myself dragged into this business.

Again I see Sarband, facing his son, calm enough, save for that nervous human movement of the hands. Anyone who has seen a man tried in a court of law will have noticed that the human hands give the 'criminal' away much sooner than his face. He stood like a man in whom some vial has broken, understanding in one lightning flash whither he had been drifting.

Children of Choice, as they were, they did not break faith with their mates because they wanted to. The thing happened. They were human. It happened less frequently because property never entered into their relationships. It happened less frequently because their matehood was much more an intellectual and helpful matehood than ours could be. But it was happening.

It was their way of facing catastrophe which gave them their right to calling themselves Children of Choice. Sarband faced his son.

"My son," he said to the young man, "this is not your concern. Your mother and I loved before you existed. We did not even come together, thinking of you. We belong to ourselves, even as you have asserted that you belong to yourself. Let Youth sound its own cries. We do not interfere with its rights. But it must leave us *ours*."

His lips were compressed as he finished this sentence. I saw the younger Sarband open his lips; but he did not speak. To assert that he wanted Messeia would have been to muddle things and make them worse.

I saw Arlene go over to Sarband. She was pale to the lips. She took his hand in her own, and laid her cheek against it.

"You will have to choose between us, Sarband," she said. "I will try to choose; give me a little time. It is very terrible to be left to live one's life alone. You must choose which of us you care for most. I will choose if I can let you go even then."

He gripped her hand in his own.

I saw that they had more left, even in their wreck and ruin, than we often had to start with. They had been *great comrades*.

"You choose *now*," young Sarband told his father. "By Evolution! You choose now. You do not keep her on the rack. You do not keep yourself on the rack. You do not keep Messeia on the rack. This you owe to them both—to me and to yourself."

"Do not dictate to me, even in your compassion," said Sarband, swiftly. "You are a young man—a very young man. You, who have not known how mysteriously love comes to men and women, how mysteriously it departs, so that they can scarcely tell when it began and when it ended, if, indeed, it ever does end, utterly, since we are not brutes, hold your peace. If you must know the worst—I recognise that it is the worst—take it! I am unable to choose. I love them equally. That is the truth, as it appears to me at this moment, this mad, fantastic moment, with chaos closing in on my public and private life, with grief at my heart, with desolation falling on my hearthstone, and Insurrection creeping up like a tide, vainly as I have tried to avert it. I am not asking for your tolerance. I am showing you the whole facts, as they appear to me."

Sarband the younger gazed at him appalled.

"Why don't you let the Insurrection come?" he asked. "Why should you be down, a self-chosen *slave*, under their feet? By Evolution: Slavery gets into the blood."

"They are divided," said Sarband. "*Till the tide swings, swung by the Mass, up from their deeps, not ours, I can only express the Progressive half. I can only point out to that reactionary mass which follows Heldon that it is wrong to stay where it is, wrong and unsafe. The peoples at the ultimate hour have ever been the voices of Destiny. All else is another tyranny. That is Democracy, as I understand Democracy.*"

Young Sarband approached his father.

"Well," he said, ironically, "I can tell you that it in coming, Death—and the fear of Death swung the Masses forwards under Capitalism. Death, and the horror of seeing it self-chosen, will swing Heldon's reactionaries over to you.

"Dreaming in my woods, I have met other dreamers. We have decided to prove to the reactionary Mass just how Unprogressive Heldon is. We are going to deepen and widen the struggle. We are going to die. We will see how many deaths it will take to break down a worn-out machine. I did not think of striking now. There was a little dream, a very little dream, stood in my way. Now, it is gone.

"I leave you to your problem of my mother or Messeia. You can consider yourself the symbol of the Progressive mass. We will do your work a little more quickly. You can sound the trumpet at the end, when Bureaucracy falls." He was rushing from the room. Sarband seized him by the shoulders.

"My son," he said, gravely, "have you considered that you will bring this system down with a crash?"

The young Sarband laughed.

"The other cannot grow till this is gone," he said, simply. "We will help it to decay. Mother! Prepare for them. They will all be here in an hour."

He grasped his cloak and went out in to the streets.

I left Arlene and Sarband standing by the window, hand in hand, facing their problem, and facing it together. The sunlit, noble years of fulfilment lay behind them. Across them a shadow had fallen—Messeia.

I see them still, hand in hand, looking dazedly at each other, the cry of one heart being, "She is still so much to me, I cannot choose"; and the cry of the other, the cry of the simple faithful of all the ages, "He is all the world to me. I shall be left alone."

I closed the door softly behind me and turned my steps to the Temple where Venensley lay awaiting the last rites. As I went up the wide steps, I met Messeia, leaving.

"How do I get in to see Venensley?" I asked.

"I will go with you," she said, and turned back.

Messeia and I stood in the great Temple. Upon the walls we saw the story of humanity's struggle for knowledge, for Reason, for Courage, for Bread, rolling out in wonderful paintings.

Here was the cave-mother, crouching by her fire, child in arms. Here was the cave-man who *won* his mate by a blow. Here was the picture of the discovery of fire, of the nomads wandering the earth, of warriors capturing men of other tribes, women of other tribes, to be their slaves.

Here Greece and Rome rose in glory and sank into insignificance, built on Slavery and Power. Here was Wat Tyler, with his thirty thousand rebels, foiled by the Fascists of their day. Here was Joan of Arc burning at her stake, the woman called 'witch' because she had heard 'voices' which were not the 'voices' of tradition. Terrible, beautiful, noble pageant of the martyrs for Science, Reason, Dreams, new Societies—murdered by the vulgar superstitions of their age.

In the centre of all this pageant of man's triumphal march, a little speck in that great hall, was the body of Venensley on a marble table.

He was in a leaden coffin.

The light of the afternoon fell on his face. The 'accident' had spared it. It was calm.

"He looks very like himself," I said in a low voice to Messeia.

She spoke back in quite her ordinary voice.

"Very. I am afraid there was very little of him left," she said. "Yes. He is very like himself, the dear old star-man. I will go and sit over there (Shallon painted that picture) whilst you say good-bye to him."

I saw Slave follow her, and lay himself down at her feet, looking up in her face.

I stood looking down on old Venensley.

I looked on the mystery of death without fear for the first time. One only realised that there was peace here—peace, the end of all dreams, the end of all struggles, leaving Youth to spring up and carry the torch on and on till the rocks melted and the seas ran dry.

"Good-bye, you old star-gazer," I said to him.

I turned, with one more look, and crossed over to Messeia.

"The sun will soon be setting," she told me.

We went out into the streets. There seemed to be more people about than usual at that hour. They were standing about in groups, conversing animatedly. There was an air of excitement which in our society had told that something had happened, either a war, or a murder, or a pit disaster, or a wreck.

Someone saw Messeia, and came towards her—a tall, white-haired man, with a scholar's face. He said something in the tongue I yet only half understood.

"English," she said, smiling.

"Oh, Pilgrim! Greeting, brother!" he said. "Well, then, have you heard? Great news! Just flashed out. The New Progressives are taking things in hand. Sarband's son and nineteen others are refusing to live under this Bureaucracy."

"Sarband's son!" said Messeia.

Then I saw that she recalled him.

"Oh, yes, I remember him. I once rolled him down a hill for telling me I was *only* a girl," she said.

The scholar laughed.

"So that will save Sarband," said Messeia.

She sighed, as though a big stone had been rolled away from her.

"Possibly," said the scholar. "The meeting is in Sarband's house tonight. This will test Heldon."

I plucked his sleeve.

"Do you mean to say a score of deaths, self-chosen, will topple a Bureaucracy over?" I asked.

He wore glasses.

His quiet eyes looked at me.

"Less than a score," he said, "if I mistake not. But one never quite knows. The measure of Unprogression may be guessed at by the lives it costs to topple it down."

I gasped.

"It would have taken a million in ours," I said. They would just have taken us up in Red Cross vans, prayed for us in the churches, stuck up memorials, called us heroes, and gone on just the same."

"Ah!" he said, "things were very bad with you." Messeia stood talking to him. All about the streets people were talking in groups. I could see the river, shining redly in the rays of the setting sun. A procession went by, very quietly, marching down, with its banners, touched by that red light. One banner caught my attention. It waved in the winter's wind.

'The Unevolved is as sacred to himself as the most Evolved', was that democratic watchword. And that banner was carried by the hands of an Intellectual.

"I suppose it means—" I said to the scholar.

"That Intellect is not worth the Aristocracy it has flung up from your Proletarian Mass," he told me, quickly. "The service of the least is as worthy as the service of the most gifted. Had that been taught wholesale in your world before the crash came, it would have changed the whole of our evolution. You see, your people were utterly unprepared. You revolutionised the State machine. It became a custom. The best intellects took charge of the chaos in your society. They swept its evils away. They became the new Power. They outstayed their use. They are going now, after five hundred years. Nothing lasts for ever. Their work is done."

Messeia talked a long time with him.

None of the groups in the streets seemed to wish to go home. I grew a little tired and cold. My poor blood congealed whilst they stood talking, warm and vigorous and electric.

"Are you going to Sarband's house," I asked Messeia.

She paused a moment.

"No."

So I went alone.

Arlene was busy with a great room which I had never seen opened before—a room capable of holding two hundred people. I assisted her. So did Sarband. The younger Sarband had not yet returned with his friends.

Chapter 11

Never shall I forget them, as they came trooping in, young Sarband and his gay friends, filling his mother's house, having brought *their* friends with them to share in the proceedings. Arlene, flushed and radiant, showing nothing of her own sorrows, received them. They greeted the elder Sarband playfully, taking, as I heard one of them tell him, 'power out of his gentle, valiant hands'. Grieved to the heart, he saw that they meant their threat. They were prepared to die. Nothing could be done with them. They gathered round him, and he listened to them, stunned and yet attentive.

"Why should we leave it all to you, brother?" asked one of them of him. He had no answer. In the middle of the arguments, and the flash of enthusiasm which caught even me in its spell, Heldon arrived. He stood in the doorway, looking in on the gay and valiant and wonderful galaxy of Youth and Beauty, Brains and Productivity.

Sarband went to meet Heldon with outstretched hand.

"You have heard?" he asked.

Heldon nodded.

He had a grimmer face than Sarband.

"So you are determined to bring the society that has given you all you have, and made you all you are, to the dust?" he asked.

A chorus of laughter went up from the New Progressives.

They clustered about the two men.

"It's *you* who are bringing it to the dust," said the tall scholar with the glasses. "We've a majority of the People who see it's going, Heldon. Can't you put yourself on one side?"

"I represent a minority, however small it is. We will fight you to the last man. I must be true to them."

I saw that all Reaction, in Leaders, draws its reactionary *power* from the masses. I saw that all progress, in leaders, draws its progressive *power* from the masses. There is no power for reaction or progress but what is in the rank and file. Otherwise it would soon go.

Then Heldon walked up to one of the gayest of the New Progressives.

"You, Carlton!" he said, bitterly, "will you throw your life away?"

Carlton laughed.

"My blood will be on your head, you old Unprogressive," he said. "By Evolution! Shall posterity say, 'Carlton, the sculptor, was an Unprogressive dog, who placed his dreams only in stone?' I shall haunt you, Heldon. I shall haunt you. You will pass my magnificent sculptured groups in the streets and say, 'I killed Carlton!'"

Heldon's face grew dark.

He wheeled round on Sarband.

"Their blood be on your head," he said, ominously.

The New Progressives suddenly shouted altogether, "No, no, no."

Heldon's eyes flamed.

"I say that if you had given in, Sarband, if you had only compromised—"

He was checked by a burst of laughter.

"Why, Heldon, you know your self compromise always leads to ruin," said the tall scholar. "Don't give us such stuff as that."

"I say I am prepared to talk things over with you, Sarband, to spare their gallant lives."

The New Progressives laughed again.

"If Sarband flinches the Mass will rise," said a young girl. "I can tell you that."

Heldon stood, a 'cornered' man.

He looked at them all, then he said:

"Who have chosen these deaths?"

Carlton the sculptor took a paper from his pocket. The room suddenly grew hushed. He read into the silence the names of those prepared to die for the idea the majority of the Mass held.

Heldon listened with whitening lips, darkening eyes.

"The flower of the island!" he yelled, suddenly. "Curse you, Sarband! Their blood be on your head!"

And as he dashed from the room, I recognized that it was, indeed, the old spirit of Unprogression, which would not take responsibility for the rising up of the people against their inequalities in every age.

Yet all that was needed was that the small minority of the reactionary mass and its leader should just stand out of the way.

When they had all gone, when Sarband and Arlene and I were alone, I turned to Sarband.

"What do you think Heldon will do now?" I asked.

He turned his calm face.

"His worst," he said.

"WHAT!"

"A tyrannical minority, fighting at the last ditch, always does its worst," he said. "A progressive minority always becomes a majority.

"Arlene, where are you going?"

She had put on her thick outdoor garments.

"I am going to the shed in the wood," she said. "I shall sleep in there tonight. I wish to be alone, to see if I can bear it."

I realised her position.

She was to see her son perish for an idea.

She was to see herself left quite alone.

Sarband held out his hand.

"Do not go," he said. "I am tired. I make my choice. I—we stay as we are. If it cannot be quite the same—we—yes—we have had the best."

Arlene grew pale, then her eyes flashed.

"I cannot accept resignation in place of joy," she said, forcibly. "No, Sarband. You must choose. I will return then."

We heard the door close with a solemn sound—solemn and sad, and echoing. I turned dumbly to Sarband.

He was sitting in silence. I said, "Why on earth can't you choose?"

He looked me full in the face.

"Ask the thousands of loveless individuals in your own society why they cannot choose," he said. "Edmund, let me confess it. Far back, somewhere in the people from whom I sprang, were two miserable people who lived on without love. We are made up of cells. I must have got those traditional slavish cells in me. In all things else I can choose. There I think I shall go down. I cannot surrender Arlene. I cannot help caring for Messeia. We have not done, even yet, with the miseries of your society."

I gazed at him, stupefied.

Chapter 12

The week that followed was very quiet. Everything appeared quite normal. The wheels went round, and the machines transported 'production'. I saw the whole of the population, saving those under 20 and those over 50, go forth to produce 'for the whole', and no man took of the fruits of their labours, saving those who had produced 30 years, and those who were yet unskilled and ungrown.

No scholar or artist here could say: 'I cannot produce because Slavery and Art do not go together'. It was all skilled work here, and did not absorb all a human's energies.

The fields were not ploughed with ploughshares, which had changed very little since they ploughed the fields before Rome existed. The guns had rusted. The plough had marched on. There was an inscription on their ploughs. They had taken it from Blake, 'mad Blake', who had said in his madness these remarkable words:—

"When gold and gems adorn the plough,
To peaceful arts shall envy bow."

Outside in the streets a few groups of men and women talked 'about it and about—'. That was all.

I went once through the snow to Arlene's shed, and brought away a memory of courage, saying stubbornly: "Edmund—he can't have us both." She went from the woods to her mill.

She lived in that simple shed, with its hammock, its rude simplicity, its armful of books—the sheds

158

that were put up for the 'dreamers' who wandered thinking out their dreams before they went back to build them in stone, or books, or music, or poesy. By working 'double time' in actual production they earned these holidays.

I went back through the snow. I took that simple message down to Sarband in his workshop. He received it in silence. He knew he could not have them both. There were no arrangements here which favoured double flat systems and a monogamous-polygamous society.

The Assembly was not gathering its antagonists. Everything was very quiet. We missed Arlene. But she could exert no tyranny over us by withdrawing herself to a shed in a wild wood carpeted with snow. The machines brought our meals. A young woman who would have worked anything from 10 to 14 hours a day, in our society, as a 'servant for the rich' came in, and with applied science vacuumed us and aired us, and 'did' the dishes in an hour every evening.

Usually, after she had gone, we went for a walk, my brother and I. Then we would come back to the silent house which Arlene had left till Sarband could choose. And I grew a little bitter against Messeia.

I went out one evening to the 'ceremony' which was poor old Venensley's 'Exit'. There were a few hundreds of his friends there. Messeia was amongst them. I heard the most glorious 'Dead March' Whitman set to harmony, the same that Messeia rolled out under the room near the stars on the organ. I watched that little body of the old, old man carried by his dearest friends, who had loved the constellations. I saw it pass into the crematorium, and come out, a little clean white dust, such as the stars are made of. The little dust, the precious dust, was placed in an urn, and carried by one of his friends.

I followed the throng. Outside were the machines. Messeia motioned me to come into one. We left Oxford behind, taking with us that little nothingness of dust, and talking of Venensley.

"You know, he would have been tickled to death," said a fellow scientist, "to know that we thought so much of him. I've left an eclipse in Spain to see the last of him."

And I realised that in our society he would have been buried like a pauper or a 'dog', for his 'genius' would never have got the chance to 'out'; or, in our society, he would have been a 'demand', supplying the science for a war-mad world.

The salt air of the sea came to us. The machine descended. I saw the dim shore, where the last receding tide had left its marks. I heard the surge of the crying seas against the rocks. There was a little boat. They placed the urn upon it, and the voices of Venensley's friends sang the glorious chant beginning, '*O Democracy of Death! Sparing none, claiming thy own, immutable and beneficent, take this, our friend!*'

They stood on the wave-marked shore, reluctant, as humanity ever is and ever will be, to lose its loved. Then Messeia, stooping gently, stepping out into the water, pushed the boat off into the great sea. I heard the surge of the waves against the crags. We watched the dim speck on the waters till it faded into nothingness. The storms, in their splendid majesty, would decide the fate of that little pathetic handful of human dust.

Silently, we went back to the machines. He had lived with the stars. He was not given to the worms.

Messeia stepped out when I did, as the machine descended beside Sarband's house.

"Are you coming in?" I asked.

She shook her head.

"Then, you ought to," I said. "Arlene is not here, Sarband is alone. In fact, he is alone because he can't make up his mind whether he likes you or Arlene best."

We stood staring at each other.

Paler and paler grew Messeia.

The light that had sprung up into her eyes faded.

"I will come in," she said. "Terrible! Terrible! Am I nothing, then? Am I considered to be a mere automaton who waits for a man to choose? Besides, who said I wanted Sarband to have to walk over another woman for him? Have I not been considered at all, then? Am I *nothing*? By Evolution!"

I realised that our sordid marriage failures which half-filled our newspapers had been sordid because they were simple, and simple because they were sordid, and blocked by economic considerations.

She swept in past me. I followed.

"What is this thing Edmund tells me?" demanded Messeia. "Where is Arlene? Why have you let her go?"

Sarband rose out of his chair.

He was very pale also.

"She is in the shed—where you first met us," he told her calmly.

"And—you have allowed her to remain there?" she asked.

"Certainly. Could I thrust myself upon her?"

I saw they had quite forgotten me.

"You and I would not get on together," said Messeia, quietly. "Oh, you must know it. I spend hundreds of hours playing with *sounds*. I forget people. I am happiest alone. I'm utterly selfish, Sarband. I'm unsympathetic. The only shake up I've ever had has been my love for you, and—joining the Progressives. I'm dogmatic. I should forget your existence most of the time. Then, one day I should look up and say,

'Hallo!' and your eyes would say, 'Yet, l've been here all the time. Have you just discovered the fact?' That's the truth, Sarband. By Evolution! *It's the truth.*"

I realised that it must have cost her something to tell that truth.

"Choose, Sarband," she said. "I have made my choice. Tell me yours."

They were both very pale—paler than ever I had seen them, paler than ever I saw them, until—

There was a pause.

Then Sarband turned his face.

"I feel you are right, Messeia," he said. "I should miss—*mothering*. I feel that you are right. I—Arlene has ruined me. She has always thought of me."

She laughed her little, ringing laugh.

"I wanted," she said, slowly, "to see how great you were, Sarband. I find *you are not great enough to walk over another woman for.*"

But I think she felt it keenly—that so much should have depended on being 'thought of'. Just then, relieving the awkwardness which I felt very much, a knock fell on the door. I think Sarband's thoughts flew to Arlene.

He went down the passage.

"Is Messeia Guilippio here?" asked Sarband the younger's voice.

"Here!" announced Messeia. "Who is that?"

He came into the room.

"This," said Sarband's son, "is Sarband the second."

Messeia looked at him.

"I have brought you a message," he told her.

He held out his hand. She placed hers in it.

"Fate has been very kind, Messeia Guilippio," he said. "Our names have been drawn together. You and I are the first on the list."

I saw her take her death sentence.

An almost imperceptible tremor stole across her lips. Then it passed.

He watched her, and a little smile crept into his eyes.

"Fate has certainly been very kind," he repeated.

"I don't see that it matters who one dies with," said Messeia. "One always faces it, I think—*quite* alone."

"Fate has been very kind," said young Sarband. "It is better to die with a Dream close to one's heart than to leave it to perish—alone."

He handed her a paper. He showed her his own. They stooped over the table.

"Carlton drew the things out—blindfolded, so that no one would be jealous," he told Messeia. "Well—good-bye, father."

I saw Sarband's face turn the colour of ashes.

He laid his hands on young Sarband's shoulders.

"Good-bye," he said, steadily. "I think—Youth will not go down alone. Good-bye. Messeia. Oh—what about your mother?"

"I am going to see her—now," said young Sarband.

They went towards the door.

"Stay!" called Sarband, the elder. His hands took Messeia by the shoulders.

"You are both very dear," he said. "Very dear. I thought—I would like to—look at you again—that's all."

He gave them a long look.

"I am very proud of you, Sarband," he said "I suppose it is the only way. Good-bye."

His look clung to Messeia. Then it turned to his son and clung there.

"Now—go—" he said, suddenly. They went.

"What are they going to do?" I asked.

He turned his face upon me.

"Starve to death," he said, simply.

"What!" I yelled.

"Just starve to death," said Sarband. "It's the only way. They won't shoot people—here."

"And will that—?" I began.

"Brother," said Sarband. "It is a very terrible thought for Heldon to carry about with him—that two people are starving to death for a dream—while he eats on. Particularly—as—Messeia happens to be his daughter."

Chapter 13

Sarband was restive. I knew he was waiting to hear Arlene come back. I wished irritably that she would come back. Then there would be a chance that when I spoke to him he would hear me. He tried to be attentive to me.

"I suppose you think that it's very terrible that we should have to adopt these methods here?" he asked, referring to the two who had gone out.

"I do."

"Well—you see—humanity as a whole has progressed to this point; whatever their differences men won't kill each other. They just won't. It would be impossible—were I tyrant enough—to say to the Majority: 'Go and tear Heldon out of his house, and throw him into the forces we use to disintegrate the bodies of blind dogs!' They would be appalled."

"Yes?" I said.

"In your society—when the whole struggle was a brute struggle for bread, and power—of course, a minority could hold a whole mass down by threats of death. That has gone. In your society, where your papers, even the capitalist papers were full of murders, and suicides, and wars, and strikes—two people choosing starvation would have left no mark at all.

"Life *is* sacred here, even the life of an old Unprogressive. The whole struggle-ground has been lifted on a higher plane. It has been a fight of mind forces. Some of your idealists used to think they could start there before the bread-struggle was over. With the Masses under the feet of Power, Grab, and Possessions they used to try to bring spiritual forces to bear!

"And of all the classes the Proletarians were the most moral. They were so Moral they stood there and let themselves be robbed, murdered, and inflicted with starvation—diseases! If morality had decided it, they would have been the victors.

"Their lives were cleaner. They suffered agonies. But the moralities which we have, the simple virtues of truth and honesty, and the simplicity which got them downed every time, came, in the main, from that great suffering class. It was less lustful. Its men and women who suffered martyrdoms together, loved in spite of the garbage they ate, and the grime and sweat on their bodies.

"They had none of the *trimmings* which keep sensuality alive. It was Love—pure Love, great Love— dragged them through the sewage of life, broken and blasted and half murdered—but it was Love. You knew you could face all kinds of things together, and faced them. *That* was Love. If Love and Morality and Spirituality had decided it you would have walked like gods, and the other clans would hate crawled like worms. "And I tell you, Edmund, when Capitalism fell—you were nobler in your *chance* victory than they were with their *planned victories.*

"No reign of Terror began. A reign of Terror had ended. You searched their houses for weapons. You segregated them—isolated them—and destroyed every article of destruction they could use against you, knowing it was the only way to save *blood,* even *their* blood. The first Statute in your House of Assembly made weapons illegal, whoever possessed them. *Your first blow was to destroy Force.* You were sick and weary of it. Woolwich Arsenal was blown up. You collected the Scientists, and said: 'Now, you serve Life, not Death. You've a world to win. Start in and conquer the secrets of Cancer, Consumption, Syphilis, Insanity. Serve the People.'"

I stared at him.

"Then, Revolution?" I began.

"In Europe—did you say it was Europe?"

"Yes. The whole lot."

"Did not go on Russian lines?" I asked.

He looked at me in wonder.

"How on earth could a highly industrialised Europe follow the lines of a country made up of peasants living under Feudalism?" he asked.

I stared at him and him at me.

"Do you mean to say you thought Europe would follow Russia?" he asked. "I gave you credit for some sanity."

"But there were people—" I began.

He laughed.

"Revolutions generally take the form of the country whose conditions they arise out of," he said. *"So do Counter-Revolutions.* In England, Edmund—it was a legislative, political, industrial Revolution. In France it was French, *very* French. In Italy—it was Italian. In Germany it was German. In one particular it took the same form in all countries. *It destroyed Force.* You see. you had all been faced by the pleasant Fear of Extinction. *You realised that every gun was a blasphemy against the sun.* Yes, in this Island, the Revolution took the form of the conditions it was born in. They always do."

"You are upsetting all my ideas!" I said, peevishly.

Sarband laughed. Then he said: "Was that the door?"

But all was still.

"The women are damned proud here, Sarband," I said, watching his restlessness.

"Yes. They bred *us*," he said. "They are not slaves of slaves. This is my punishment. I suppose I had better go and meet her half way."

I felt, restless, too.

I walked with him.

The quiet stars shone down on us. The lights shone from the windows. The cars went past. They went above us. We parted at the corner of a great building where child players were playing an ancient play by Toller.

I felt very much alone. I believe for the first time I desired to return to Binkers Court—just to see them all, just to know what was happening to them. After all, it was my world and those were my people. But— to *stay* there—I could not bring myself to face it. I walked along. Two people were standing—talking. I glanced again. It was Messeia and the younger Sarband. He was laughing, and I managed to make out what he was saying.

"Don't be so conservative," he was teasing Messeia. "You know I'm a better man than my father. Let's go to the Temple—*now*."

"I tell you, I should forget you were there—half the time," she told him.

He lilted a few bars of a song.

"I should forget you were there half the time," he teased her. "Queer if we both forgot when the other was remembering. Besides—three weeks to live! Besides, it's all theorising. You're half-crazed with your *Music*. Try *Life*."

She pondered.

Breathlessly I watched them.

Did people here just walk away, out of the streets,

without any fuss, and get married? He laid his hand on her sleeve. She frowned at him.

"Don't coerce me," she said.

"Thou who die and have never loved are nonentities," said young Sarband.

"I won't be coerced," said Messeia.

I realised it.

In the back street of a slum she might have got murdered—rebel slave of a rebel slave. In Park Lane she would probably have had quite a competitive crowd of masculinity, which would have competed for the holy joy sportsmen feel in breaking the spirit of a wild young ' thoroughbred'.

"Please coerce me," said Sarband.

"Please go away," said Messeia, distractedly. "I can think better."

"You're afraid of me," laughed Sarband. "Messeia! You're lost. You're afraid of me. You're afraid of me smashing up your plans, your music. I know it's beautiful. But so am I."

Then he ceased teasing.

"Very well, good evening."

I recognised the same old 'stunts'.

"Stay, don't go off like *that*."

Same old immortal stunts.

"Well, we'll just walk down as far as the river."

Same old stunts.

The world had changed. Humanity was very much the same. I am ashamed to say I followed them.

It struck me that though I kept quite close to them by hurrying, they did not see me, took not the slightest notice of me. But then—I had *never* loved. Horror of horrors! I had lived twenty eight years, a flesh-and-blood human, thinking only of bread, bread, bread—or else 'How the devil could I keep a woman?' I might as well never have been born. Their voices drifted to me, Sarband's little rugged sentences, Messeia's voice, sweeter and clearer. I saw her place her hand reluctantly on his arm, and look for the first time into his face.

"The first time you ever endeavour to *crush* me," she told him, "you will *lose* me."

Remarkable words. Very. Strange words of surrender. Young Sarband smiled.

"You need not tell *me* that," he said.

They turned round.

"If it is a day, or a week," said Messeia, passionately. "You understand?"

I saw in him suddenly the gentle calmness of his father.

"And why should anyone, man or woman, wish to crush what he loves beyond himself?" asked he, half-jestingly, half-earnest.

Crushed creature from a crushed class—I knew I could never forget those words.

"I don't know. I suppose these fears die hard in us," said Messeia. "I suppose—they are race-memories of a time—when men and women crushed each other and crushed their children, and were all crushed together, by priests, and soldiers, and hungers— and—*laws*. There! I could not be a tyrant, Sarband. I refuse to have one, even in Love's name."

She held out her hand.

It was trembling a little.

He bent his head and laid his lips against it.

"Dear little hand," I heard.

Why did I remember blundering into the Jones' room, to borrow a scrape of margarine, when first they came, newly wedded, to Binkers Court? Then I saw that they were walking away. I followed. It simply could not be. People could not walk off like that to get married! Outside the Temple of Evolution Messeia paused.

"It will soon be over," Sarband said, encouragingly.

I couldn't help it.

I had never been in love.

I floundered up to them.

"But—haven't you bigamy wholesale here?" I asked.

"Hang it! If people could walk off the streets like this in our world! We had to make investigations!"

"Edmund!" said Sarband, "please, please, go away."

Messeia turned her head and smiled faintly.

I realised the old femininity; calmer, always facing love, birth, and death, sometimes the three-in-one, in our society.

"What is bigamy?" asked Messeia, on steps of the Temple of Evolution.

I think the younger Sarband felt as much like murdering me as a man in his society could.

"We have only ten minutes," he said, coldly, "and there will be crowds there. Go and read the 'Industrial History of England' by Gibbons! Go anywhere, read anything. But—go!"

I fled.

I could not throw my shadow there, nor darken the ground their feet would walk over—their free, proud feet—their happy, noble feet.

Chapter 14

As I sauntered along, thinking my own thoughts, I ran into Mrs. Biers. I scarcely recognized her at first. Clothes do make an enormous difference.

She had left Sarband's house two months ago because she would rather live where there were some children. So they had sent her where there were half a dozen. The greatest change I noticed in Mrs. Biers was that her expression had lost its up-in-arms-against-the-world look.

"Well, how's the washing going on?" I asked her.

"Oh, cheese it," she said, Mr. Sniggins!" She answered. "It's all right. I'm a-sitting with the children learning all I can. Geography, an' all that! 'Ow the maps have changed! Lord, Mr. Sniggins, when I looks at the children here, and things how they have been banged into shape in Binkers Court—I feel 'eart-broke, fair 'eart-broke,. The questions they ask the poor teacher, jumpin' up all over the place. And, you know, they've got to get answered fair straight or they comes back to the point like a lot of bluebottles round a honey-pot. Askin' how it is twice wun isn't three, and 'ow long 'as the moon been here, and why the earth was governed by policemen and soldiers and kings in the Middle Ages, and why so many people had to be kept walking about just because they had money they had not worked for."

I laughed.

"'Arskin' me," she continued, pathetically, "'ow it was I didn't know nuffink, when there was all the universities there was—till I'd got to tell 'em the universities was only for us to smell at, just to catch the flavour.

"Arskin' me how the ladies could be so cruel as to go on knittin' when men was being a-smashed up with guns. Seems they've seen some picters of 'knitting parties during the Great War'. I'd be 'appy here, Mr. Sniggins—*if* only I could get Joshua outer my head. Where are you goin', now?"

I told her that it had been my intention of going to see how Sparkins was going on. She agreed to accompany me. We walked along to Skeeley's house, passing a procession on the way.

"They do say," whispered Mrs. Biers, "as how there's goin' to be a social change here, and how it would happen quite natural if only Heldon would get out of the way—him and his little minority. What'll happen in our world, Mr. Sniggins—when the Majority wants a change an' the others stand in the way?"

I did not desire to discuss it.

"You see," was all I allowed myself to say, "when they are legislated out, and all the representatives of the people are legislated in—the capitalists have got force in their hands, unless that is legislated out of their hands, too. Anyhow, I suppose the workers will link up together to stop the next war. If they found out how to do that, I expect Capitalism would not have much of a leg to stand on. Now, don't laugh at Skeeley, Mrs. Biers."

"I'll try not to," she said.

We waited on the mat whilst Skeeley let us in. He was in very high spirits.

"Come in, come in," he urged. "My friend, Sparkins, is *great*. We've just taken Baghdad, and resurrected Napoleon and Alexander, and set them up to bring unity into the lives of the Masses. We're just having a revival now, whilst Napoleon and Alexander settle which of them is going to be dictator. If they don't make up their minds soon we shall have to bring the Pope back."

Mrs. Biers winked at me.

We followed Skeeley.

Upon the table was his glorified dream of the Middle Ages. We sat down and watched a toy air ship dropping little objects upon the 'populace', and Sparkins directing an ambulance van and picking them up.

We watched him and Sparkins for an hour, then Mrs. Biers nudged me, and, taking the hint, I told Skeeley we hope that it kept him happy. Sparkins gave me a peculiar look. He told us in the passage that Skeeley was the greatest man on the island, and if Skeeley had his way, the folk would not be processioning in the streets.

"Well, it does no harm *here*," I said. "Though I think he'd be safer shut up. Have you got your passport, Sparkins?"

He snorted, and said something about they would maybe wish they had granted it to him.

Mrs. Biers left me and went back to the house with the six children. I don't know how I came to be wandering past Heldon's house, but I recognized it. The air was rather cold. I was going as quickly as I could, when I saw two figures sitting in Heldon's doorway.

"Greeting, brother," came the voice of the younger Sarband.

I turned.

They were both sitting there, one cloak about them.

"What are you doing there?" I asked.

"Waiting," said Messeia, calmly.

"But it's so cold! You can't mean—?"

"Yes," said Messeia, "we shall sit here till he gives in."

"But won't he have you thrown off the steps?" I asked.

"That would be brute force," said Messeia.

"So you'll just—"

"Yes. Sit here—till he can't bear it any longer," said Sarband.

"And am I to go home to a bed, and fire, and food, and leave you here?" I asked, bitterly.

Even as I spoke I recalled that we did it in our society. I ponder the while. Then I turned away. I realised I was seeing the conditions of utopia, and our own terrific struggles transplanted here, without force to combat them. As I walked away I met Sarband, the elder. I watched him sit down by Heldon's door. Then Carlton came up, whistling gaily. I watched him sit there, too.

It was very terrible to know that they would sit here, waiting, till they died, but never give in. I went back to the house. Arlene was weeping.

"What are you?" I asked.

She turned her wet face upon me.

"I am Human Love," she said. "I am going to die with the rest. Let me pass."

I stood aside, dumbfounded.

"Good-bye," I called.

When I went to the door she was gone. I was alone. All the people I had loved—*if* they were people, and not symbols—were dying out there. And I was allowing it, doing nothing. Well, had it not been so in my own place? *What had I done as an individual to fling my weight however small, on the side of Progress?*

Let me pass over it quickly. I used to walk past Heldon's house, and see my brother starving to break down Unprogression. I saw Arlene, her face getting sharpened into the look of other women I had seen in our society, the eyes growing sadder. the energy fading, dullness creeping over the beings I had loved. Messeia! How like she was to the spirit of Genius in the Masses 1 had left, sinking into despair. And always the younger Sarband, with his turbulent face, like the face of the youth of our society, when it was going down under Greed, Militarism, and Hunger.

Sometimes 1 would sit with them, and their voices would answer mine, saying, "It cannot last long now, Edmund". Once I saw Heldon open the door. He argued with them. He held out Compromise. Carlton laughed. Sarband the elder always shook his head. Then Heldon would go in, saying, "It is your own fault".

One day I sat by Messeia and Sarband the younger.

They were sitting close together, hand in hand.

When next I passed they were dead.

It was I who made the outcry.

Heldon came out.

His face was wan in the light.

"Take them away, quickly!" he said, and staggered into the house like a drunken man. I sat by Sarband and Arlene and saw them die. Again I saw them taken away quickly. Then Carlton. Others passed up and took their places. They were laid in the Temple. Loneliness and horror and desolation fell on me. Then one night the streets were full of people.

"This is enough," said their feet, tramping through the streets.

Heldon came out.

He looked like a maniac as he staggered down the steps.

"I am not fit to live. I have killed twelve people," he shouted. "Take me. Take me and do with me what you will."

I followed as they took him. I walked beside Heldon. All the way as he went he was mumbling about "Twelve people".

It was Unprogression, but nothing to that which we had, which took its toll of hundreds of thousands every year, and justified itself from every pulpit, Press, in cultured words, and in the words of military men. I realised the truth. Heldon had killed twelve people. He wished to die. The Unprogressive had become Progressive. He had no Interests. He had only Opinions. He had even to let them kill themselves. Yet he did not wish to live. The battle was won.

I had seen the two Sarbands and Messeia, and then Arlene, laid in the Temple of Evolution. I had seen the great throngs giving them love and reverence— who had left them to die. I had seen one lot of people pass from the steps and another lot take their place. I had seen the whole tragedy repeated. I had seen the dust of Sarband and Messeia, the elder Sarband and Arlene cast out to the great tides, drifting into nothingness.

Loneliness and desolation fell upon me. I had seen destruction sweeping away the best of the race. I had seen Skeeley playing with his 'toys', and Sparkins aiding him in his fantastic schemes—moving soldiers and emperors and statesmen about—whilst the great creative impulses of humanity went down to death.

And then—just when I had lost all hope—I rushed out of the house to see the masses, the divided Intelligences, rushing into the streets, heard their voices, and knew that this was the beginning of the End. How I got down through the crowds I do not know. But somehow I found myself outside the Temple of Evolution, full of their dead, and knew that they had got Heldon inside, and were keeping him prisoner till they had changed things.

Then, a great cry went up. I stared upwards at the tower of the temple, and waving a rod about in his hands—there was Skeeley, master of the situation, with a rod of force in his hands which I knew could destroy them all. They had allowed a madman, with his dreams of the 'glories' of the past, to steal a march on them. Somehow I found myself climbing up the walls after him. Queer things peeped out at me as I went up. Gargoyles and devils and saints. Bishops and half starved men, motherhood skimped and weary, drudges and prostitutes, lawmen in wigs, hangmen, murderers, compromisers, insurgents, snobs of all classes, fanatics, miracle-mongers and dumped up and down amongst them all crowds of workers, listening to them, and not realising that all Power for Progress or Reaction came from them.

I looked up, and there was Skeeley, waving his rod and dancing like a Dervish! I tried to propitiate him, coax him, flatter him, threaten him, creeping up to him a little nearer all the time. At every moment I expected him to hurl that rod down, and to see the Masses destroyed. Knowing his weakness for kings I tried to get him to sit down whilst I told him the history of all the kings of the island. I became all things, climbing up the Temple, diplomat and insurgent, rebel and cringer—knowing he had got the *force*. At last I reached him. We stood face to face, I, the fool who had lived in the dream of the future, he, the knave who had lived in the dream of the past.

"Give me your rod, Skeeley," I cried. "Give me your rod and go down. The revolution's over. The people are united."

We walked round and round each other, and Skeeley suddenly threw his rod—

I leaped forwards and caught it, and found myself falling, falling—

A horrible fear that I should strike the people below almost paralysed me. The sweat burst out of every pore, and a wild idea shot through me that I would gladly return to the old world before I brought disaster to the new. I tried to shout out and warn them—but I could make no sound—and then, just as I expected to crash upon their heads—I awoke. My gaze fell on walls, beds, on a face bent over me.

"Where am I?" I asked.

The answer was civil—but, oh, how cold after those voices I had been used to.

"You are in the workhouse hospital. Don't move."

Chapter 15

*"Most of the social and political ills from which you suffer
are under your control, given only the will and courage to
alter them. You can live in another and wiser fashion if you
choose to think it out and work it out. You are not awake to
your own power."* —PLATO.
*"That is a high, adventurous teaching that has still to
soak into the common intelligence of our race.'* —H.G.WELLS

"How long have I been here?" I asked the female
attendant.

"Oh, I don't know. I lose count of the days—so
much to do," she said, casually. "About three weeks."

I saw that she was almost run off her feet, and had
no special interest in me, as why, indeed, should
she have! I heard a man at the far end of the ward
groaning abominably. The female attendant went to
him several times and spoke harshly, when he 'shut
up' for a little while. Horrible, horrible, to lie there,
weak, and helpless! Horrible to think 'I am *back*'.

I managed to raise myself on my elbow after several
attempts, and the words on a card hung on the foot
of my bed danced before my sight:

Edmund Sniggins,
Aged 29.
Cerebral Meningitis.
Diet. Farinaceous.

"If you don't stop that row I'll have you put in with
the lunatics," said the female attendant, going to the
old man again. He gave her a cowed and appealing look.

All through the night at intervals that horrible groaning went on. Once, I think, I turned my face into the pillows and wept. Brutal and horrible world! Why had I not died? Out of here—to go to Binkers Court! I thought of the houses of Equality Island! But most of all I thought of the people! Perhaps I wandered a little. It seemed to me that down that moaning of the old man at the end of the ward drifted another voice: 'Brother! Take courage! You shall find us again. Dreams never perish.' Dawn was stealing into the ward as I slept at last. I awoke to a scene of tumult. Two men were taking the old man out, the old man stuttering and incoherent—to be in a room where he would disturb no one else. He started crying and blabbering, appealing, cringing, but they were firm.

"Come on, Dad!" said the younger fellow, taking hold of his elbow.

He gave a wondering and stricken look at the ward.

Suddenly he stopped.

"I won't go," he said, stubbornly. "I won't."

"Just catch hold of his other elbow, Ted," said the young man.

"It is worse than prison. Worse than prison," suddenly came the blubbering voice of the old man. "Strike me dead, God! Mary. Mary. Oh, Mary, if you could see me *here*."

I buried my head under the clothes.

They led him away.

"Senile decay," said the man in the next bed to mine.

I said nothing.

"You're a surly blighter," was his comment on me.

I turned my face towards him.

"No," I said. "Only, I feel too ill to talk much."

He was mollified.

"Ulcers in the leg I've got." he added. "They talks o' takin' it off. Nice look-out fer me, with a wife and six kids. It's a hell of a life!"

I realised that I was indeed back in the old world. I closed my eyes, and tried to recreate again the scenes I had lately wandered in. I recalled a wide stretch of lonely shore, with the rock towering up, to which Arlene had taken me, to show me where the last man who had murdered another actually had looked his last wistful look at the sky, finding it impossible to live with another's blood upon his hands.

"Good lights, these, ain't they?" asked my companion.

I opened my eyes.

"I was thinking they were both poor and glaring," I told him.

He seemed nonplussed.

"One of them there grousin' devils you seem to be," he said.

I laughed.

"No. I've never had much to say," I informed him. "Up to now. Seems like—if I get better I shall *have* a lot to say."

He pondered me.

"Blinking Socialist or something, I'll bet you are," he hazarded.

"Yes, I'm a Socialist," I said. "Socialism is out to stop exploitation, which is the only way of bringing peace and prosperity to the workers."

"You make me tired," he said.

"Weren't *you* grousing about your life being a hell?" I asked.

"An 'ow the 'ell will Socialism alter that?" he asked.

"Have you been lazy?" I asked.

"I'll smash your jaw," he began.

"Well, observe that I did not say you *had* been lazy. Ever asked yourself the question how it comes about men work from the cradle to the grave, and can't stand a few months' illness, but have to be packed off into workhouses? Now, this workhouse has been built by working men like us. Ever see a rich bloke up a ladder, carrying a hod? Ever see one on the railway lines, or hear of one getting jammed between the bumpers! Ever hear of one 'signing on', or applying for a 'pension', or for parish relief? Why? One lot makes all, and the other nothing. But the last lot never does things like we do."

"More sense," chuckled my bed-companion. "Wouldn't you do it if you had the chance? I'd be the same, myself. No, There's no hope. Always been like this. Always will be."

"But it hasn't always been like this," I told him. "Do you mean to say the world has never changed? Do you never read? Never think? Never?"

"Oh, hell," he said, grinning, "Talkin' o' readin' and thinkin' in that hell-hole I live in. It's like a German band and a Barnum and Bailey's show. When I want to rest I goes out into the streets, an' walks about till I'm tired. There's the old woman cryin' half her time, an' the hell of a time I've had when she found out she was goin' to have another. There were eight of us to keep on one pound nineteen a week. But I votes the Tory in. Always trade when there's Tories in. You'll see, there'll be a boom—peace an' plenty. Leave it to the Tories, old man."

I burst out laughing.

"Well, maybe they'll bring revolution sooner," I acknowledged.

"Eh?"

"I mean. Unprogression, unchecked, will probably destroy itself much sooner if it's left to go on. Only, as Socialists, we've a right to have at least the roots of a new society ready, and stop the crash from being a chaos."

"You're a silly devil!" he said. "I say, your sister is a nice girl. An' she left you some cigarettes."

I stared at him.

It was the first time I knew I had a sister.

Five minutes later I was possessed of two cigarettes, handed to me by the female attendant.

I handed my antagonist one.

He winked.

"Knew it wasn't your sister," he taunted.

I felt myself redden.

"Well," I told him, "I don't know who it could be. I have no lady friends—only a fat woman married to a sand-hawker, who borrows off me sometimes. May be —"

"No. Not her. But she's been," he said.

"What was she like?" I asked.

He had a curiously indefinite mind. His evidence in a witness box would have been taken no notice of.

"Don't know her," I said, after his description.

Neither did I. After all, there are so many women with yellow hair, large eyes, wide apart, and a cleft in the chin. A train rumbled past the window. Its smoke was illumined by the glow from the engine. He pointed to the colour.

"Hair *that* colour," he said, pointing.

"Oh! "I said, faintly.

I sank back on my pillows, and pretended sleep, to have silence. *That* was the colour of Arlene's hair.

I was unable to sleep much in that place, I have nothing to say against its scrupulous cleanliness. From an hygienic point of view it was better than Binkers Court. But it annoyed me to find myself in a workhouse.

Perhaps it looked worse to me, because I had dreamed a dream. But the thing that worried me most was to be amongst sick people. When the man in the next bed was 'worse' and told me he was 'worse' I'm blessed if I did not feel *worse* myself. I found my sensitiveness to the misery of others increased a 'hundredfold'.

Though the faces of my suffering fellows were averagely cheerful—considering all things— they looked to *whimper* after the calm and generous-expressioned faces of the people I had dreamed about.

I began to pay the penalty for having dreamed a dream from the moment of my awakening from it. I had walked amidst beauty, and grown accustomed to that. Now, I was pitched back to walk amidst ugliness, to which I would nevermore be accustomed, because I had standards of comparison.

But one great comfort lay close to my heart, even in those terrible first days, when I was getting 'climatised' again. I knew that the conditions we lived under were purely transitionary.

"When can I get out of this bed?" I asked the female attendant.

"When you are told!"

I tried in vain to get her to give me an idea of when I should be at 'large' but could get no definite answer. So I tried to be as content as possible, but did a bit of 'studying', as Mrs. Biers calls it. I managed to get on the right side of the female attendant by running her about as little as possible, and very sincerely, I ask you to believe, sympathising with her when she started to pour out her grievances.

"Well, you will send another class to represent you in Parliament," I told her.

She stared at me. "I voted Labour," she said disgustedly. "And he was at the bottom of the poll, all owing to them Bolshevists."

"Put it there," I said.

What I had left of a hand I held out.

She giggled, but put hers into it.

"But you know," I told her, "that was a dodge. Knowing the people were scared of Bolshevism, Capitalism made that the peg to win what it calls a 'victory.' Bolshevism is purely Russian, and Russia is only a part of the map. From what I can gather, the people there are much better off than they were under feudalism. But every country acts as conditions determine, and they vary in circumstances the world over."

"Well, I shan't vote again," she said, in a depressed voice. "I'm not going to be told I've voted for Revolution!"

She was moving away.

"Always remember it will be Capitalism brings a revolution," I said. "The more it is left to do as it likes—the faster it'll come, and the more havoc it will work. The less people there are awakened the worse it will be. If there's blood-letting it will be Capitalism does the blood-letting. They are experts at it."

"When'll we get all the people with us?" she asked, sadly.

I smiled.

"Why, they are on the way fast—*when they want security and peace which this system can't give them,*" I told her.

She pondered.

"How many do you know who want those two things?" I asked.

"Lots!" she admitted.

"You go about amongst 'em showing they can get neither under this system, and you'll be helpin' a lot," I said.

She went away to her work.

"Somebody to see you," she told me later.

I raised myself on my elbow. Could it be, could it be the sister I had lately become possessed of? Hair the colour of Arlene's—that was something to look forward to.

I sank back as *she* came through the doorway of the ward. *Mrs. Biers.*

Still, I was pleased to see her, very pleased—after the first disappointment.

"Well, old sport, 'ow are you?" asked Mrs. Biers.

"Better," I told her.

"Well, you looks like a sort of washed-off mummy, yet," she said. "But you *are* alive, and not gabbling the stuff you *was.*"

"How are the Joneses?" I asked. "Tom got work yet?"

She shook her head.

"Awful, it is," she said. "'E's been a big-hearted one, but he's getting a bit low, now, in my opinion. Mr. Sniggins, 'ow is it there is no work?"

She banged a packet of Woodbines on my coverlet.

"Because human values have sunk to nothing—and only profit values count," I told her.

"They were as loving a pair as I ever saw," said Mrs. Biers. "They are yet—only it's different. I believe it's driving him crazy, seein' her *so changed.* An', now, Sparkins is coming, to have 'em turned out. The child 'as bronchitis, an', Mr. Sniggins, I wishes *I was* in Parliament."

I did, too.

She had a knowledge beyond college education.

I felt morose when she had gone. I sank back on my pillows, realising that if the Joneses were turned out I would be turned out *also.* For, according to Mrs. Biers, I had saved nothing by coming here. As I had left with nothing I returned with nothing. Nay, but I had my *dream,* and, a *sister* with hair the colour—What fools we all are!

I passed a wretched night, some times slipping into fitful slumber, in which, as in a vision, I saw glimpses of the land forever lost to me.

I awoke, weak and depressed. The female attendant had brought my bowl of bread and milk. The lights looked sickly in the dawn.

"Had a good night?" she asked.

"Yes. How long am I to stay here?" I asked in my turn.

"Three weeks—at the least," she was pleased to inform me.

Sudden resolution entered my heart.

"No," I told her.

"Doctor's orders," she said. "Ain't you treated all right here?"

She seemed a little piqued.

"I'm not grumbling," I told her. "But I want to get back."

"Three weeks, he said," she told me.

She sat on the foot of my bed, breaking the rules.

"Shall I hitch your pillow higher?" she asked.

I shook my head.

"Did my sister look well?" I asked.

She sniffed.

Odd how most women of our world do not like to admit that another woman looks well.

"She looked all right," she told me. "I expect *most* of it was paint. Not much like you."

"No," I allowed. "Now, I'm dark—"

"Hair the colour of a haystack," she said. "I expect it is dyed."

"Bobbed?" I hazarded.

"No, if they bobbed *that* hair, they'd have to run the lawn-mower over it. You know she isn't your sister."

I grinned.

I admitted that I had no sister. There was no particular virtue in it, as I have never been a really good liar. Even my face, Mrs. Biers says, gives me away. Still, Nature did not leave me entirely unprotected. If you are really simple and what is called elemental, she generally supplies *instincts*.

But just then she saw the matron coming, and jumped up from the bed.

All that day I pestered her to bring me my clothes. She told the doctor of it.

"If you leave this place under three weeks you are a damned fool," he told me.

I smiled patiently.

But I had made up my mind to leave it.

After three days, just to please me, she hung my clothes at the foot of the bed. She did not know I had become a Child of Choice. I'll admit it is a dangerous proceeding to try to get out of any rut. But I did want to leave that place and get back to normal life, even normal life in Binkers Court. Vaguely, I felt that when I returned I should be able to face it better than I had faced it before. I had no longer, weak as I was, that apathy which is so destructive in the individual and in the mass. When I was unwatched, I began to try the strength of my feeble limbs, doing silly little exercises under cover of the bedclothes. Once I walked several feet down the ward and back to my bed. I was appalled to find out how feeble I was.

I gave myself one week.

When the week was up there were no clothes hung at the foot of my bed. That was awkward, very awkward. Clothes I must have somehow. There was a man on the other side of me, a silent man, with the dreadful look of one who has never rebelled in his life, with the look of one born caged, without knowing it. He always lay, quite still, like a corpse—eyes wide open, staring at the ceiling. Always, when asked how he was, he said, monotonously: 'Worse'. Just that one word.

Only once did I see him rouse himself. A girl of fourteen came to see him, and I heard him ask: "Has she paid the rent?" "Yes. An' the byby's better," said the girl, cheerfully. He took no notice, but asked anxiously again, after a few minutes: "She 'as paid the rent. Lisa?"

One morning, the very morning when I had decided to quit, somehow, they found him dead. It upset all the ward. The man with the running in his leg had a lot of pain, and moaned a lot himself now. I said to myself beneath my breath: "Not another day and night in this place! You'll never got better *here*."

"I say," I told my female attendant: "Just bring me my clothes to look at, and I'll remember you when I get back to my hotel."

She hung my clothes at the foot of the bed, *just to please me.*

At two in the morning I dressed, by instalments, under the bedclothes, and stole out of the ward.

Then—I realised that I had come here in one shoe. That was a trifle awkward. Still, not insurmountable. I decided to leave the odd one behind as a souvenir of the man who had left a London workhouse hospital. How I got out beats me. I heard voices once in a room, and limped past, holding my breath.

I found a door open, and ran out, and across some damp grass, and saw, dim above me, 'old Venensley's children'. Then I came to a wall. There was the choice of a gate or the wall. I decided on the gate. A dog barked somewhere. Poor 'Slave!' When I got on the top I thought I would never get down. But gradually I found I *was* getting down. And, at last, I touched the ground. I was *free.*

Ten minutes later I was on the road, penniless, bootless, but curiously delighted with myself. I stared about me. I found my way to a coffee-stall, but I had no money for coffee. A girl was standing there, smoking a cigarette.

"Gawd! 'Ow you made me jump!" she said, and glanced at my feet.

She was a street-walker.

I took her to one side.

It was the first time I had ever spoken to a woman of that order. She laughed when I told her I had walked out of the workhouse.

"All rite. I've had some luck," she said.

She gave me a shilling.

I drank a cup of coffee, ate a thick cake, and said as I went off: "Good night, *sister.*"

"'Ere," she called.

I turned back.

She was half drunk.

"Pray for me," she said.

"I'll tell you what I'll do," I said, stammeringly. "I'll remember your fellowship to the day of my death— against *all* I've ever heard of women like you. And, you can always know, whenever I see a coffee-stall, I'll say: "*There*, I once was helped by a s*ister* of mine."

She eyed me, silent for a moment.

"That'll do," she said. "Gawd!

Chapter 16

This is Slavery. Savage men
And wild beasts within their den
Would endure not as ye do.
But such things they never know. —SHELLEY

I was interrogated by a policeman at the corner of Duff Street. He wanted to know where my shoes were. I informed him that one of them had gone in rebellion against a cats' chorus some weeks ago, and that the other was left in the workhouse. The remarkable thing about our world is that as soon as you tell the truth, the whole truth, and nothing but the truth, it laughs in your face.

"You're drunk," he said. "Now, move on, or I'll fix you up a resting-place."

"I wish you *could*. Oh, I wish you could, brother," I answered him, and went upon my pilgrim way.

It was beginning to come light as I neared the environs of my 'native land'. I recognised the landmarks—first the pawnbroker's shop, then the shop which made a living out of retailing the boiled hearts of sheep—an inelegant shop, with a cracked trencher set on a newspaper. I had eaten many a hearty meal, lifted to me out of that window. Now, I sickened as I went past it. There was the funny little shop where a grubby-handed giant of a woman, who suffered from bronchitis and gallstones, retailed highly-coloured sweets to the kids of Binkers Court. I dimly sensed the toys untidily heaped up, which could be grasped by childhood's eager hand, unconscious of the weary, ill-paid labour which had created them.

I stood on a bridge, its masonry black with smoke, and looked down on the river where the fish, if any, had long since been poisoned. 'Hideous' does not describe to you the word I felt for it all. A watery gleam of sun was coming—to stream fantastically through the city's smoke.

I went on my way. There was the newsagent's shop (he did a bit as bookie on the q.t. to help things up a bit, when there were no murders on). I stopped to read the placards.

MINERS ENTOMBED

FINANCIAL MAGNATE BLOWS HIS BRAINS OUT

PANIC IN WALL STREET

TROOPS SENT OUT EAST

TERRIBLE DUAL MURDER

BABY IN BOX

BISHOP CONDEMNS THEATRES

They were similar headings to many I had read before. But they conveyed more to me now. It no longer seemed strange that such follies and torments should afflict our society. Indeed, it seemed to me that these horrors would grow, rather than decrease, seeing that we living in an age of destruction.

These headings conveyed to me the conflicts going on in individuals because they were going on in society. They were the products of our life, 'social' and 'economic', the signs of degeneracy multiplying whilst intelligence struggled against great barriers, flung to stem it by the black hands of Unprogression. I can't say it gave me any satisfaction. Under another state of society I think I would have had a nature which turned naturally towards the 'sunny side' always.

These things on the placards were manifestations of causes—economic causes. I even felt pity for the financial magnate. It must feel pretty rotten to go 'broke' after you've been pulling strings successfully, which kept thousands of human puppets dancing on the ends of them—and find you can't control 'laws' any more. All the same, I could imagine his face, had I tapped him on the shoulder, and said: "Old man, you are a gambler, playing with loaded dice, which deals death—and will finally swing back on you. You'd be happier under Socialism, working and having no more than your mates." It would have been futile. He would have gone on, to that dark hour when the boomerang he played with hit him on the head, and with the cowardice of the man untrained to *lose all*, he blew out his dominant brains rather than be—*a wreck*, counted with the wrecks he had *made others.*

Terrible world. Miners Entombed. Not much account of *their lives*, I'd bet, I mused. Just—Miners Entombed.

I trudged on. I had forgotten my feet, now sodden with mire and wet. Same old alley. Same old words, dancing at me out of the murky dawn. BINKERS COURT. Same old communal ashpit, where we threw our empty herring-tins and banana peelings—and tomatoes, bought somewhat 'squashed' as we were 'squashed'. Two lean cats were singing a war-song over a bone with nothing on it. Horrible details of a horrible scramble life lived by millions. And, yet, I knew I was going to live here. Live! Live! Live! Not exist—but *Live*. I had left it, a child of Chance. I came back, a Child of Choice.

"My God! Mr. Sniggins! Is that you?" asked Mrs. Biers, tousle-headed, opening her door, as I meandered up the same old dark staircase.

"No," I told her. "It's not *me*. It's a new tenant."

"Now, don't you set me off larfin' before breakfast, or I'll cry afore supper," said she.

We are not very decorous in Binkers Court.

Mrs. Biers had on a tattered petticoat, and Joshua's old coat, and some old boots she had rescued from the ash-pit. Her hair was half-pinned up. She looked awful, just a*wful. England, home*—and *beauty.* Not that I felt scornful. Quite the reverse. I felt heartbroken, just heartbroken, to see her standing in these *old rags,* pathetically unconscious of the figure she cut.

Oh, be quite sure, be quite sure, reader of these chronicles, that no single word I have written against the ignominies of our *lives* has been written for bitterness, or because of personal bitterness, or as one who sits in the scorner's seat. I have learned sufficient, after much travail, only to suffer with my kind, only to share their shames, only to know that all stone-wall misery is the cause of utter hopelessness, from which they will awaken, as even I, who wasted my gifts in hopeless brooding on my own miseries, one day awoke, and became, if not a free soul, at least a living one.

Listen well, in the heart of dawns, sleepless dawns, and you shall hear the bugle of Democracy rousing her children with her glorious reveille call. Though they be dumb with agonies, they shall answer her. *Out of the deeper depths from which they rise they shall mount to the higher heights. And the measure of the heights they have scaled is the measure of the pit where they lay submerged.*

But it was not with such vigour and certainty that I entered again my sordid room. The torn blind was battering against a draught from a half-open dirty window. I wound it up, and saw the den where I had lived.

The open cupboard (someone had removed its other door!) revealed old tins, all empty of food. The fire-grate was rust red. The rains beating in had left pools of muddy water on the floor. Stuck on the wall, with a pin, was a bill from Sparkins, with the list of my rent arrears.

I found a few sticks, and lit the fire with them, including Sparkin's list of my 'arrears'. I shivered as I knelt down striking matches and encouraging the wet wood. Mrs. Biers tapped at the door.

"Some tea," she told me. "Carn't gossip. Joshua's gittin' up. He's got off the wrong side the bed this mornin'. Just as if I can get bacon-scraps *every* day outer what 'e brings! Where'll I set it down?"

"Give it to me," I asked.

"There! It's wet an' warm. It's the most can be said for it," she said.

"You're a good fellow, Mrs. Biers," I called after her.

Her raucous laughter answered me.

How was I going to face these miseries? How was I going to bridge the gulf between the future, and now? I sat in the dust, warming my hands on the sides of the pot. Finally, the fire got going. Some rancid bacon cooking told me Joshua was being prepared for. She must have found some scraps in a forgotten corner! I heard the Joneses stirring in the next room. Shortly afterwards Mrs. Jones came into the room.

"Oh!" she said, starting back.

She turned pale, then red.

"Are you—could you lend me the carvin'-knife?" she said. "I left it in 'ere by mistake. Didn't know you *was* back."

"How is the baby?" I asked.

She looked gratefully at me.

"If you'd only mind him for me—an hour, this morning," she suggested. "I'm going after work. Tom can't get any. Will you?"

Now I can play with little Jimmy, who is three. But little babies worry me. I'm afraid of dropping 'em.

"Well, not above an hour," I said, ruefully.

She found the carving-knife.

"And, can I bring it back?" she asked.

"Certainly."

I asked no questions.

I have learned not to ask the soul-sick questions. I know all they want, down in their depths, is either practical help, or *leaving alone*, not pestering with questions as to why, in their misery, they do this or that seemingly strange thing. I set to and washed the floor before Mrs. Jones brought the baby.

He howled when he saw me, which was disconcerting. But I don't blame him. After half an hour he agreed that I was passable. I got Mrs. Biers in, to explain about my dole. When I'd gone in the workhouse they had taken it off to pay for me at the workhouse.

"Well," I said. "I'll have to go an' see about how I've got to exist."

I tried to pass the baby on to Mrs. Biers.

But she was washing and would not accept him. Just as I sat comforting the baby to the best of my abilities, which are not great in that direction, I saw a figure looking in on us, passing the door.

"Hello! Mrs. Jones!" I said.

Silence answered.

When I turned to look more closely it was gone. I went to the door, carrying the baby to investigate.

"Look! You're holding him wrong end up!" said her voice.

She just reached us in time, and pulled the child from me indignantly.

"Carn't 'old a byby," she challenged.

She stood with the Jones' baby staring at her, attracted to her hair, which the sun, a watery glimmer through the roof-window, touched. I went close up to her.

"Wot are you starin' at?" she asked.

She turned her face.

It was close to mine.

A beam of uncertain sunlight touched it for a moment, then faded. I recalled having seen her at close quarters once—was it years ago—beside the ashpit.

"Arlene!" I gasped.

Like, yet unlike! Bitterness of bitterness! There was paint on her cheek—young and well-curved as it was.

She stared at me.

"Take the damned byby," she told me. "What's the game? Take it. Go on. Take it. Are you mad? What are you staring like that for?"

"What's your name?" I asked.

She glowered at me.

"Nothing. To *you*!" she said. "Nothing, to *you*."

She pitched the baby at me, snapped finger at thumb, unlocked her door, and banged it, as if she shut me out.

Why *nothing to me particularly*? The eyes were wider apart than the average, but not so wide as Arlene's had been. She reeked of cheap scent! Complexion was only to be guessed at by it being covered up. A handkerchief lay at my feet. I picked it up. I read across one corner the name, *Minnie*. I thought once of knocking on the door, but did not. I threw the handkerchief down outside the door, on the dust of the threshold.

That girl, Minnie! That the Arlene I was to find in Binkers Court.

Chapter 17

Looking back, recalling that first month I spent in Binkers Court after my passage from the workhouse, from 'Equality Island'—which was only a dream (the city not yet built by hands), I think the most terrible part of my torment came from my inability to find out how to build a bridge which would span the gulf between the dreadful Now and the Progressive Future.

It is so difficult with discord and ugliness about one, concrete reality, to cling even to the vestures of a dream. The first price one pays for any dream is additional despair! It looks so far away, so utterly unattainable. The ugliness seems so much worse than it did *before* the dream.

Exteriorly none of my neighbours saw that anything had happened to me. I went in, and I went out. Dole had stopped. I took a tin from the 'communal ashpit' (strange that they are not against our sharing ashes together, but don't like us sharing bread and *dreams!*), carried it away by stealth, and scraped it out, late one afternoon. I found a crust little Jimmy had left on the stairs. My hunger was greater than my aesthetic vibrations.

Then I went to sit by the window.

The grate was fireless, the rain coming down. Somebody knocked on the door. I opened it. A sleek, well-clad man stood there. I did not know him.

"Could you tell me where Mr. Edmund Sniggins lives?" he asked.

"I am Edmund Sniggins."

Wild hope flashed into me.

Drowning men so are said to hold out their fingers to clutch passing straws.

"Oh, may I come in?"

"Certainly."

Time was when I would have been ashamed of the hole I lived in. I now considered it Society's shame.

"Cold day!" he said.

I saw that his quick gaze took in the firelessness.

"I say, old man. I'm sorry you're so down," he said.

His manner had fine tact.

"So am I!" was my rejoinder.

He met my glance.

"To tell you the truth, I saw a letter of yours in one of the papers some time ago. Now! If you can do some articles *for us* on those lines, but with more humour in them, of course, we could put you in *Easy Street*!"

I collapsed upon a chair.

I felt that a stone had been rolled away from me.

"Four guineas a column," he said.

I felt all the sensations of one coming up out of a pit, rescued. Then, swirled away by this almost terrible hope as I was, I asked him the question:

"What paper do you represent?"

He told me.

It was the vilest paper, the dirtiest weapon against the aspirations of the Mass!

"No," I told him.

My manner at a crisis is always hesitant. He mistook my nervousness for caving in.

"Six guineas," he said, blandly. "Come! Why should you rot here?"

It was a question I had often asked myself.

"No. I'd rather not."

"Come. Think of what this world means to *you*!"

"No. I'd rather not."

My manner was still hesitant.

"You're a fool, if you'll rot here, when we could help you and you could help us. You have what we call 'the common touch'. It is all too rare. It has a market value. I'll take chances on offering you eight guineas. Now. Take a week to think it over. The people you could help, old man."

"No. I'd rather not."

"You'll stay here in this hole, then?"

"Yes. I'll die here, rather than serve *you* and your interests," I managed to stammer.

"Come. Let's talk together like sane men. Try a cigar!"

"Mine's Woodbines," I told him. "Picked up in the streets!"

"More fool you," he said. "Come! You Socialists are like other men. *You are living under Capitalism.*"

My gaze wandered round the wretched room. I could walk out of it—to-morrow! Ill-clothed, famished, sick at heart, almost friendless, alone, with only a dream! My eyes fell on a piece of a book back I had pinned up, quite as a fancy, yesterday. It was off the book Voltaire had written. The title stared out at me. Translated it meant 'It is necessary to *Choose*'. It certainly was. "*I will not*," I told him, still in my hesitant stammer.

He recognised at last that that hesitancy was not my moral weakness, but only my nervously hesitant manner. I did not offer to kick him down the stairs. Indeed, I look him a light, so that he would not fall down. You can be quite revolutionary in speech, and quite reactionary in crisis. It was sufficient for me to refuse his offer.

At the foot of the stairs he looked up at me, still holding the candle.

"Sure—*yet*?" he asked.

"Sure yet," I answered. "Also, many thanks."

"For what?" he asked.

"If I can be used against the people, I can know I am good enough to serve them against you," I told him.

He laughed.

Then he hurled his parting bolt.

"Think the Labour Press will take you up?" he jeered. "*We* get the men they are not wide enough awake to find."

"Good afternoon," I told him.

As I went into my room I caught a glimpse of a figure dodging into the next room but one. But I did not take much notice. I was going back to hunger—chosen for the first time. Deliberate poverty, for once. *Il faut choisir.* (One must choose.)

I sank upon a chair and buried my head in my hands. When I looked up, I saw a loaf, set on my table, my rickety table. I saw a note beside it. I made out the words.

"*I got it easy. You can share.—Minnie.*"

I stood staring at the loaf, and then at the scrawl on the paper. Minnie! 'Arlene' dumped down in Binkers Court—offering me bread. I had eaten little Jimmy's crust, after the cats had possibly forsaken it. I had scraped out the dust-covered tin from the communal ash-pit, but I did not feel I could eat that bread.

She must have guessed what a plight I was in. Somehow, she had guessed. I wondered how. It was almost dark in my room now. I lit a candle, my last.

I took up the loaf. It made me feel hungrier than ever to hold it in my hands, so near and yet so far. I wavered once. Wasn't it damned silly, I agreed, to be taking it back? Ungracious, too? Was not it as clean bread as lots of other bread? Was not prostitution rife in all sorts of professions other than that of sex?

I found myself knocking on her little door. She opened it. I got a glimpse of a room with a lamp—a lamp with a pretty, coloured shade, and the walls had nice pictures on them. There were flowers in a glass. There was a bed with an artistic coverlet on it, and a book, and her hat and gloves, just as she had thrown them down. She leaned against the doorpost and surveyed me. She looked tired and worn, yet child-like, too, in her sheath-like dress, short-skirted, her silk stockings and brogue shoes.

"Oh, have you brought it back?" she asked. "I damned well thought you would."

She spoke two languages, it seemed. One was the lingo of Binkers Court. The other was English—picked up from books. Possibly she used it in her 'trade'.

"Yes, I—I don't really need it," I told her.

"Oh. well. If you're so proud, you need not lie about it," she said. "Hand it here."

I gave it back into her hand.

She came out with the loaf in her hand.

"Well," she said. "I make a practice of never taking anything back that I've given. See?"

By Evolution! The light from the open doorway was on her face, with that fugitive likeness which I knew so well stamped upon it. Her eyes, wider apart than ordinarily they are in the faces of folk in our world, surveyed me with scorn. They were scarcely less beautiful than Arlene's eyes. She was smaller, flatter-chested, sharper, wiser and sadder in miseries, less intelligent in joy and full living—and with something of tragedy in the compression of the lips, which gave them a strange curve as of habitual endurance of existence.

"No. I never take anything back I've once given," she reiterated. "See?"

I held out my hand to check her.

But it was too late.

The loaf was pitched over the banister, and from below came old Sparkins' voice.

"Who the devil's throwing bread about?"

Then we heard it 'bump, bump, bump', as it hit the filthy stairs.

"Me, I'm throwin' the bread about," said Minnie, as he puffed up the stairs. "Me. 'Ave you anything to say against it? Ain't it my own? 'Aven't I paid for it? Can't I do as I likes with my own, you old humbug? Ain't the pore got to be as spendthrift as you, *if they wants?* What the 'ell 'as it to do with you, so long as I pays my rent?"

"Now, now," said Mr. Sparkins, soothingly, in his best churchwarden voice. She glared at him like a wild cat and quite suddenly licked her tongue out at him, turned, and banged the door in both our faces.

"If the world was not so wicked," said Mr. Sparkins, "I think we would have it different. Don't you, Sniggins?"

By Evolution! What an abomination he looked in his checked suit, rent-book in the fat hand, and that smug self-satisfaction on his face. Beefy of countenance, dead of soul.

"Good bread wasted!" he sighed, as I was silent. "Thrift! That's what wants preaching to the working classes. Thrift! A sense of values. Just a sense of values. Don't you agree, Sniggins? Thrift—and decent citizenship. Eh?"

Time was when I would have nodded—just to save myself the trouble of arguing the point.

"I'd like to see some of the rich live here for a week—just for a week—living as we live, and send a committee to them to preach thrift. It would be rather fun, wouldn't it, Sparkins?"

By Evolution! I thought he was going to choke. Then he snorted.

"Since when have I become *Sparkins*?" he asked.

"Since I became *Sniggins*," I told him.

Dash him! Did he think I was going to lick his boots, because he lived by filthy property not fit for humanity to live in?

Queer how I could survey him so calmly—so 'impartially', so impersonally, when he had the power to turn me out of my shelter anywhere, nowhere—to the gutter or the doss-house. Queer—how old Sparkins could make me fear no more!

"Have you got the rent?" he asked.

"Sorry! I haven't. I've been ill, you know. Haven't worked for going on three years now. Know anyone wants a man, Sparkins?"

We eyed each other.

"No. I don't know anyone wants any labour," he said. "But I want my rent."

"You're on dole, are you not? Single man. Only this one room to pay for. I've known men able to live on several shillings a week."

"Here," I stopped him. "Come inside."

He walked in, disapproving of standing for a few minutes in the den I had to *live* in all the time.

"We'll work it out on paper," I said.

I got pencil and paper and stood by the rickety table.

Item by item I took the sordid details of my daily necessities.

"I'm not saying you've much," said old Sparkins.

He began to edge towards the door.

"Here, that won't do," I said. "Come back. Now, I'm going to show you that unless I half starve—that's when I'm getting dole—(I'm not now) there's nothing for you. Besides, looked at from a business point of view, *is* this room worth five shillings?"

"Oh, it's not a bad room," said Sparkins.

"You would really let a man go short of food, which only keeps his body fit to work—when work comes—if ever it does, to pay *you* five shillings for a hole like this?"

"I've got to live," said old Sparkins.

"From a moral point of view," I began. "And you're religious, too. Now, here's Binkers Court. Your father bought it for a mere song. He left it you in his will. What had you done to own it, anyhow? You let these rooms out to the poorest of the poor, five shillings a room. What do you call it? I call it *robbery*. I consider you a thief. Just a low down common thief, with the law behind you. Now, the time's coming when some of us are going to alter those laws. In the meantime, what about *you* and *me*?"

Mr. Sparkins went various colours.

"I want my rent," he said.

I whistled cheerfully.

"And I've had nothing to eat for two days," I said, stopping whistling.

"Good God!" said Mr. Sparkins. "Is that true? Are you sure you couldn't get something, Sniggins?"

"Well," I told him, "seeing it's so easy to get, and you are a man of influence, I suppose it might be done. But there are over a million *out*. You're not going to insinuate, are you, that there are over a million men who *won't* work, in this country?"

He pondered me, gloomily.

"After all, I've got to have my rent," he said. "That's my position."

"Then—there is *you*—as a class," I went on. "You are the top dogs. You haven't a policy to shelter the people, feed them, give them peace. You've had your chance. You've had your day. So soon as we start in to break your chains, your dominance, you're kicking up a dust and going into hysterics. I say, did not you have some shares in a Bible factory before the war, when the girls had to go on the streets to eke out their livings? What are we going to have to do with your sort of human nature! Tell me *that?*"

As I talked I advanced towards him. He retreated. We landed on the staircase.

"Insult! This is insult!" spluttered Sparkins. "I say this property is mine, legally mine, and I've a right for some return on it. As for altering the laws—we'll show you. You'll pay your rent or go."

"Chuck him down the stairs, Nibby!" came from the doorway where *she* stood.

That fetched me to my senses.

"Think I want to swing for an object like that," I asked, bitterly.

"Unless you're got the rent in seven days I'll evict you," was Sparkins' last shot.

'Arlene' rushed to the head of the stairs.

"An' if you turns him out, I'll smash up your 'appy home," she called. "Do you 'ear? Wot O! Decree nisi. 'Ow'd you like that? You turn him out, an' I'll do it! 'Ear me, you blighter!"

I stared at her. Then I felt the landing turning round.

She managed to get me through my own doorway, and sit me down on the disguised orange box.

"Let me get you something to eat,'" she beseeched.

We surveyed each other.

"Nibby, I've a cupboard full," she said, eagerly.

"Don't want it," I told her. "Sorry to hurt your feelings. But it'd choke me—Arlene."

"Gawd, Nibby!" she said, wonderingly. "*What for?*" Then she said sharply." And who's *Arlene?*"

"Nothing," I said, wearily. "'Only a dream!"

We stared at each other.

A dull flush rose to her face, showing even through the paint.

"It's 'cause I gets it that way?" she asked.

I nodded.

"If you're going to be so particular you'll ha' to starve," she said. "You're a silly blighter, Nibby. Well, I 'opes you'll be better. Ta-ta!"

She was gone.

I sat on in that horrible room until it was almost dark. Then I went down the stairs. I met Tom Jones coming up.

"Got anything?" I asked.

"Nothing."

The hopelessness of his tone was a condemnation of society.

"Couldn't lend me twopence?" I asked.

"Broke," he said.

I went down into the street. It was pouring with rain. The lights danced before my eyes. I had got to raise a few coppers, somehow. Otherwise, I was going to be 'found dead'.

I carried a parcel for a man, and bought some meat scraps, took them 'home', and boiled them, borrowing a handful of coal from Mrs. Biers. Whilst they boiled I sat and wondered what I was *going to do*? And as I wondered, from the Jones' room came the voice of Mrs. Jones: "Tom, I'm at the far end. I can't go no further. What are we going to do?"

The words, in Mrs. Jones' heart-broken voice, rang in my ears all through that night.

It was the despairing cry of the semi-submerged, going a little farther down all the time, struggling against the tides.

I rose at the first sign of dawn. There was nothing much to get up for. I rose from force of habit.

A knock came to the door.

It was Mrs. Jones.

"You haven't a drop of milk, have you, Mr. Sniggins, for the baby?" she asked.

The light through the dirty window fell on her face, her hair, her eyes.

"Terrible!" I cried suddenly, vehemently.

"What's the matter? Are you ill? Oh, you do look ill, Mr. Sniggins," she said, in a frightened voice.

By Evolution! As she stood there, with the little cracked jug in her hand, asking me if I'd a drop of milk for the baby, I had recognised *Messeia*—Messeia the beautiful, Messeia the gifted, Messeia the lion-hearted, who *could find courage to starve to death by choice to break down a system she felt was wrong*. I recovered.

"No, I'm not ill. I've no milk. Haven't had any milk for months—before I went to the work-house."

She gave a sharp breath of disappointment.

"Well, it can't be helped," she said.

She was turning away.

I heard the baby crying in the next room.

"Isn't *life awful*?" she asked, suddenly. Then she laughed, a shaky little laugh, and ran in. Ten minutes later Jones tapped and came in. He sat down on the orange-box.

"I've heard of a job thirty miles away," he said. And I've been to the Labour Exchange. They think I might have a chance. God! Sniggins. If only I could get it," he said, anxiously. "You know, *it's killing the wife.* The kid, too. She—you didn't know her, Sniggins, did you, when I fetched her here, first? Only place we could get. Thought we'd get out soon."

"I remember stumbling into your place once, when you came first. You were holding hands by the window," I told him, smiling a little.

He smiled too.

"Yes. So you did. It's frightful to love a woman, and see her dragged down like this! She isn't one of the crying sort. I almost wish she was. Sits there, you know, old man, staring at the baby, and wishing she'd never had him. Gets on my nerves. I seem to be all nerves, lately.

"Queer there's no room for men like us, isn't it? Something terrible wrong *somewhere*, Sniggins, don't you think, when we have to be like this, eh?"

He had got up and we were facing each other.

"There is something wrong," I managed to gasp.

As the grey light fell on his grey face, his sad, strained eyes, on the tongue licking his dry lips as he unburdened himself to me, I almost staggered against the dirty wall. Sarband—Sarband the younger!

"Yes. There is. Sure of it. I mean to find out—when I get on my feet. Sort of knocks all the *old ideas* out of you, this sort does. Only, you can't think it out. You get dazed. Just dazed. Well, I've got to get to that place. Mrs. Biers—she's a good sort—lent me two bob on the strength of it. I say, old man, you haven't seen our carving-knife, have you?"

He looked at me anxiously.

I felt my blood run cold.

"I haven't," I said.

"You know, she gets so crushed with it all," he confided. "When I *missed* it, I wondered if she'd hid it." He shuddered. "You get some queer thoughts in your head when you get driven right down," he said.

I sat on the orange-box for some time after he had gone, hearing in imagination the thousands of feet in this city, trudging about suffering *these things*. I went out to the Exchange myself, after getting Joshua to lend me his No. 12s, just for the trip.

I came out without any hope. Over the doorway I read, "Join His Majesty's Forces." I limped away.

When I got back, and as I was passing the door, I saw Mrs. Jones, baby on arm, knocking at Minnie's door.

Now, I had never seen Mrs. Jones speak to Minnie. Mrs. Jones was respectable.

Minnie was *not*.

I wondered what she could be doing there.

"Hope Tom gets that job, Mrs. Jones," I said.

She nodded.

I saw that she had no hope—no hope.

Hope is one of those dreams that die in holes like these. I went into my room, and heard Minnie's door open, heard her surprised, "Oh, yes. Come in." I felt worried something was afoot here—Tom Jones and I had never had much to say to each other. But we had always, I think, respected each other, noticed each other's misery, helpless as we were to aid each other. I believed I was justified in learning what was going on inside that room. They had left the door ajar. I crept up to it, and peeped round the doorpost. They were standing near the window. The light such as it was, smoke-fouled, fell on Mrs. Jones' face. She was rocking the baby about in her arms, and I heard a voice, appealing, strained, saying these dreadful words. "I can't see the baby suffer any more. How do you get 'on the streets'?"

I leaned against the doorpost.

Minnie's voice came to me.

Its tone had a ring of wild purity that had survived even the mud of the common streets.

"Woman! You'd better drown yourself than do as I have done."

Then I got into a panic, thinking Minnie had seen me.

Stealthily I crept back into my room, closed the door, and helplessly banged my head against a wall. The physical pain numbed the other a little. Life, Love, Beauty, dragged through the dust, the great immortals. And for what! Profits!

To uphold a system that had no room for manhood, womanhood, childhood—but only for machines which could make *Interest*. And the Economic Theory of Socialism was Materialism! And the 'Spiritual preachment' that all was well in this best of possible worlds was held as a great Ideal, as Law, and Order, and Progression. If only I could get on my feet—I pledged myself to pitch myself into the battle against Unprogression, whatever noble ideal it waved to cover its debasement, its unspeakable debasement, which nothing could cloak.

***

It was late when I went to bed, though the candle had long guttered into darkness. I heard Jones' return, and the sound of feet made me wonder if he had got the job. It was late when I awoke next morning. I wondered again if Jones had brought good news last night. I remembered that he had said something about giving me a hand if he got the job: it would not solve my case, though. The fellowship of the worker to worker is a priceless thing. With the bulk of the world's workers living from hand to mouth I knew it could only stand as a token of fellowship yet to be. That the comfortable should go about looking for miseries to alleviate was equally futile to solve the social phenomena.

The human element appeared to be fast passing out of the scheme of things. We were in a mechanical age, wonderful, titanic, liberating force after force, discovery after discovery—and humanity passing, in greater and greater numbers, ignored as such, only not ignored in the realisation that absolute starvation would spring the whole fabric of Society.

Every day newspapers revealed increases in insanity, suicide, crime, the human element registering its perversity in being unable to accept its relegation as 'scrapped machinery'. New theories of how to deal with its inabilities. Nothing to get to the roots. Terrible and remarkable. Ability to produce as never before—inability to consume proportionately. I lay in the dark thinking about it until my head swam. I picked it up next morning where I left off, and was still doddering round it when Jones knocked at my door.

"Hello?" I asked.

"It's me," he answered. "Can I come in?"

"Do," I told him.

I flashed one look at his face.

"You've got the job," I said.

He laughed—queerly.

"I *think* so, Sniggins! Sniggins—I've to go again. They must think I've got to have it, eh? I've never slept all night. Fairly can't believe there's a *chance*, after all this time! You sort o' let go, and give yourself up—after all this time—an' I heard an old fool in the train telling another some of us wouldn't take work if it dropped on us. Talked like we were rolling millionaires. 'Struth, old man. Bit my lip and sat back in the corner. To be able to get out of this hole. The wife's talking about what she's goin' to buy the baby. 'Hold hard', I said to her, 'It might be a false alarm'. Put new life into me, it has.

"It has been a time, Sniggins, but I feel if I get on my feet again, there's things I've got to find out, and then tell others about. Had any breakfast?"

I grinned.

"They say there are a lot dig their own graves with their teeth," I jested. "We ought to be a healthy lot. Here, where are you going?"

He went out.

"And the wife says there's some more tea," he told me when he came back.

He sat down on the 'dais'—otherwise orange box.

I ate the bread and margarine, and the rancid bacon of the 'rolling millionaire'. He lit an inch of the end of a 'fag'. He had very fine hands. I noticed them as he lit the cigarette. They shook a little, unnerved by this sudden 'uplift' of his. He was leaner, more haggard. But the fugitive likeness was there. The younger Sarband's link—yet in this dark Now.

"Queer how you get it into your nut things will last forever, eh?" he asked. "You know they can't. But it does seem so."

Somewhere in the distance we heard a woman calling to someone to know if he were going to lie in bed for ever.

"That's old Viner she's callin' of," said Jones. "Six she has, and now the old man. They're talking of the workhouse for him. Seems to have worked hard all his life. Queer how they soon shunts you off as soon as you give a bit of trouble. Was it all right, old man?"

"I was hungry," I told him. "Thanks, brother."

Almost mechanically my hand moved towards his. Almost mechanically his hand crept towards mine. They met, awkward, masculine, restrained, and blundered away.

"Seems like these things should not be," said Jones, in a muffled voice. "Well, I'll get that train. Wife's doing the room out. Not that we shall stay here long, *if* get it. And I feel I'm going to get it, Sniggins."

He was leaving me.

"Old man."

I raised myself in bed, my elbow poking out of my torn shirt sleeve. He turned. I can see him yet. Less than the Sarband of the turbulent heart, feebler, more irregular of feature—the man whom I dreamed forward! Pale, harassed, puzzled, no dreamer of the woods, no defier of authority, yet with something stamped upon him that gave him the look of one who held dreams too deeply crushed down to be easily revealed.

"I wouldn't build on it," I warned him.

"No, no; I'm not doing," he said. "Only there's the *chance*. I've to go again today. Must think I'm to have it."

When he had gone I dressed.

I went out, in Joshua's boots, and hunted advertisements myself in the newsroom. There was one advertisement that stuck in my mind.

Man for Sale, Body and Soul.

Educated man. Will go anywhere, and do anything. Must have work.

Chapter 18

It haunted me all the way back. It haunted me even in my problem of how to get stamps to answer the adverts I had written down. Just as I neared the doorway of Binkers Court, I met the sleek man coming out—the man who had asked me to write *humorous* articles on the underworld!

It annoyed me to see him.

"You don't mean to say —" I began.

"Yes! Thought you'd have thought it over."

"Same yet," I told him. "Only *more so*. I'd thank you not to come again."

I banged past him, and up the dark stairs, nearly knocking him over.

As I went into my room, I heard Mrs. Jones—singing. She heard me come in. She came and knocked at the door.

"Mr. Sniggins, I think he is going to get it this time," she said. "Oh, won't it be a relief?"

I nodded.

It was becoming a monstrous nightmare to me that I was to witness beings I knew had the germs of untold generosities, nobilities, intelligence, loyalty, affection in themselves, driven between hope and despair—and for what? Nothing more than secure lives, with sufficient bread, clothes, and shelter.

I tried to warn her that he might not get it.

"I feel sure he'll get it—this time," she said, and ran away.

I spent the afternoon tramping about.

I managed to get a couple of parcels to carry. The proceeds provided me with a bottle of ink, two stamps, and paper. I answered advertisements until tea-time.

Then I heard a hullabaloo on the first floor.

Things were bumping about. I went down to investigate, and found a family in the process of eviction.

"But—where will we go—and what will we do?" sobbed the mother. Two kids stood pulling at her skirt. It was a widow who went out 'washing' when neuritis would permit. As I stood there with them, amongst the pots and pans, the door of the room opposite opened, and, hobbling on his stick, old Viner came out.

"Y-y-y-you," he stammered, pointing his stick at the evictors, "g-g-go!"

His white hair hung long on his head. His shirt-neck was open. His eyes held all the fire his poor tongue could not convey. I drew a deep breath. Old Venensley! Fancy dreaming old Viner into Venensley.

"We're on the right side. We have the writ. Chuck the stuff out, Bill," said one of the men.

"Come in, or you'll be bringing another stroke on," said his daughter, wearily, opening the door that had closed behind Viner. She drew him in, objecting, protesting.

"Only till to-morrow," begged the widow. "It's raining so. And—"

She closed her eyes suddenly, and then covered them with her hand.

"Well, leave them there," I said, suddenly. "I'll shift 'em. They can go up in my place."

"And where are you!" asked one of the men.

"I'm on the top floor. Fifty-two."

The men grinned.

217

"Oh, we're coming on to you tomorrow," said one.

"Well, I'll shift 'em there for tonight," I told them.

A door had opened.

Minnie, in all her war-paint. She stood staring at the things.

"Old Sparkins ordered this?" she demanded.

"Doctor's orders," said one of the men. "We starts at the bottom and clears the lot!"

"You don't touch a thing—till I comes back," she told him.

The door opened and banged behind her. I ran out after her, limping. She heard my panting, and turned. The whiteness of her face showed through the streaky paint. She told me what she was going to do.

"But, dash it, Arl—I mean Minnie, it's *blackmail*. You're stopping him getting his rent by—yes, it's blackmail."

"Blackmail! *Do I care what you call it!* Let him turn us out in the streets! I'll get his wife the divorce she's after. She's been once to see me, but I was mum. No. I holds the key to Binkers Court. An' if he doesn't get the rents, his son'll know why! Educated, he is."

"But I say they could imprison—" I began.

"Do I care?" she asked. "What'd you call me if I let poor folk be turned out—when I holds the key?"

And as we stood talking, somebody came wearily along the alley,

"Jones!" I said.

He looked at me like a man in a nightmare.

But all he said was, "Missed it, Sniggins".

Then he passed us.

"Gawd!' said Minnie, suddenly.

"What?" I asked.

"I—I left a note for 'er, pinned on the door, arskin' her not to go on my hop, even if he didn't get work. Gawd! What if he finds it?"

218

"I know all about it," I told Minnie. "I must get in before him, somehow."

"Run, Nibby, run," said Minnie.

I looked back once in my flight, and she waved a terrified hand at me.

I caught Jones halfway up the stairs. "You must buck up, old chap," I told him.

If only I could get in front of him.

"Yes, I missed the job!" he reiterated, heavily.

Five more steps, then we should be at the top. I must keep the unhappy man from getting that note on the door—if it were still there. It would not help him much to know that his wife was ready to sell her soul to feed the kid.

I gave a sudden groan.

Jones stopped.

"What's to do!" he asked, dully.

"Cramp," I told him. "Just go down the stairs, old man, an' get Mrs. Simms to tell you what's good for cramp."

To my great relief he went down.

I slowly crawled up the steps, groaning the while, and limped to the door of the Joneses. The note was there, staring ghostlike out of the gloom. I ripped it down, tearing my hand on the pin, and shoved it in my pocket. Then I groaned away for all I was worth and leaned against the wall. Mrs. Jones opened the door in surprise. She had the lamp in her hand. Their gas, like my own, had been cut off. The radiance fell on her face, wonderfully bright and hopeful—waiting for Tom to come home with the 'great news'.

"What is it, Mr. Sniggins?" she asked.

"I've got cramp," I said.

"Oh, dear. Can I do anything?"

"No, it's passing off, I think."

"I'm glad. Tom hasn't come back. Perhaps he's *started*."

Then I heard Jones coming up.

She heard him too. She set the lamp down inside the door, and bent over the old banisters, peeping down at him.

"Have you got it, Tom?"

He came gloomily up the steps, without a word. I heard her catch her breath. 1 saw the wild fear leap across her face.

"Tom!' You *have* got it, Tom?"

I breathed a fervent prayer of thanksgiving. Was not I thankful, even in my wretchedness, that no woman would stand there looking thus and asking that question. I tried to drag myself away. But Jones was on the landing now.

"I *missed* it," he said. "They thought it would require more strength than I have got."

I saw her rally herself together.

She slipped her thin hand with the heavy wedding-ring through his arm.

"Never mind," she said. "Never mind."

And suddenly, out of the silence, I heard him gulping, saw the twitching of his face, as she picked up the lamp.

"Never mind. Never mind."

Their door had closed upon 'the end of a perfect day'. Jones had forgotten my 'cramp'. I crept into my own room.

I sat again in the darkness, on the old orange-box, with the optimistic mice doing little scampers after grub in an 'Englishman's castle'. Some silly lunatic, away at the end of the landing was playing 'Rule Britannia' on a mouth-organ!

"And Britons *never, never,* never shall be slaves—" came from the end of the landing in a woman's shrill voice.

Suddenly, I found I really could not stop myself from laughing.

Mrs. Biers came to the door.

"Mr. Sniggins, are you ill?"

"No."

I started off laughing again.

"Mr. Sniggins, they can hear you all over the top floor!"

That made me worse.

"Joshua!" she called.

Joshua clomped cut, clay pipe in his mouth, and into my room.

"Sniggins can't stop laughing. What'll we do?"

"Lettimlaffon," said Joshua.

I really became hilarious at that. The tears were running down my cheeks—tears not of sorrow, not of cynicism, but of pure laughter, at the utter absurdity of men living as we lived—and enduring it.

An hour later someone knocked at my door. I opened it.

"Gawd! Are you sitting in the dark?" asked Minnie.

"Seems so," I told her.

"I seen Sparkins at his office," she informed me. "Nibby! Let me lend you a candle?"

"All right," I told her.

A minute later she was back, struck a match and lit the candle.

She stood by the orange-box drumming her fingers on it.

"I seen Sparkins—he daren't go on—leastways, not yet. He's got to hang on to his wife, for she's got the dibs. Lawks, Nibby. It was funny. But he'd like to have murdered me all the same. Only he daren't."

I nodded.

"Horrible cold in 'ere, Nibby," said Minnie, shivering. "Say! Let me lend you a few coals."

"All right," I told her.

She looked at me.

"And—a bit o' supper? Something hot—and nice—you look blue, you know, fair blue."

Three minutes later she came in with a little tablecloth, two plates full of steaming grub, and the lamp with the coloured shade on it. I lit the fire.

"What's that?" said Minnie, suddenly. Again: "What's that?" she asked, in a weird whisper.

She was staring at the ceiling above our head.

"What?" I asked.

There was something, something dripping above our heads.

We rose from the table and stared at each other. I made for the door.

"Nibby, don't leave me!" cried Minnie.

She grabbed my sleeve.

I dragged myself from her grip.

I tottered to the door of the Joneses and knocked.

Mrs. Jones opened it.

"Is Tom in? I asked. My fears that Tom would never come in again were ice to my heart.

Mrs. Jones shook her head.

"He's gone out for a cigarette," she said.

I backed away. The door closed. I went into the Biers', without knocking, which surprised Mrs. Biers.

"My God! Mr. Sniggins. You do look sick," she said.

I went over to Joshua.

"There's something dripping through the boards of that room where old Harrison used to store Bibles," I said. "Biers! I think it's blood. And—*Jones went out a bit since*, and hasn't come back."

Mrs. Biers dropped her iron, and slithered into a chair.

"Wait till I get me boots on," said Joshua. "You don't go screaming round the place." This to his spouse.

"Oh, my God!" said Mrs. Biers.

On the way along the landing we picked up Teddy Michell. We whispered to him.

"Better get the beaks," he said.

"Best get up and see what it is," said Joshua.

We went up the staircase. As we went, Minnie came flying after us.

We came to the room where old Harrison used to store Bibles and sell them out by instalment.

"Gimme the candle, Sniggins." Joshua tried the door.

"Locked," he said.

Teddy Michell, Joshua, and I got our shoulders to it.

The banging we made brought people out of their rooms. Peaked-faced children, brought crying from their beds, in their mothers' arms, women in their shoddy rags, pale and sickly with half-starvation and hopelessness, jostling up to us.

At last the door burst.

"Gimme the candle, Michell," said Joshua. "Keep the crowd out."

We left Minnie to do that.

She stood against the doorway.

Joshua's cry met me as I landed in the centre of the room.

"Don't go an' look, Sniggins," was his injunction.

"Is it—Jones?"

"Jones all right."

"Dead?"

"I don't know," he said.

I turned, irresolute, then walked into the room where Joshua had warned me not to look.

Jones was there, lying on the floor.

"Don't touch him till the slop has been," came a warning in a woman's hysterical voice.

I knelt down beside him.

I tried to focus my attention on his eyes, and keep it away from his throat. They were wide open—staring—staring.

I felt at his heart. It gave a feeble beating.

223

His hand, the razor fallen from it, was stretched out, listlessly lying in a great widening pool.

"Jones—old man," I said.

His fixed gaze never changed.

His boots were stuck up, the worn soles showing where he had tramped about. I gulped suddenly, scrambled up, and went and stood against the wall. Were they never coming? Then I heard them—heard the crowd moving back, and then, into the room like a wraith burst Mrs. Jones, her hair down her back, her cheeks bloodless, her eyes staring—staring.

She gave one glance at the figure on the floor, ran to it, threw herself down—

"Tom! Tom! Tom!"

She lifted up his hand and rubbed it between her own.

I saw her stagger to her feet suddenly, stare round the room. Then the air was torn with a terrible shriek, then another, then another—and the crowd came in. I felt myself sliding gently down from the wall where I was leaning, overcome by the horror of it all. I heard the candle drop.

***

When I opened my eyes my first sensation was of a load creeping back, creeping back. Then I saw that I was not in my own room. Vaguely, slowly, I began to realise that it was Minnie's. There was a terrible noise in the next room. Slowly out of the mists the horrible details of what I had seen began to come back. I managed to trail across from the bed to the door, and went and knocked on the Joneses door. Minnie opened it. Her eyes were swollen and red. She took me back into her room and sat me on the bed.

"What's happening in there?" I asked.

"Crazy! She's gone crazy!"

"No?"

"But she has! The baby had got out of bed, and tumbled down the stairs whilst she was out. After someone came and told her Tom had cut his throat! An' they've ta'en him to the horspittle, and she's crazy. We're waitin' for the thing comin' round to take her away."

Soon after they removed her.

The message came in the morning.

Jones died six o'clock. Baby slightly improved. Minnie knocked at my door to tell me about it.

She sat down on the orange-box.

"What do you think about life, Nibby," she asked, suddenly. "Think there's any meaning to it all?"

"Yes. I think there's some."

She glanced at me with wild hope.

"What do you think it is, Nibby?"

"That the strong will come up, out of a struggle like this, and struggle with the strong who would keep it as it is," I told her. "Men have made this world, Minnie. Made these holes we live in, these laws we live under, and yet life could be clean and happy, and worth living.

"Human nature's good enough. It only hasn't got room. Anyhow, I've made up my mind I'm going to get out of Binkers Court—if I've to walk out and live in the woods."

She looked across at the window, the dirty window, the dirty sky.

Then she said: "Couldn't you take a pal, Nibby?"

"Do you mean it?" I asked.

"Sure!"

And suddenly she ran out of the room, sobbing like a child. When I got to her door I found it locked.

"You can get yourself ready, Minnie," I called.

There was no answer.

"I shall be ready in an hour," I warned her.

No answer—only that terrible sobbing—the agony of one who had passed through the sewerage of the world.

After about half an hour I heard Minnie's door open. I was shaving myself before a bit of broken looking-glass propped against a jam-jar. She came and stood in the doorway.

"How can you go out with nothing?" she asked.

"Same as you can stay with nothing," I told her. "Course, if you want to stay—stay. Yet—you can't say you haven't the pluck to take risks. Come and try some big clean 'uns."

She fired at that.

"What would you ha' done if you'd been starvin', and threatened with no roof over you at seventeen? That was how I started, if you want to know."

"Well, I didn't an' don't. Your past is nothin' to do with me. What I'm after is a fresh day—and Binkers Court behind me."

"There's half an hour to make up your mind," I went on. "I'm going out in ten minutes. Business. I'll be back in twenty, after that."

I went forth and returned with a decent pair of second-hand boots on my feet. She was sitting on the orange-box, kicking her heels.

"But where are you going, Nibby?"

So I told her a little bit about it.

I spread my worldly wealth on the orange-box, beside her.

Nine pounds, fifteen shillings!

"We'll buy a donkey for about ten shillings, strap a basket on his back—and off we go." I said encouragingly. "I've burned my coffin behind me—sold my death insurance papers. I'm for the roads. If you want to come, say so. It'll cost me two pounds for a special licence."

She nearly toppled off the box.

"But there'll still be seven fifteen."

She came up to me with a little moved look.

"Nibby! You'd never marry one like me?" she asked incredulously.

"Oh—it's all in a life's march," I told her. "Don't let's get sentimental. It would merely be convenient to tell the children that are buying balloons we are strictly and honourably joined together. Pity you weren't a boy, though. It would save two pounds."

She looked at me for what seemed an interminably long time. Then she said. "Nibby—I'm on."

"You take nothing with you," I said.

"I leaves all the stuff in my place?" she asked.

"All the damned lot. Make your bank account—if you have one—over to Mrs. Biers—anybody. And you promise me. If we say good bye—you don't come back here, and you don't pick up where you left off."

"Gawd!" she said, in a choked voice. "I'll never come back."

She sat on the orange-box whilst I put my rag of a tie on.

In all my miseries I had still clung to a tooth-brush. I put it in my pocket with the book of Whitman, and another of Thoreau.

"Nibby," said Minnie suddenly, "I'll go as a *boy*."

"All right," I said.

"Then it'll save two pounds," said Minnie.

"Ok—no—I'm not travelling round the country on that hop," I said. "It'll cost at least ten more shillings if you go as a boy. You'll want a suit."

"Oh!" said Minnie, in a funny little voice.

Mrs. Biers drew near.

"My God! Mr. Sniggins! Are you hopping off?" she asked.

"H'm. Last night put the tin lid on here," I said.

"But where are you going?"

"I am going to see a bit of my native land," I told her. And that was all she got out of me—excepting a bob—which she borrowed. Minnie followed me down the stairs. Two hours later we left a registry office. We went into a second-hand dealer's and bought a suit for a boy of seventeen. I carried the parcel. We took a bus, and took another, and another—and then we walked miles. The sun was dropping as we came on the outskirts of Rundean—with the rolling commons out on each side of us.

"You can change into a lord of creation here, Minnie," I told her—and walked on, leaving her in a little wild hollow where the pool would soon be full of stars—full of stars!

I heard someone running after me. She was laughing. She had tucked her hair under her cap, and she looked like a devil-may-care jockey.

"Now," I said, taking her by the shoulders, "You're Peter. Peter—remember! Mr. Peter Shallon, and I want to tell you—so that your mind'll be easy on the matter—I've not brought you with me for anything at all but just to go along with me, and get your damned trade out *of* your blood. Hush! Let me go on. Forget we're *married*. Forget I'm one of the same damned fools who think they buy women for so many shillings, or pounds, or thousands—or millions. If we get to like one another—well, but just now—we're journeying along, you and me, and we've seven pounds five to knock a living out of. I'm asking for nothing."

"I ain't ever dreamed there was men like you," she said faintly.

We went along till we entered a village street. 'Peter' followed me in through the inn door.

"Could you give us a rattling good meal?" I asked.

"In the kitchen," said the landlord.

So we had tea, and later we borrowed a pair of scissors from the landlady and clipped Peter's hair short, behind the barn, made a parcel of it, and went out for a stroll. I tied a stone round the parcel and dropped it in a pool. Poor Minnie! But it was no use grieving. We had set out to get out of a rut, and we were going to do it. We found out all the rooms were 'full up', but they could put us in the barn.

I pulled a lot of last year's bracken about, and piled hay on it, and we rolled ourselves up in it.

"How's this striking you?" I asked Peter. "Honest! Do you want to go back to Binkers Court? Honest— all the time—Peter."

There was a little silence.

"I never want to see Binkers Court again," said Peter.

Then out of the hay—some time after—

"I lived in the country till I was nine."

I sank into oblivion.

Next morning we bought a donkey, and managed to get a basket to fit his back.

Then we purchased two pounds worth of handkerchiefs, stockings, smallware of all kinds, in the next town, at a wholesaler's, and trundled away toward the farms.

The morning was raw, and blue and white, and the celandine leaves shone like dark green satin in the cold sunshine.

We passed a cottage with a porch. On the porch roof grew a yellowy sort of moss.

"I always thought I'd like to live in a house with a porch and moss on it," said Peter. Funny, that, I thought. To wander all through the mire of the world— and never forget that you once thought you'd like to live in a house with a porch that had moss on it.

We made our way down to the house of the porch with the moss on it, and finally took refuge in the porch. There was a little stone seat on one side of it, and still as I write I see her there, a little shadowy figure, a little tossed mind thinking who knows what thoughts, in the shadow of a childish dream come true. I can see the chimney pots as they appeared against the sky, as I went to look up at the house, and heard the crunch of the ground under my feet, and as I stood looking to see if the bill in the window really could mean to say the house was to be let.

"It is to let, Minnie," I told her, as I went back into the little porch. "There must be something the matter with it, but at least it's shelter. We'll go round to the next house and see who considers this is his private property."

"You go and see, Nibby," said Minnie. "I sort o' like to sit here listening to the wind."

So I went to the next house.

How funny it was to hear them undoing locks, remembering the open, free houses of *my dream*. Funny to see 'em drawing back bolts and chains and what-nots they kept round their minds, too, as though they were always on *guard*, and not used to open speech, fearless and free, but had to open the doors of their minds *by degrees*, and see how much it was wise to show. I asked how much they wanted per week. More humming and ha-ing, till I got frantic, as I always get when it got to grovelling among shillings and pence! So I offered them five bob, just to escape from the sordidness of it all. Then the old chap brought a lease out, and the middle-aged daughter a bottle of ink, and quite frantically I signed to take the house for five years.

Then the daughter got a key and came out with me and unlocked the door. There was a slate off here and there, it seemed, and the copper boiler ran, and the walls were a bit damp. I nodded my head in acceptance of it all.

"Anyhow, Minnie," I said, "There's some moss on the porch roof. We've to take our dreams where we find 'em."

I looked at Minnie where she sat on an old bucket turned upside down—souvenir left by the last tenant. Minnie looked up at me, where I stood with my back to the grate.

"Like you took me," she said.

"And you me," I told her.

"Oh, but you was different," she said, slowly.

"And how the hell was I different?" I demanded.

"Oh! You was good, Nibby," she said in a shaken little voice. "I've seen you sitting with your books, an' puckering your face up, an' I always said: 'Well, I think he's good, but you never know,' and now I *know*. An' I can't help thinkin' of the difference, an' how it'll always be there, Nibby, always there between us, makin' me feel like I'm not fit to be here, Nibby."

And quite suddenly she burst into a storm of passionate tears.

"Oh! Nibby," she said, struggling with herself. "Why wasn't you a devil? I think I'd have felt happier, not so like I'd never catch up!"

We managed to sit down on the bucket together, and tried to talk things over, and I placed the evolutionary theory before her, rooted in the good old earth, out of which we had all come, and tried to show her that goodness and badness are relative terms, subject to necessity, and that as a matter of fact I'd only been what she called good because I'd been afraid of the consequence of being otherwise, just preserving myself, and how I did not judge her, and so did not see why she should judge herself.

And I told her that somewhere in each of us was a very weak place, and I sort of knew how weak I was, for I'd experienced it *in a dream*. Then I tried to point out to her how some time nobler folk than we were would love each other with a greater love than we could, and that we were the bridges between the gulf that seemed unspannable now to us, sitting here in this old house with the winds blowing round it.

I dried her tears on one of the handkerchiefs that were part of my 'stock'. I pressed her little sallow, unpainted face to my own, and laughed at her for looking back when every little child has the art of letting yesterday go by, and gets up each morning to a new creation, a new epoch, a new age.

"But, Nibby, the farther I gets away from it the worse it looks," she cried.

I got desperate at last.

"Oh! Minnie, *forget it*," I cried. "Sex is overrated. Much overrated. It isn't the most precious thing that's sold in this moral world of ours. By Evolution! Let's be happy, Minnie. If there's any immorality in the world it's being miserable about our damned skids and making others miserable about their skids!

"Let's be happy and defiant of all that makes and keeps people wretched. We'll try to smash the necessity that drives people into all sorts of corners and then dumps a lot of moral codes on 'em and sends 'em into lunatic asylums to prove how we dream *one set of dreams* and *live under conditions that don't allow us to make them real.*"

Hand-in-hand we left the cottage, the key in my pocket. The winds were big and free. The sky was clear and blue, the bright sun was shining, and we went back through the wood to the inn. Only the dead leaves were rustling under our feet, and about them—the leaves of yesteryear. Next day we moved into the house with the moss on the porch door, with four chairs, a table, pots and pans, and a bed. But it did not look so bad when the fire was built up. And as we stood by the windows looking out on the stars I remembered that this bleak wind blowing outside was blowing on some humans who had not even a roof over their heads!

After two thousand years of morals and spirituality there were actually human beings left out in the shelter-less night to huddle in holes like wild animals! I wanted to get settled down, settled down so that I could go out and rouse the unburied dead! To preach Justice not Charity, and Equality of Material Things, as the basis of moral and mental equalities. With poor, blind, groping hands, I was reaching nearer to the man I might have been had the worst been the best.

Chapter 19

In the new old house we commenced our new existence.

Minnie had returned to her woman's garments. She was unconvincing and ill at ease as a 'boy'. But she had not returned to her old habits of thought. Existence was, indeed, new to her.

The lighter, longer days were coming. I turned the old garden over. I set blue lupins, and sweet-scented stocks, and mignonette and pansies, purple and white and yellow pansies.

In the evenings we went out, but no man said as he passed me in the starlight, "Greetings, brother. A glorious evening!" In the daytime the donkey and I went up the winding white roads to the little farms. When I returned, there was always the lighted window, and then Minnie at the gate, saying in a whisper, "How have you gone on to-day, Nibby?"

Sometimes it was five bob, sometimes it got to ten. But even a crusty loaf of country bread and fresh butter and a brown-shelled new-laid egg looked delicious to me, with the lamp light aglow, and the fire burning bright—and Minnie had made me a pair of slippers out of some old soles the last tenant had left, and we set to work to make a rug for the front of the hearth. Minnie working at one end and I at the other, and Minnie used her old 'suit' for the purpose, and bought rags off the rag-cart for the rest.

It was a funny, transitional period, with Binkers Court receding, but yet standing out more distinctly for all that it went further away. Curious and transitional, too, to have to be thinking about some other individual than myself, wondering 'Would Minnie like that?' or 'Would Minnie like this?'

A farmer's wife to whom I confessed we had just 'set up', and had no pictures, presented me with a pair of old pictures which had been varnished, and I used to sit smoking the pipe Minnie had bought me (as a wedding present) and stare at the sheep going over the bridge, and the other one of the cows standing in the summer water, till I nodded, and Minnie would say it was time to go to roost.

We had no clock. Funds had not run to it yet, so we used to stand at the door and count the chimes from the old church clock, and in the mornings we could guess it to half an hour from the light. Outwardly, our lives were very dull, but we had got out of the rut of our old, terrible existence. By walking out and facing what looked like nothing, we had achieved something and it was something better. It used to amuse me to hear Minnie say the old 'naughty' words she had used in Binkers Court, if the bacon got on fire, or when I could not find my tic. But Minnie was changing, too. It was nothing you could take hold of—concrete. Yet it was there. She would sit and listen to my reading with her hands on her lap, and frown at me when I said, "Do you want me to stop?" and say "No, carn't you see I'm a-listening?" Once she looked at me and asked, "Nibby! Do you think we shall live here for *five years*?"

"Fed up, already?" I asked, in alarm.

"Don't be so s'picious like," she retorted. "When I'm fed up I'll *walk out*. Because I've learned if you can walk out of one place you don't like, you can walk out of another."

Dangerous creatures, women, when you let 'em know their power! Sometimes we discussed the trade she had left, and I was always very suspicious lest she should ever suppose I'd married her for anything but to be a pilgrim journeying along with me, and sharing every 'possession' and every 'freedom' I claimed for myself.

It was at the end of April that I got the first shock which had entered my new existence. When I got back from my journey, just as I turned the old lane, giving the donkey little encouraging pushes, I saw that the house was dark. There did not seem to be any firelight even. But when I'd disposed of the donkey, by putting him in the shed where pigs had once been kept, I peeped in through the window and saw that there were a few red embers flickering in the grate.

I found the key and went in—with all sorts of panic in my heart. Had I married a woman who could not stick to any man? There was my tea on the table, the bread covered with a plate, my cup set, and the leaden spoon—and the tea-box by the side of it, and a plate of cress, with hard-boiled egg and slices of onion on it. And—there was a note set by my plate.

With trembling hands I lit the lamp, and read the message:

Dear Nibby,—I have gone back to Binkers Court to fetch something what we left behind. Don't worry, it's quite rite.—Minnie.

The woman next door said she had gone early in the morning, and had stacked up the fire. There were no trains but one that came within four and a half miles, and the last one would get in at nine o'clock.

I spent a horrible two hours, and then set out to walk four and a half miles. Queer if she *never* came back. Perhaps the life had been dull for her. I realised vaguely that women's lives were dull, pottering about with pots and pans—and we had not so many of those, either. I wished I had taken her out with me, with the donkey, till things got more comfortable and we had made friends, and were not so cut-off.

The roads shone white in the starlight. I went over quiet fields once. I tried to think what I should do if I were left alone. Yet I had lived alone before, or, at least, existed alone. I realised that one could make laws for one's own nature, and over-look the needs of other sorts of natures. And I worried because I had left the old donkey without his feed, quite thrown off my balance by finding Minnie flown.

Never shall I forget watching for that train coming in, watching people step down out of it, one after the other, with my heart sinking lower and lower.

Then I heard—

"Nibby! Did you think you was a grass widower?"

For the first time I realised what she meant to me.

"But, whatever—" I asked.

"It's Tom Jones' kid, what they'd taken to the workhouse, Nibby. Mrs. Biers had heard you was livin' here. Her cousin works at the brewery, by the village. So—I collared some money, Nibby. You don't mind? And I went and fetched him out. His head's nearly better. Take hold of him—right end up!"

She started laughing.

There was something absurdly happy about her tonight.

"You—you are going to keep him, Minnie?"

"If—if you don't mind, Nibby!"

"No—I don't mind, if we *can* keep him," I said.

And as we went along the fields, with poor Tom's evolutionary link with the turbulent young Sarband, the terrible thought struck me of what Mrs Bier's cousin working at the brewery could mean! He had seen me on the roads, and must have recognised me, having seen me in Binkers Court three times when he had visited her. He would have the whole story— Minnie's story—it would follow us round, follow us round.

"Is he heavy, Nibby?" asked Minnie.

"No."

We trudged on.

He was not very heavy, poor little chap. He was asleep. Minnie unlocked the door. It was eleven o'clock. We heard the church clock strike. If only Mrs. Biers' cousin had worked in any other brewery than—But I pushed the thought away, and helped Minnie to undress little Tom.

So concerned was I to think of Mrs. Biers' cousin working near here and knowing of poor Minnie's dreadful past existence, I lost no time in going down to see him. I left the house with a picture in my mind of Minnie, feeding little Tom with bread and milk whilst he stared solemnly at her hair, now curling all round her head again, its bright colour taking his savage's fancy. I asked for Teddy Biers, not knowing Mrs. Biers' maiden name, but they found him, as only one Teddy worked there. There was the smell of the brewery on him as he come out to me in the yard. How I stumbled through the telling of it I don't know. I saw that he had heard it all before.

"Well, what about it?" asked Teddy.

He was a little, thickset man, heavy of look, and with a most peculiar resemblance to a horse. I think it was the length of his face.

"I want you to keep your mouth shut," I told him. "I've got to knock a living out selling at the farms round here. My goods are as good as any other man's. But I know the drawbacks of a moral world that advertises buying and selling of everything—calls it practical, and allows it on certain conditions and not on others.

"If Minnie had been knocked down by an auctioneer's hammer to one man, whether she liked him or not, they'd have put it in all the papers, and they would have legalised the transaction in Westminster. But because she did the same thing, without the bell and the book, and did it wholesale, it might stop us being able to live. We're happy here. We're not hurting anyone. We want to forget the things we have endured. Minnie's my wife. She's also my pal. I'd have picked her up from whatever hell Chance had pitched her to, and whatever she'd been. So just keep your mouth shut. That's all I'm asking."

He half opened his mouth and shut it again.

Then he nodded.

"All right," he said. "I admires you, Sniggins. But I think you're a fool all the same. It won't get known with my telling. All right, Bill. I'm coming. Morning."

He turned and left me, but looked back once— then, just as I thought he was coming back to say something more, he evidently changed his mind.

I went back to the little house I had left with lighter heart. There were little shoots of green coming up in the garden.

I called Minnie, and she stood up with the Jones' baby in her arms, staring at her hair, just as we were staring at the garden. Then I got the donkey out, and started on my pilgrimage.

The road ran on and the sky got blue. They were sowing the fields at H——, and I recalled how man had been a reaper before he was a sower; how he had found wheat growing wild and pounded it for food, and then how some 'lunatic' (pioneers are always 'lunatics') had sowed some of it in the earth just to see what would happen.

And as I jogged along by the old donkey I thought of all the sacrifices, human sacrifices, that the priests had made to help the wheat to grow better, and, later, to get in the tithes. And still there was blood on our bread. Beggars whined for it; artists sold their art for it; women sold their bodies for it;

bread fights raged around it; millionaires cornered it to become billionaires; parsons gagged themselves so that they could go on eating—just eating. The whole of the earth's inhabitants were chained with chains of bread.

The honeysuckle leaves were quite full. I saw the flower of it, too, at little B—— ready to open out at the first good warmth of the sun. Celandines galore, little yellow stars set in the green of the earth—celandines that had fought their way up, whilst countless generations of other flora had been extinguished by glacial periods.

In the dim of the evening I came back under the moon and stars, encouraging the donkey. Good to see the lighted window as I turned the lane. There was something fresh about the window to-night—curtain shadows. I could hear the bubbling of a well as I gave the donkey his fodder and shook his bedding up. Minnie stood waiting for my surprise as I stepped into the kitchen.

"Got the wallpaper off Miss Anmell," she explained. "They'd had it years. Ain't the little pink roses nice, Nibby. An'—I made you a little bookcase, Nibby. How 'ave you gone on to-day, Nibby?"

"Take the wages of barter—holy barter!" I told her jocularly, and threw seven shillings on the table. Little Tom was in bed. I went up to look at him, shading the candle with my hand. He was curled up like a dormouse, and I realised I was getting a bit fond of him, and should miss him if he wasn't there. Then I came down and admired Minnie's wall-papering a bit more. Then I got some fodder, and helped Minnie wash up the pots, because that wall-papering had taken her all day, and she was as fit to sit and rest as I.

We sat whilst I read bits out of Wells, the great history of the world, which makes our own little egos seem so ridiculous, and our patriotism such provincialism! Whilst we sat there came a knock at the door. It was raining heavily now, and must be eleven o'clock, at least.

"Could I shelter till this lot's over?" said a man's tired voice.

"Come in," I told him.

Whilst Minnie made him some tea we talked.

The steam from his wet coat was rising round him as he sat by the fire. After work. He looked more like a sanatorium. But he was after being exploited. Journeying by the spikes, but he found it hopeless, just *hopeless*. Still, there might be a chance. He had heard they were starting a reservoir at H——, and would get along when the rain stopped. We tried to persuade him to stay the night, but he said he was dirty, going along from spike to spike, and he would rather not. He would get in some barn for the night, and in the morning there might be a chance.

Very reluctantly we let him go.

I tried to get him to come in till morning, as we stood by the gate, but he said it was fine again now, and he'd 'get on'.

"Buck up," I said, haltingly, "a system of society which can't feed, clothe, and shelter its workers *can't* last very long."

He turned by the gate.

"I'll give it about ten years," he said. "I'll maybe be kicking the daisies up, but I'll give it about ten years. They can't hinder it, mate. And they can't bring it. It'll just come. But I think I'll be kicking the daisies up, so what's the odds to me?"

We heard him coughing his way along into the night. Orion was shining The eyes of the serfs had stared at these same stars. The eyes of the waged slaves were staring at them now. And after we were gone other eyes would look up, and other lips say, 'I wonder what they thought, the people who looked up *yesterday*'. We went in, and only the knowledge that all this misery was transitory gave me calmness enough to sink into sleep. In the dawn I woke up. Minnie was lying staring at the sunrise flooding the window, and we heard the cocky little proletarian hoppers, the sparrows, chattering and cheerful.

"What are you thinking about, Minnie?" I asked.

"Nothing," she told me.

Isn't it odd the way we have of shutting our hearts up and saying 'Nothing', when we are thinking a lot?

It was a bonnie May Sunday, and I remembered that all over Europe workers were celebrating May-Day. So I helped Minnie make sandwiches, and we wrapped up little Tom and set him on the donkey, and went down to celebrate it in the woods. We had not the money to journey to London, so we just went down into the woods; and how the old man next door did stare to see me with my bit of red in my buttonhole.

"Red for danger, Mr. Sniggins," Miss Anmell had called, as we went past.

"Well, it has been a dangerous colour for them who wore it,' I had chatted her. "But we won't take it out for all that. There must be millions wearing it to-day. And they call each other 'Comrade'."

But we sat in the woods, and the earth was warm and everything was still. You could almost feel the earth breathing, moving, as you lay there, staring up between the larches and the beeches. We had tied the donkey to a tree; but he had a long rope, and was nibbling away at the new grass. Young Tom was one of those kind who don't keep you watching him all the time. Minnie gave him some fancy grass she found, and he occupied himself pulling it to bits. It was so quiet, so warm, so youngly green and delicate, and the leaves seemed so to hang on nothing, it scarcely seemed real.

Gradually, I fell asleep, with the voice of Minnie in my ears, talking to little Tom. He had got to putting his hand up and stroking her hair now. I suppose those who passed by must have thought us a shabby lot. But we had a most glorious day in the woods on May Day!—May Day! The symbol of the coming of the People's dream the world over. We took primrose roots back with us, to come up in the garden next year.

That night, just as I was taking 'Wells' out again, when we had got Tom to bed (as happy as a drunken fiddler, with a bit of colour in his cheeks. and overcome with sleep), came a knock at the door. There was Teddy Farrow, just as he had called after church. Thought he'd look in at us a bit, he said. I can't say I was too pleased to see him. I wanted to get on with the reading, and Minnie was getting interested, too. But I put the thought by as unsociable. Minnie made him some supper. He had had a letter from Mrs. Biers.

Old Viner had gone to the work-house. Sparkins had evicted half a dozen families. I saw Minnie's eyes flame at that. But it made us both unhappy and uncomfortable to be talking about Binkers Court. I wished he had not called. We were glad when he went, though I was glad we had made him sufficiently comfortable to have him say he would come again whenever he was round that way.

"What are you doing, Nibby?" asked Minnie next morning.

"Counting my worldly wealth," I explained.

"What for?"

"There's a cart being sold—a light cart at a sale. I think I'll go up and get it. I could put more stuff on and sell at the houses along the way."

I got it two days later.

It certainly increased my sales. We got a carpet for the floor. It certainly began to look less like a ship-wreck and more like a home. And in the town I bought an unframed print of Dante and Beatrice on the Bridge, and another called 'An Idyll'—a romance, with a brown man kissing a pale, moonbeamy sort of woman in a field of poppies.

And we dreamed of what the house would be in *five years*. Funny little dreams you get—living in a house with yellow moss growing over the porch door—with a sort of new creation growing up around you, and getting the smoke and dinginess out of your blood, and the hope back in your heart, every day that dawns. And the idiotic sort of things you say! As 'How much do you love me. Minnie?' And Minnie, saying nothing much but showing it by her eagerness to run upstairs and hunt for a collar-stud, or any thing I've lost, till I say 'Minnie, don't do it. I don't ask for a *slave.*'

Chapter 20

As I went to and fro between the house with the porch that had moss on it and the farms, I got to know people as I had never known those of Binkers Court. They revealed (by chance) fragments of their dreams, often revealing them in uncultured language which in no wise detracted from their progressiveness. Some of them would almost have gone into hysterics, these commonplace women who purchased 'remnants' from me, had I informed them that their little outbursts revealed in themselves a resistance and challenge to the society they lived in.

One man I talked to by the roadside made more terrible charges against our Bureaucracy than anything I have ever heard from either Socialist or Bolshevist. But he was quite unaware of where his thoughts were leading him. I left him to find out at some future time.

The great thing to me was to discover that the hidden dreams of the people (some of them hidden so deep they scarcely realised them themselves) were alive. Their desires were common desires. Perhaps the ideas of the old pioneers had permeated further than we knew—reaching these people I talked with on the lines of their struggling lives.

And amidst all this I watched the swallows come back. In the lengthening evenings I would notice on my way home the kingfisher who was building under the little bridge; hear the chaffinch's 'tink tink-tink' in the boughs of the sycamore, where the leaves were coming out like fairies' fans now!

Larks went up in the silvery dawns and in the fires of the sunsets. The may-blossoms were white and red, and, after showers, their scattered blossoms on the ground lay as confetti for Puck and the little folk to whom Shakespeare had given 'souls'—dreaming of them, no doubt, long ago, walking in the woods, with a blade of grass between his teeth and the romance of youth in his blood. There was a vibrant life all around that made one quiver to it.

So irresistibly did it grip me, that, riding on the cart past the hedges, when I have seen the grass blades moving, I have jumped off and looked to see what was behind them, and found it was only the invisible and gentle wind.

A wonderful month to me, that May! Warmer than many a June. It was as though I also awoke with the earth. I, the creature made of the same elements that ran in the streams, that shone in the stars, that lay in its deep, unplumbed depths. Always I took home some handfuls of new blossoms or flowers I had found.

Then I discovered that the sea was only twenty miles away. We had had no orthodox 'honeymoon'. Minnie's eyes sparkled when I proposed a wholly unorthodox one—to journey to the sea, on the cart, taking little Tom with us, and a tent we could hire for three-and-six a day. We would be away three days. It would be three days' loss of 'wages'. But we set out, though we should come back 'broke'.

We rode through lanes all red and white, and the sun shone all the time, all the time—shining life down on us, warming us, cheering us, as though he said, 'This for you, also, children of the dust, even as for monarchs and magnates and the elect of the earth'.

Sometimes we sat down on the fragrant grass, where the cattle had trampled the wild thyme which flung up its sweetness. Minnie cut hunks of bread, saying at intervals, "Go' blymee, Nibby, you surely carn't eat no more!"

But the tent was best of all. And the people we passed on the roads that run all round the world and home again—home again! Never again would I see them. I knew it. Silently we passed them and they passed us—each with our dreams in our hearts.

I recall still two men, looking like marionettes, high up on a quarry, who waved their hands to us and shouted as we passed. What they shouted we could not tell. But we waved our hands back, and little Tom made us laugh by waving his, clumsily.

Old men we passed, bent with toil, whom the great trees seemed to reproach as they passed beneath them, saying as they swung their new leaves about. 'Why are you bent of back and dim of eye? Look at us! We are straight still—and a glory to behold!'

And to say at intervals, "Are you happy, Minnie?" and hear, "Ain't you? Well, I am, then." The great earth that had flung up the rocks, and demolished cities, and thrown the sea on the dry land, and built up the continents below the sea, was very kind those three days to Minnie, and little Tom, and me.

At Fairfax there was a steeple-chase. Just as if it had been waiting for Minnie's 'honeymoon' and mine! We left the tent (with the food hung up by a contrivance of mine so that dogs could not get it), and journeyed in the early morning to Fairfax, where they brew beer and sell hand-made baskets.

I recall the man hawking strings of onions; the gipsies in their print frocks, and the subtle freedom in their faces (also travelling on a cart which we scraped past on a narrow road where we saw the first wild rose).

The medley of humanity at the steeplechase, the riders in their satin coats, gay and shimmering in the sun. 'Gentlemen' and the 'sons of gentlemen', doing nothing a year. Still, it was our 'honeymoon', and they were entertaining us for once.

We wandered up and down amongst the bookies. 'Five to one on Horralus!' I can hear it yet—over the murmur of the crowd. And the chap who was doing the crown and anchor trick on the grass; and the way people packed together and stood tip-toe when the horses set out—horses worth more, in market value, than the folk who were watching 'em.

And the scraps of conversation in the crowd. "That chap riding Horralus is going to marry the woman what owns the hoss. Her 'usband ran away with a girl worker in his silk factory. They say 'e ran away because she used to kiss the chap what's riding Horralus—"

And "I've sixpence on White Star."

Suddenly Minnie plucked my sleeve. I turned.

"Ain't you putting anything on?" she asked challengingly.

So we put two shillings on 'White Star' because the odds were against him, like the working classes. And after all he won at five against him and we got as excited as the Wall Street Gamblers' when they are making a corner that 'corners' the people.

"That was 'cause he was ridden by a man that wore a red shirt, Minnie," I told her.

Pleasant to be jogging along, jogging along, all in the scented evening, under the wide sky, and the little silver-grey moths a-dancing about, come early because it was warm. But the donkey was tired, so I walked, and at the inn where we saw the man drinking the ale, I fetched out a tiny glass of wine for Minnie, and one for myself, and we drank it outside, and I said as I lifted my glass up: "To Minnie and little Tom, and the workers of the world." And Minnie laughed and said, "To Nibby. Here's 'is 'ealth." and suddenly handed me the empty glass and started to cry because she had been so happy, she said afterwards. Three happy, happy days.

Then we went back to the little house with the moss on the porch door, and Teddy Farrow came, rather aggrieved because he had been three times and found us gone out each time. That night I started the thing that had been stirring in my blood all these weeks.

"How's that for the title of a book?" I asked Minnie. She pored over it.

"'Dreams of a Wandering Pedlar'," she repeated. "Well, it ain't a book I would buy with a title like that." I had to wake her up by the time I'd done writing, and as she roused to consciousness the dim and fugitive likeness to Arlene—Arlene, free and beautiful and proud and joyous—Arlene without 'shadows' stared me in the face.

I knew Arlene would not quite have said what Minnie had said about my title. But it did not matter. I was as far away from being Sarband as Minnie was from being 'Arlene'. We were only their prototypes. I slipped my arm around her neck and kissed my dream.

Life was pretty crowded for us all that summer. Little Tom was learning to walk without falling down. Minnie was making up 'remnants' into garments to increase my 'sales'. The house had not so much in it, and allowed her time to sit out on the little rustic bench in the garden—sewing.

The stocks and asters and mignonette and pansies came up—and the sun burned my neck and face brick-red in my pilgrimings up the roads. Minnie was getting brown, too, and Tom was like a berry.

Once the parson saw the three of us, paddling in a deep, clear stream, and how he did stare, but finally lifted his hat, and we saw him pass out of sight on the path.

And as I went paddling in the clean, sun-warmed water, little scenes of the dirty river bridge near Binkers Court—the 'communal ash-pits', etc.—would drift into my mind, and somewhere from the city streets I heard the echo of the tramping of thousands of feet, and saw the banners demanding the right to work, and knew this was only a pleasant backwater of peace and joy and beauty, from which I should some day walk by choice, to fling in my small weight on the side of the great dispossessed. I realised it would not be much—my weight—but was content to dream it would count a little, and be on the right side.

In the country, too, I saw the ignominy of the rural workers' lot, and realised struggle here, organisations here—all lining up—lining up in the bloodless bread-battle.

We sent Mrs. Biers a box of new-laid eggs, and butter with a cow stamped on it, and I did my 'Pedlar's Dreams' every evening, Minnie sitting watching me, the lamp between us shining on her hair—the colour of Arlene's.

"Don't it make your head ache, Nibby?" she would ask sometimes.

Always now she put the cork in the ink-pot, and handed me the paper grip. After she had heard little Tom 'swear' after her, she stopped herself. There was a bit of natural colour in her cheeks, now. She was quieter, but sometimes I heard her singing—singing—and I cut off a bit of her hair once, when she was asleep, and hid it away without saying a word.

Teddy Farrow did come round a lot. But then, he was in lodgings. We asked him once if he was coming paddling with us, and he stared like a stuck sheep. Comical fellow, Farrow; always jingling his money round in his pocket, like he liked to hear it.

And I quarrelled with Minnie once because she propped the leg up with Wells' 'Outline of History'! Little Tom called us 'Nibby and Minnie'. Miss Anmell thought we should get him to call us 'Uncle' and 'Aunt', not being 'ours', and whenever she came in she always had a good look at the picture of the brown man and the white moonbeamy nymph-woman kissing in a field of poppies and said: "*When* are you going to take that picture down?" and quarrelled with me because I told her she liked the picture, but was afraid to admit it.

She sulked at me three days, till little Tom toddled up to the chained and bolted door, kicked it with his new boots, and said: "Unky Nibby's sent dis"—this being a bunch of white dog-roses.

She told Minnie afterwards she thought I was a nice husband—odd as I was—and Minnie surprised me by showing a spark of jealousy, and got angry when I sat down and laughed, and laughed, and finally gave me a push which made little Tom cry, then snatched him up in her arms and got jealous again, and said: "Now, you push me, and see if he'll cry." So I pushed Minnie, and he cried again, and we both laughed, and stood all three together, he in Minnie's arms, and mine round the pair, laughing, and yet pathetically glad that we meant so much to each other, we three, flotsam and jetsam of the great world which had found no use for us, and looked at us down its nose.

Just as we stood there, Teddy Farrow came. He had got a motor-bike and a trailer, to seat two, and he planned wonderful trips for the lot of us—into Wales and Scotland and Evolution knows where—and Minnie heard him with a strange look on her face. So that I got a bit jealous, but put it away and trampled it down, as unworthy of a man who had dreamed a dream and seen a vision.

He took us around the Hump that evening, and we knocked part of a wall down, though we were only going five miles an hour! Minnie had enjoyed it—even running into the wall. And I felt a little jealous—for women have a way of overlooking the fact that you are trundling up and down, like a donkey, just to bring grist to the mill, and that it is not your fault that they are stuck amongst pots and pans all day.

So I wove some wonderful plans of where we would go when 'Dreams of a Pedlar' came out, and Minnie watched me, with a stranger look than ever, and suddenly said, "Nibby—you don't trust me!"

I was startled.

"You think I'm gone on Teddy Farrow!" she said. "Nibby, if it's anything of a consolation to you, I could have gone off with the old fool up the road. Him what made 'is money with backing horses. He's gone abroad, an' he would have took me with him. But I says, 'Not me. I've sampled all your sort 'as to give -- an' it ain't much!' Nibby, if you like, I'll hot the poker and lay it across my face—if it'll make you trust me more!"

By Evolution! She rushed at the poker and plunged it in the fire—pale and trembling all at once—and I knew she would do it if—I was such a fool!

And Minnie said, after a while, "And I'm glad you're jealous, Nibby, in a way. You've been—terrible good to me—Nibby—and I'm glad—you can get jealous when there's no need—for it makes me feel more equal like."

It was when the leaves were falling and the swallows had followed the route of the sunshine that my 'sales' began to fall off.

Teddy Farrow did not come now, and would pass me with a curt nod when I met him in the lanes.

Minnie would be standing by the gate in the shortening daylight as I came home, and say in a strained whisper: "'Ow have you gone on today, Nibby?"

Sometimes it was almost nil. I put it down to a lull, and tried not to get down-hearted. Minnie would look at me if I got to staring into the fire, and say: "Never mind, Nibby! You'll do better tomorrow".

People were always polite when they did not buy. I never suspected anything until Miss Anmell stopped coming in, and then, as little Tom and Minnie and I were coming back from a walk one evening, a little country lad threw a stone, and it hit the wall, but I knew it was meant for us.

"What was that for, Minnie?" I asked.

She burst out crying in the lane, and the lad ran away, frightened I think.

"Here, dry up. There's Miss Anmell coming," I told her.

I felt Minnie's violent effort at composure as Miss Anmell came up to us, face to face in the lane.

"Nice to-night, Miss Anmell," I greeted her.

"It is," said she, and hurried away as if *afraid* to be seen exchanging words with us.

"Don't ask me now. Wait till Tom's in bed," said Minnie. So she gave him his bread and milk, and I carried the candle up in front. Downstairs again, Minnie leaned against one side of the fireplace.

"It's Teddy Farrow, I think. I told him I'd tell you if 'e came when you wasn't in, playin' the fool, and 'e must 'ave told round the plice what I been, Nibby. Arter all, you can't expect 'em to be as ready to give one like me another chance as you *was*, Nibby. Where are you goin', Nibby?"

"If I don't publish Teddy Farrow to this village as a would-be fallen man (and woman can't fall alone!) I'll eat my cap! Give up moanin', Minnie. I'll give Farrow the best hiding any descendant from the man-like ape has ever had in this sanctimonious village, where there are half- a-dozen imbeciles walking about, through inter-marriage, to keep money in the family. They can starve us out if they like. I'll leave our mark here against their damned hypocrisy!"

But—"Oh, Nibby, don't!" sobbed Minnie, and clung to me.

I sat down and regarded her desperately.

"Oh! Nibby! If I went away they'd let *you* live," she said, wearily. "I've felt it would come, Nibby. It's only to be expected—"

"It is," I said, "in a mad world like ours, where they justify the system of buying and selling of all things so long as it moves on orthodox lines. I'll try not to hit Farrow *too* hard. Give us a kiss, Minnie. I'll be back soon."

I kissed her trembling lips. "You'll not 'ave a chance against Farrow!" sobbed Minnie.

Not have a chance! I tore along the lane, saying it ironically to myself. Just let me get him.

I could see myself and Farrow struggling together, and see the rain of blows, and myself jumping on him! Just a primitive child of imagination and passion picturing me and Farrow—Farrow and me.

Then I'd call round on the parson and ask him to send Farrow into a home for fallen men—Magdalene Hostelry or Judas Mansions, or something of that ilk, where he'd be told he was to save his immortal soul by scrubbing floors and reaching a state of penitence where human pride in the possibility of climbing up must be cast out!

And through it all a remote figure, with childishly trembling lips, I heard Minnie saying: "Oh! Nibby! If I went away they'd let *you* live!"

I passed the ale-house and heard someone roaring out one of the 'dirty songs and dreary' our moral world so loves. Wouldn't I bash Farrow. Then I saw the church where they had the figure of Christ, whose blood, they said, washed away the sins of the world, and yet they would jump on poor Minnie!

"Night, Sniggins," came a voice.

It was like a bad dream.

But that was Farrow's voice, and Farrow himself, and he had a woman with him.

"I want to speak to you," I told him.

"Wait, then, Nancy," he said.

He came up to me, jingling his money round in his pockets.

"Want to buy a bike, Sniggins?" he asked.

I got my face close to his.

"No. I want to give you a jolly good thrashing," I said. "Get your coat off. Put your fists up. You've told all round about Minnie. You should have told *why* you told, you rat. You've stopped our bread supply. You've told Minnie you loved her—ha! ha!—Love! love! You *Christian*. You *Judas*. Off with your jacket or I'll tear it off your back!"

The woman Farrow had with him was approaching.

He staggered back from me.

"Sniggins! Have mercy! Don't let her hear!" he groaned. "Sniggins! You—don't let her hear or I'm done. I'm sorry, Sniggins. I'll give you fifty pounds. She's coming. Don't say anything. Sniggins, she's promised to marry me. Sniggins, for God's sake, Sniggins."

He got hold of my sIeeve.

"She's all the world to me, Sniggins," he said hoarsely. "Don't let her know what I am."

I snatched my sleeve from his hand. I drew a deep breath.

I could smash his 'dream' with a word or two, as he had smashed ours.

She was moving up to us. Terrible, terrible struggle, but not on the lines I had dreamed. Away in the cottage I could see Minnie, with her lips trembling weakly and childishly.

"Whatever is the matter, Eddie?" asked the woman.

Chapter 21

She was younger than Farrow, comely, and quiet spoken, with something rather rigid in her manner.

"Nothing, Nancy. Only a few—a few words over some money I owe Sniggins," said Farrow, eagerly. "Isn't it, Sniggins?"

"You're an unevolved creature, Farrow," I told him shortly. "I suppose you don't know any better. Against your 'religion' you can set my 'manhood'. I'll look over it. Good-night."

So I left them.

He came running after me a few minutes later.

"Sniggins, I'll be down to-morrow. I'll bring fifty pounds," he began.

I spat near his boots and turned my back on him.

I did not make for the house with the moss on the porch door right away. I felt so distressed that I wanted to be out in the night.

So I struck over by the heath. Its spreading wilderness did not seem (one local writer had so christened it) 'God-forsaken' to me, for I knew the living things of the earth were here; also, the heather was blowing and the gorse-bushes shaking, and the little pools were full of stars.

Somehow, in the walking to and fro, I worked out the problem with which we were faced. Then I set out to walk back. But there were clouds covering the moon.

The rain came in torrents as I blundered on; but at last I found the road by following running water, which I recalled always went down to the valley. I hurried, wondering if Minnie had got worked up and what time it was.

There was a lanthorn moving about, and, to my surprise, Miss Anmell's voice came out of the night.

"Mr. Sniggins, is that you?"

"It is," I told her.

"You're wife's nearly crazy. She's been seeking you all in the rain. She left the baby, and she's been all over. Do go in. I'll tell her you've come. She's in our house."

Which surprised me somewhat.

The rain was running off my coat, and my boots were soaked, and the fire was nearly out. Miss Anmell, to my surprise, had followed me in.

"You know," she said, haltingly, "I've been right sorry for *you*, Mr. Sniggins.

"You'll never be able to get a living now," she said. "Unless you get right away. My father'll wipe out the lease. I've brought him to it, because I've known what trouble is, myself. You see, it's s*elling* you're in, and if you could get some sort of work in the towns, away from these backward places, where they never lets by-gones be by-gones, you'd have a chance. I've saved five pounds. It's taken me years; but if it's any good to you, I'll lend it to you. And, if you never can pay it back, don't worry. We're here to help one another, and I'm sorry I've kept away, whatever they have said."

Before I could say anything she had gone.

Minnie came in, with Tom under old Anmell's topcoat.

"Oh, Nibby!" she said. "I thought he must have killed you."

Wretched as I was, I could not help laughing at that.

I helped her to get Tom to bed. He was cross and tired at this upheaval in his calm life. He refused a drink of hot milk, and sent the spoon flying; but we quite understood, Minnie and I. So we got him to bed, and got the fire up, and dried our sodden garments, and Tom's crying died away into peace, as all our crying dies. Minnie kept shivering.

But we got warmed through at last, and then at one o'clock in the morning, we started packing up.

At three o'clock we went upstairs.

The rain was coming down in torrents yet. It dripped through the slates before morning.

"Your hands are hot, Minnie," I told her.

"It's all the upset!" she answered. We got up at seven.

I went out and looked at the little garden where the wind and rain had ruined the last of our summer flowers.

Sadly the dawn was stealing over it as though this was the end. Yet next summer others would live in the house of the porch with the moss on it, and the things we had set would some of them come bravely up and the new tenants say: 'Why, what's this coming up?' The donkey was braying for his breakfast, so I went and fed him.

By ten o'clock all the furniture was packed up. We left it till we sent for it. Old Anmell was very kind now we were going.

Miss Anmell gave us some sandwiches, and I handed her the key. Just as we got up the lane, Minnie and Tom sitting on the cart, Farrow came running after us.

"Sniggins!" he said, "I meant it last night. I've brought the cheque-book. I'm sorry. It was something came over me. I just drifted. At first," he looked at Minnie, "I was just testing her. I couldn't believe, after what I knowed, it could be real. Then I got wild, and yet I didn't mean to tell. An' then I did. I'd have given anything to stop it—but—I couldn't. An'

Sniggins, you're a better man than me. Now—call it compensation."

"Drive on. Minnie," I told her.

Minnie pulled at the reins.

He came running after us.

"But—man—I can't let you go like this—"

There was a crude agony in his tone.

"Pull him up, Minnie!" I said.

Minnie pulled the donkey up.

"What is it you want, Farrow?" I asked.

"Just to ease something I'm feeling that's all," he said.

"With a cheque-book?" I asked.

I could see the mountain-ash. The berries on it were reddening. The leaves were fallen from the oak.

"Just so you'd forgive me a bit easier, Sniggins," he said.

I felt the sort of pity the people of 'Equality Island' must have felt for me, but with me, less developed, it was not wholly untouched with scorn. With great cost I held out my hand to him.

"Don't want the money," I said. "I think barter is all vile. And a man can't buy or sell these things. But there is my hand. You can book it against all you've ever heard against Socialists."

He looked at me in a staggered way.

Then he said: "You—you do forgive me, Sniggins?"

I pointed to Minnie.

"There's the one you've injured," I told him. "Ask her."

Minnie turned her face.

"No," she said, fiercely. "Not for what you've brought on Nibby. No, I 'ope it'll come back to you—you what wouldn't let us be 'appy where we was. I 'ope you'll remember 'ow you've driven us out to nowhere."

With that she pulled the reins.

I saw Farrow looking after us.

There was something on his face—something written there I had once felt in my own heart—in a dream—Regret. Pain. Disgust—for himself.

And so we passed up the road, Farrow watching us out of sight, the poor child of Chance, who drifted, feeling things 'come over him'.

Chapter 22

When we reached the crest of the little hill where the road wanders towards H——, the rain was beginning to slant down, and, looking back, the village we had left appeared blotted out. Minnie and Tom were under the tarpaulin. How it slashed down, fairly dancing on the road, whilst the fields, as we saw them through the palings, smoked again. The donkey plodded on, and I by his side.

If we could only reach H—— I thought we might find somewhere to creep in until morning, and then, if I heard of work near by, we might get lodgings. But H—— was two miles away. Sometimes a motor-wagon or car passed us. I had to keep a sharp look-out for them, for the road to H—— twists and turns.

I felt a pang of regret as we passed the fine pine trees, where I had often eaten my bread and cheese lunch when out on my rounds.

"The straw's gettin' wet, Nibby," Minnie informed me.

So we stopped the cart and tried to pull the tarpaulin nearer the sides. But there was no help for it. There was a little stream of rain soaking through the straw. Minnie tried to keep little Tom dry, and I tried to keep Minnie dry by piling up the straw into a sort of high chair, all in a heap, for her to sit on where the rain did not gather.

"You're cold, Minnie," I told her, for I could hear her teeth chattering. It had come down, that rain. I offered her my coat, but that was soused nearly through, so maybe it would not have helped *if* she *had* taken it. But the worst blow of all was when we got to H—— and found even the inn 'full up'. It had been an old-time 'house' once, but it had a garage now, and the garage was full of motors, and the place full of motorists, having half-crown dinners.

The landlady, however, took pity on us, and sat us down in the kitchen, and we partly dried ourselves by the big fire whilst she looked after the motorists. And at last she gave us some big pots full of hot tea, and thick slices of home-made cake. We stayed until we were ashamed to stay any longer. It was so warm in there; but the rain was nearly over.

As we came out, there was a fading rainbow, which little Tom managed to see after he looked everywhere for it except where it was—as is the way of those dreamers, even older—and I wondered vaguely if in years to come he might recall, like a dream, the first time he had seen a rainbow.

It was beautiful enough, as we went along, for a dozen artists to have made pictures from. There were big blobs of silver rain on the grass by the wayside, sliding down as you looked at them, and trembling on the edges of red and brown and yellow leaves the wind had yet spared. But the uncertainty of whether we would get in anywhere and our half-wet clothes, and the sense of responsibility I had for Minnie and Tom veiled it for me, though afterwards, when I looked back, I could see it all again—that tremulous, after-the-storm Beauty of the Earth. Even so, we retain the glimpses of all dear delights, and perhaps they go on and on down the ages, until, at last, from such as us, some poet leaps, singing with nightingale tongue the things we only felt.

We sat in a cake-shop at little B——, hearing the rain again; but the donkey was out in it all. We went on as soon as it slackened. I could hear of no work anywhere. I began to get apprehensive when it got two o'clock, for the cold and darkness would close in soon. Minnie's teeth had ceased to chatter.

She sat on the cart, very still and blue with cold, and I began to think she would be warmer walking; but Tom would not sit in the cart without Minnie. The sun made a valiant attempt to shine once, and half an hour later there was thunder, and Minnie cowered in the cart when the lightning blazed, and, seeing her afraid, little Tom began to cry. We came to another village.

"We are getting in here, somewhere," I vowed.

In the teeth of another downpour I took the donkey to the inn and they put him in the stable. I left Minnie and little Tom by the inn fire, amongst a lot of sheep-farmers returning from a market fair, whilst I went to hunt us a corner to creep in.

I spent an hour hunting all in vain. Two women would have put me up, but as soon as I spoke of a wife and child down came the shutters. I limped back to Minnie, and told her to stay there till I got somewhere.

The inn had no accommodation. We must have looked a raggle-taggle trio. I went about from door to door. Darkness was creeping over the earth. We had not where to lay our heads. As I was thinking this I nearly collided with a parson. I tried to pin some responsibility on to him, but he would not receive it. We stood talking, and he did seem a little uneasy after some of the things I said.

"Wait a moment. Let me think," he asked.

Finally he pointed a gloved hand towards a light shining in the distance.

"There's an old crank lives over there—he might find you shelter," he told me.

I felt rattled.

"Thanks. I'll try a crank," I told him. "They are the things that make Revolutions, you know, or at least, deal with 'em when the other side has made 'em."

"Oh! Then you are not a stranger to these parts. You know him?"

"No, I don't. But there's always a bit of hope from 'cranks'," I told him.

So I trudged on to the light.

When I got to the door I could smell something burning, and I heard someone just finding it out, and saying things on the subject. I knocked till he realised someone was knocking. Then he came and opened the door with a toasting-fork in his hand. I explained our plight.

"Bring 'em in. Bring 'em in," he said, peering out into the wet gloom.

I explained that they were not there, and, jubilant, thankful beyond words, warm at this warmth of heart I found in this arid plot of orthodoxy—went to 'bring 'em in'.

The rain was still falling when I brought Minnie and Tom to the haven we had found.

"Come in, come in," called the 'crank'.

The place was still pervaded with the odour of burnt toast. The kitchen had a higgledy-piggledly look usual to men's sanctums. But there was a large atmosphere of freedom which I felt when we had been in a few minutes.

He did not fuss over us, merely told us to take off our sodden outer clothes, and pushed a bowl of unburned hot milk across the table for 'the youngster'.

There was a picture of Walter Crane's on the wall. 'The Triumphant March of Democracy'. I stood looking at it, whilst the steam rose from my garments, brought out by the oven-like warmth of the kitchen. He took meat from the oven and began to baste it, talking to me all the time about the picture I had been looking at and its artist, and William Morris, whose portrait hung by Crane's wonderful draughtsmanship. I let him go on, taking me for 'raw material'. Unexpectedly I dropped a remark which made him drop his spoon.

"Dammit! You're one of us," he said. "Why didn't you say so? Well, we meet everywhere, we dreamers, we madmen, we brothers of the times that are not yet. What's your particular brand?"

He picked the spoon up from the rug, placed it on the table, and got another.

"International Socialist," I confessed, with a smile, "of the robbed at the point of production type, with sympathies for all the struggling clans of Democracy, believing that we shall pass through a Socialist state and travel towards the liberation of the individual and be fit at length to govern ourselves."

"Come up and get some meat," he invited. "I'm an Anarchist. I'd start where you left off. Glad you came, though, Mrs.——?"

He turned to me.

"Sniggins," I told him. "Minnie, draw your chair round."

Then I felt embarrassed, realising that I had acted as freely as though that table had been mine. He noticed it, and his eyes twinkled.

"Everybody does it that comes here," he said. "It's my fault. So soon as they enter that door private property ceases to exist. It's my fault. I'm a corrupter—a base corrupter. Come up, Mrs. Sniggins. It isn't very dainty. What's your first name?"

"Mine's Edmund. Hers is Minnie. That's Tom."

I pondered him.

He was lean, agile, thoughtful, big, and had a sort of pouncing style of argument that threw me into no end of corners before the night was out. We were dodging in and out of 'em for two hours after that meal.

"Nibby! I think I'll go to bed," said Minnie. "I don't feel quite myself."

The old Anarchist looked at her.

"You don't look well," he told her. "Edmund, take a candle, make up the bed in the first room, and I'll get a hot bottle ready. Have a drop of whisky, Mrs. Sniggins. You've got a chill."

But Minnie shook her head.

"I do feel all queer-like," she said, "but I only had some wine once, with 'im—with Nibby—on our honeymoon——"

Strange though it was, it was true.

She had followed her calling in her sober senses, fearing to go 'any lower', and facing whatever wretchedness she felt in her sober senses.

I went up and made up the bed in the first room. There were pamphlets littered on it. And as my shadow bobbed about on the candle-lit wall a dim premonition was growing in my mind. I threw it off. I went down and almost carried her upstairs. I only realised then how thin and sharp-boned she was— the life of our streets. She sank upon the pillow with a weary sigh of relief.

"Good of 'im, ain't it, Nibby, letting us come here!" she said.

As the candlelight fell on the moved gratitude of her look, her eyes made more gentle by it, once again, far-off and beautiful, I saw 'Arlene', as gentle as proud, because life had been gentler and prouder, and kinder.

"You does love us a bit, Nibby?" she asked, pathetically.

I took her hands in one of mine and kissed them. They were burning.

"I know I ain't much," she said, sleepily, "but you does love us a bit, Nibby? Sit here till I drop off, Nibby. I feels safe when you're by." So I sat on the chair, on the pamphlets, till she dropped off. Then I went down, and the old man and I fished up some bedding to make little Tom a bed on the wash table in the room he had given up to us. I took him up. He asked where 'Minnie' was. You could scarcely see there was anyone in that great bed.

He went to sleep happily, singing to himself 'Wee Willie Winkie', the only song he knew. Then I went down again. Cranshaw told me his name, and said we must stay till I got something definite. He made me feel more as if I was near the people of 'Equality Island' than anyone I knew. Before I knew, I came out with the whole story. He laid his hand on my shoulder, the dear old 'crank'.

"There, comrade," he said, "this is a sordid world; but there are still 'bright veins of glory that run through the mire', as Stevenson put it. And 'the smooth shall bloom from the rough'. You must bring your sticks here, and have the upper room next to yours. It is empty."

And that was how he told he was going to sleep on the couch.

I went upstairs several times, breaking off our argumentative duels, and listened to Minnie's breathing. It was sharp and irregular. She looked like a bit of marble, with a rose-flush on the cheeks. The candlelight turned her hair into red-gold. She seemed a thing nobler than the life she had had thrust upon her—infinitely more noble than the chances she had had.

"That you, Nibby?" she murmured.

At dawn she awakened me, coughing. I had to open the window. She sat up, fighting for breath. The wet glimmer of the dawn on the grey fields rushed at me, and then I was back, holding her burning hands. Cranshaw ran off for the doctor before breakfast, and the house seemed to change, change, to grow fearful and wailing, and full of wind-echoes because my mind saw it so. How the wind blew that morning! 'Oo-oo-ee', through the lock, and away round the house like a long sob—and 'oo-oo-ee' in the chimney. Whenever I hear the wind like that, always that room comes back to me, and Minnie, Minnie, fighting for her breath, her gaze fixed to my face, as though she was silently saying "Good-bye."

All through the nights and days that followed I sat in that room. Cranshaw had Tom with him, and sometimes came up to keep me company when the child was asleep. Sometimes she wandered in days and times before she had known Binkers Court, its language, its dust, its misery, and its 'bright veins of glory'.

Sometimes she laughed, staring up, like a child swinging under apple-boughs. So it seemed to me, sometimes she travelled through the dark places— once thinking she was fighting some cad who would not 'pay up'. Sitting there, grievous-hearted and oppressed with my own helplessness —pitying, aiding, weeping sometimes—all the little mosaic fragments of poor Minnie's life cohesed together and became a pathetic whole. Sometimes she knew me, stroked my face, and said: "Poor Nibby!" and then went wandering off again.

I defied the doctor, and attempted to get nourishment between the babbling lips; but it trickled away, rejected and soaking the pillow besides the hair that 'came over with the Vikings'. Whilst we seemed to be in an eerie circle, set round with the blowing wind, crying 'oo-oo-ee' and the swirl of the falling leaves.

Nerves taut, I sometimes wished irritably the wind would stop for a little while; but it went on, went on. Cranshaw said it had done a lot of damage all over the country. But all that mattered to me was that it should only stop for a little while, so that I could think quietly. The doctor held out no hope. There was no large reserve behind the body, he said. Tom would be brought up every night to look at 'Minnie'. A child judges by what it has received, so long as it remembers.

It was on the dawn of the fourth day, as I was watching the glimmering square of the window which made my sleepless eyes feel sore with its brightness, that Minnie became conscious.

"'Ave I been ill, Nibby?" she asked.

I nodded.

"Poor Nibby! 'Ow tired you look!"

"I'm not."

"Where's Tom?"

I told her.

"Oh, yes; we did come here," she said, vaguely.

"Try to sleep, Minnie."

She surveyed me with grave wisdom.

"Seems like I'm goin' to leave you, Nibby."

"No," I said, firmly.

She surveyed me with the same grave wisdom.

"Seems like—I am, Nibby," she said. "'Ow queer the walls look, Nibby, like they was going further away. Then they comes back agen. Glad I can see your fice, Nibby. You do love me a bit, Nibby, don't yer?"

I buried my face in the clothes and sobbed aloud.

She tried to reach my head, but failed, so I lifted her hand and placed it where she wanted it to rest.

"If you'd a been the first I ever walked up to, Nibby," she said, calmly. "you'd 'ave arsked me what brought me to it, an' sat down an' talked to me, an' 'ave given me something from your own pocket for mother, an' talked to me; but it didn't 'appen so. *It was my luck.* It came awful hard at first, Nibby. Then you sort o' settles down to it, gets hardened to it. It was that *Sparkins.*

"I got out at the laundry, an' they sent me summons-papers for what I owed, an' it seemed to me they sells everything in this world. Maybe it's better as it is, Nibby. You might 'ave seen as 'ow it 'ad got in my blood. The walls is goin' away again, Nibby. I feel I can breathe better, then. Then, they come back. Don't cry, Nibby."

Then she grew sleepy again, and I held her hand. She slept very calmly, quietly, too.

Cranshaw came up on tip-toes.

"I shouldn't be surprised if she recovered, comrade," he said. "Whilst there's life there's hope. There's a change. I'll run round for the doctor."

"Twenty-four hours," said the doctor.

So fell my poor little dream back to the earth.

"Just drifting out," he said at noon. "You want a little sleep, man, or you'll be crumpling up."

It was at sunset that Minnie awoke.

"You don't go away, Nibby, do you?" she asked.

"No, I'm here all the time."

"'Cause I feel *safe*," she murmured. "I can feel when you've 'old o' my 'and when I'm asleep. Don't go away, Nibby."

I saw Hesperus through the purple evening glimmer—star of the early shepherds. The house was very still.

"Light the candle, Nibby. Then I can see your face," she said.

So I lit the candle.

"You can tell old Farrow I waved my hand," she said once. I told her I would.

"And old Sparkins—I forgive 'im," she said later.

I promised.

"Talk to me, Nibby, about where we went them three days."

And so I talked of it, with a hand feeling to clutch my throat at times—the hand of my own bitter sorrow. I had often seen a string and little packet hanging round her neck. She asked me to take it off.

"You ain't never arsked about it, Nibby," she said. "Take it when I'm gone, an' tell my relatives I'm finished with. You'll remember I arsked you, Nibby?"

She looked with a strange look into my face.

"I'll remember," I promised.

At midnight she passed very quietly, like a sad, soft wind suddenly ceasing, so that one can scarcely tell when it does come. I was left alone with those last faint words still in my ears. "Ta-ta, Nibby. You're the first—I ever loved a *little bit,* Nibby."

Chapter 23

We put Minnie into the ground on a calm, sunshiny day, sending little Tom into the woods with a girl of 16 who sometimes ran errands for Cranshaw. It seemed to me that I had followed a dream which had ended in nothing.

I sat in the mellow sunset, by Cranshaw's kitchen window, watching the yellow leaves fall down, sometimes singly, sometimes in twos and threes. The old torpor which had been mine in the 'old den' in Binkers Court, the old brooding apathy, the old question, "Why, why, why?" came back again. The earth looked brown and large from Cranshaw's window. I watched the low moon arise.

The bitter sorrow of loss was upon me. Cranshaw never interfered with me, never trotted out any of the usual platitudes. I was grateful for that. Minnie had looked very young, almost childishly young, and even beautiful in that first glance and last I took at her on the first day after her death. One who had not known would have said: 'Here is a body that has known no stain, no grief, no struggle.' That was very strange, I thought, and recalled Maeterlinck saying somewhere that some souls could pass through all things and still retain a purity which was not smirched, which still went aloof, elusive, crying: 'This of me yet remains incorruptible.' But the earth felt very empty.

I think my greatest consolation was to remember Minnie's little revelations, made from time and time to me, after we fled from Binkers Court. "If I'd met you, Nibby, a long time since"—and "You know, Nibby, I always hated men till I saw you with your nose over your books. You know, Nibby, they was only my trade."

And sometimes to hear again in memory. "I never thought this luck would come my way. You do love us a little bit, Nibby, don't you?" Little Tom, after some weeks, ceased to ask where Minnie had gone.

I went out along the road with the donkey, leaving Tom with Cranshaw, quite contented, quite adapting himself to new conditions, new associations, with Cranshaw answering all his questions in the gravest manner; questions such as: "Does the moon walk with me and Nibby, 'cos it moves, so 'as it got legs on?" Cranshaw trying to explain earth motions to a child under three years of age made the funniest, tenderest picture. But it was always 'Nibby' he greeted with an excited "I wouldn't go to bed till you come 'ome, Nibby."

He was a dogged child, with one of those foreheads that make you wonder—large and fleshy, and calm. Always as I looked into his eyes the soul of Tom Jones—as it had been when he was young—seemed to stare out at me.

He was not very demonstrative, only when he was tired. Then he would hitch up close to you. He used to sit whilst Cranshaw and I discussed all the horrors that arose from an unnatural state of society, turning a toy horse about and about to find out how it was put together, and he certainly pulled a lot of stuff to bits to find out how it was stuck together. Gradually he began to fill a big part of my life.

He was not my flesh and blood, but we had somehow got dumped together, and sometimes I used to wonder just how I'd feel about it if Mrs. Jones got cured and came out and took him away. Mrs. Biers, however, wrote me that this was not likely.

I looked forward to the spring and summer when he could travel with me along my routes, sitting on the cart and asking me questions. The winter set in, and somehow I picked up the broken task of finishing 'Dreams of a Wandering Pedlar'. Such winds shook Cranshaw's house that winter, blowing as if they would like to tear it up by the roots.

It always sounded mournful now as well as wild, for always I would associate it, I thought, with poor Minnie, as I had heard it blowing round the house when she lay dying.

Cranshaw would calmly discuss prostitution and all the vices peculiar to the race, as "Reactions, you know, Sniggins, reactions against being crushed down. Rebellion that has taken the wrong turning, because it was not conscious. So it is bedded in the system after all," and little Tom would eye us gravely, and pull something to bits in his destructive, constructive way.

'Dreams of a Pedlar'. I wrote that last part often dog-tired with beating my way through the winter rains, chronicling the scenes I saw, the humanity I passed on the roads, the little bursts of sunshine I saw on the marsh, the odd drifting thoughts that come as one is passing along, passing along, and only knew that it eased me of my sense that I had followed a dream that had led to nothing. Cranshaw would argue with me about some of the passages, then he would ask me not to alter them.

He helped me with the spelling of words I was uncertain about, and saved me going to the dictionary. Our housekeeping was a great joke, and we muddled along somehow, but we got on very well, Cranshaw and I.

And gradually the winter got over, long and dark and wild, and I was not surprised to find spring in the air, for I had followed her path all through the heart of winter's blackness—yes, all through the loss, and the lack, and the pain.

It was on a warm May morning that in turning out my drawer I found the little packet on the string Minnie had worn around her neck. It was not that I had forgotten it. But I had flinched from going to see Minnie's 'relatives'. The wound was closing. I had faced my grief like a child of Choice. The blossoms that hung like magic beauty on the boughs that had been black and bare gave me their message. Because I had lost a poor little dream was no reason why one should utterly despair.

I could see no plan to my life. There was Tom and me—and me and Tom. There was a little book no one might print. There was Cranshaw getting old and looking for me as I came in through the door. And at some time, some place, I should find my place in the struggle. Than I came across the string and the little packet. I opened it, and the light fell on a faded photograph of two children sitting on a wall together, their hair blown in the wind. Two bits of hair tied together with a thread, and a paper which bore faded, proletarian writing: 'Minnie's hair, aged three, Eleanor's hair, aged seven'. And in Minnie's writing the address of the house where her 'relatives' lived.

Miss Hales, The Nest,—and the village, down in Sussex.

"Yes. It will do you good to go," Cranshaw told me.

So I went in the spring to Sussex-by-the-sea, with that little string and packet, and the news of Minnie's death.

Chapter 24

"Could you tell me where Miss Hales lives?"

He was a countryman with rosy cheeks and quiet eyes, leaning his elbow on a wall by a springing field of green corn just flaming through the earth.

He directed me, and if I had encouraged him would have accompanied me. He looked askance at my black garments, an inharmonious note in the setting of the awakening earth. He was very curious with the pathetic curiosity of those who have lived in a narrow world without any chance to know what lies beyond it. He was one of the village grandfathers, unlettered, and full of scorn for all modern procedure, as I proved later.

I followed the rutted road between the hedges. The warmth of the sun streamed at my back. Walking along one could smell the salt in the air. I hurried, anxious to get this interview over, asking myself why I had not come before and had done with it. Minnie had been a poor little dream, without any links, and perhaps I had had some sort of dull resentment that her people had left her unaided and unsustained.

At the turn of the rutted road I paused in delight—fresh, warm delight which gave me a feeling of guilt, that foolish fantasy bred of our orthodoxy that we should not dare to enjoy the beauty of the earth when it returns to us because other eyes have closed on it. The sea!

There it was, an indescribable colour, with little flashes of white here and there, and far out a white sail glimmering against the mysterious horizon. Upon the crumble-soiled cliff, where wild grass waved against the blue of the sky, a garden flamed into sight.

"Miss Hales' nursery is there," a schoolboy told me, swinging on a gate.

He pointed at the house, small and old, and deeply eaved, still in the distance miniature, clear-lined,

"Cats or babies?" I asked the boy.

He had the look that divided him by untold ages from the quiet-eyed old yokel I had seen by the wall. I realised that the scientists were right—that we are rushing to either the end of civilisation or its noonday. Here was a boy swinging on a gate who knew about wireless, aircraft, and heard echoes of rumours of world-wars. His eyes were alive and restless, and active.

"Flowers and vegetables," he astonished me with. "I'll go with you to the gate. One gate is always closed."

I read upon it 'The Nest'.

I was going to offer him sixpence. He flushed, said "Oh! no."

Then he looked at my pocket.

I followed his glance.

Poking out was a book, and its title 'The Sleeper Awakes'.

"Would you like it?" I asked.

He nodded eagerly. He had heard of it. I gave it to him, and parted from him still looking back at me every few yards, and then I saw him take the book into his hands and walk on with his gaze fixed upon it.

I opened the white gate and passed up the cobbled walk, and noticed the scraper at the door. The little windows were all agleam but curtain-less. A bee buzzed out of a flower and went past my head. Whoever lived here was old-world. I thought, getting a glimpse of two bee hives.

I rehearsed my little message. "Minnie is dead. She asked me to tell you she was finished with." It sounded a bit bleak that. Perhaps they would feel it, Miss Hales and whoever else of Minnie's relatives dwelt in this pleasant old house.

I knocked.

No one answered.

I knocked again.

Then I heard an inner door open and someone coming into the passage *whistling* 'The Red Flag' in a way that told the person was unconscious of whistling it, so much was it part of herself. I knocked again feeling I could have been knocked down with a feather. That clear whistling of the hymn of 'The Dream' told all.

A door within was flung bark.

Then the door I stood beside opened, and I stood staring at her. I pulled myself together.

"Am I addressing Miss Hales?" I asked, feebly.

The cobbles felt to be moving and doing a hop and a jump under my feet.

"I am Eleanor Hales," she told me. "Won't you come in?"

I followed her in, still dazed. Not *quite* Arlene. Not quite. Still with something on her face, in her eyes, in her bearing that stamped her as a woman of this generation, which had known bread-struggles and heart-hungers, and cares which *it* had passed by, to greater struggles, nobler hungers, and diviner cares. Yet, as she turned her head, the sunlight from the curtain-less window streaming on her face, where virtue sat, a warm and human beauty, intangible, and like the perfume one smells without being able to grasp it, as her clear eyes looked questioningly into mine, frank and comradely, and brave and gentle, I felt suddenly stunned. Far away I seemed to hear

Sarband saying, as he raised the green wine: "There is no dream which ends in nothingness."

"Oh, I'm sorry. The room is warm," she said, with quick intuition. She crossed over to the window and opened it, and the tang of the chill sea-air came into the room.

"I came to give you these," I stammered.

I fumbled for them, found them, and heard her quick breath as she recognised them.

"Where is Minnie? Where is she?" she asked. She came over to me, as I stood by the window. I looked out on the shining sea and at the little sail that was now blotted out in the mists, aglow and a-glimmer. "Where is Minnie?" Little Tom's question; my own question; the question of the bereaved, and unanswerable, quite unanswerable, rounded with mystery, wide as the universe, pathetic human question which, as Ingersoll said, is unanswerable to the honest man.

"She was your sister?" I asked.

She nodded.

She looked at my garments and put out her bands, like one warding off a blow.

"She is dead?" she asked. "I have sought her everywhere. She is dead? I can hear now, when she is dead!"

"Yes."

"What, what were you to her?"

She was pale, and the tears stood in her wonderful eyes as she asked it. How thankful I was that I could say, "I married her," and not stand for ever classed as one who had made even poor Minnie my 'fancy'. Even whilst I realised that this was only tradition, like my black clothes, and my feeling that I ought not to have awakened once more to the beauty of the earth, Minnie being dead. For such poor creatures are we, we of this generation, we must seal everything with a seal, when the seal is so little and the thing sealed so great, so very great!

"Sometimes," she told me later, "I have got close on her track, then lost it again. You see, she was given to someone else. My aunt took me. I suppose, had she been here, and I there, she would have been the one who sought for me!"

I told her the pathetic little story.

She walked back along the rutted road with me, a creature the sea-winds kissed, pure and strong, who would perhaps have even kept her soul through all the troughs of the storm. The wind ruffled her hair, shining and beautiful, like the flame of the sunset cloud. Everyone seemed to know her. She introduced me to the old yokel as her 'brother-in-law'. And as I rode in the train I saw the dip of the sea, with the little sail somewhere in its expanse, like a lost dream, which had led to a greater, to one so great I knew it would be quite beyond me ever to reach my hands to it.

Chapter 25

In August, to my great astonishment, a publisher decided that he could risk publishing 'Dreams of a Wandering Pedlar'. I signed an agreement 'between one Edmund Sniggins, author of the before-mentioned— etc.,' and quite a good London publisher, one of the old school who specialise in belles-lettres.

It was quite astonishing to me that people made a fuss about it. I received a letter from one dame asking me, if ever in London, to come along to dinner and bring my pedlar's outfit with me! It was called 'pagan' and called other things, and wiseacre critics who sat on the heights wearing their midnight bags, said it would probably be the last. Cranshaw and I had some fun reading the reviews. Then, to his horror, I lit the fire with them. He damned me shamefully, but he did not know how little store I could set on such trifling tributes to one's ability to push a pen, for I had never told him of my dream of 'Equality Island', where the greatest of a greater civilisation had held them as worthless baubles. However, he forgave me, and we set out for the Normandy trip I had promised him, if 'Dreams of a Pedlar' ever got into print.

"And after," asked Cranshaw, "what then?"

"After that the battle," I told him.

Sun-drenched, leaf-shadowed, beautiful Normandy! Yet there, still burdened peasants, and all the visible signs of social inequalities one cannot escape from— no, not anywhere. Forever the same, I saw the types akin to the English rural workers, forever the same I knew I would meet them in all the countries of the earth, arcadian or industrialised. But to read Whitman there under the fruit trees, in the long grasses, rustling softly as one reads messages like this:—

'What do you suppose will satisfy the soul except to walk free and own no superior?'

Rustle of grasses, shadows of the leaves, and to read on:—

'Those that look carelessly in the faces of Presidents and Governors, as to say: 'Who are you?'

Warmth of the earth, and the smell of it, and to read on:—

'I want the people to have their own. The people, forever the people. Not the polished persons, not the factors. The people. All of them. Good and bad no matter. The people. The eternal, fraternal, people.'

To walk back in the twilight with the bells swinging, carrying words like those in the heart. So we wandered, Cranshaw and I. I happy because in some little way I am paying him back by giving him forever the leaves and earth of Normandy to remember, for that great and wonderful gift of brotherhood which he gave to me when he said: "Bring 'em in," and flung his door wide to the "likes of us."

Still, there, in Normandy, to find myself pursued by a 'dream"—glory—crowned with bright hair, with brave, pure-set, clear eyes, and to find Cranshaw saying dryly, "This is the third time I've spoken, and you have not heard me." But I do not explain, that thought being unlimited by the body. I have been from Normandy to Sussex, walking on little white rain-washed cobbles, near beehives, and then into a sunny room, where the window looks on the sea, and then along the rutted road between fragrant hedges, with a green dress that was almost the colour of Arlene's, passing along by me, criss-crossed with shadows of trees in the wonder of a sunset near a blue and darkening sea.

So the pleasant days pass—the lull before I plunge into the storm of that conflict against Unprogression which will only cease when, like the little sail, I pass into the mists. Strange to think how once I, who flinched from all struggle, can walk resolutely into it now, knowing it has brought all Progress.

Deep in the eyes of the 'eternal, fraternal people' to read their dreams like to my own—like to my own—and, if not alike wholly, to realise that that also is a point of variation which will travel down the ages, and make further progress until, perchance, at some hour, some Place, the individual dream of each man, each brother, meets, wonder-faced and beautiful, saying calmly, "Greetings, brother. We have come far. Greetings, brother."

Pleasant days, with these wandering thoughts—fitful, elusive—saying silently as one passes the peasants. "Greetings, brother." Then back to the house where we muddle through our housekeeping, Cranshaw and I, and Cranshaw sells the donkey, saying unamiably: "You don't need to be going round the place with a donkey *now*." And still to find my thoughts wandering away, as I work, to an old house, and one day to find myself knocking again there because Cranshaw is getting married, and I don't know exactly where I am going to choose to plant myself and Tom.

And, after all, I say nothing about Cranshaw getting married, and wander back along the rutted road, dolorous and tongue-tied, talking about geology, of all things, and Eleanor gives me her hand on the little station where flowers spell the name of it.

And Cranshaw looks into my face as I come in through the door, and says: "Well, I'm damned. You've been all that way for nothing".

"Seems so," I say.

Conclusion

I lay down my pen. I can hear the surge of the sea, immemorial, coming up from the foot of the cliff. There is the glow of lamplight in the room beyond, and a child's voice asking questions. That is Tom, brown-haired, sturdy, calm-browed, incorrigible Tom, and that is Eleanor's voice. "Hush, you'll wake Arlene. Try not to shout, Tom dear." Sunset and the stars will soon shine over the sea.

Pleasant rattle of tea-cups. The figures are those of the Dream, and those not yet, and those who are of reality, Sarband and Jones, Minnie and Arlene, pass in the dim sunset hour, beckoning to each other across the gulf of time. And Eleanor comes into the room.

"Edmund?"

"Yes, I know tea is ready," I say, "Come and sit here just for a moment and we'll watch the sun set."

So we sit just till the sun dips.

"You've got be at the Hall by seven, Edmund."

"Yes."

I can see the glimmer of her hair even in the darkening sunset, and the same glimmering radiance has found a lesser brow in the room beyond. "Like two wands of ivory tinted with gold for awful kings."

Yet not for 'awful kings', so it seems, but even for me, known now throughout this Island of Inequalities as the Pilgrim. And in the room beyond Eleanor says "What is Tom doing? That's the milk-jug".

On the walls of the room beyond is a drawing an artist friend, a Socialist, has drawn from my description of Peter Shallon's statue of another Pilgrim. Clever draughtsman as he is, he has not quite got it. Who can touch a dream beyond the horizon of his age? Who can say what Love will be like when he is grown?

And Eleanor and I run down to get the train, and I see the moon shine on the hollow of the sea as the train swings round the old curve.

And as I run up the steps of the Hall when we arrive at the town, I catch "It's the Pilgrim", and smile, recalling the familiar name. 'Pilgrim', then burdened with my sad memories, in the country where all were brothers. I lift up the banner of their Dream, here in this Island, here on this star-set world, pilgrimming itself through the Universe, crying boldly. 'Behold it! The Banner of the Dream! The Eternal, Immortal, Storm-Tossed Dream, which challenges all Inequalities until they are no more'.

And the night is large and calm and quiet as we return up the deeply rutted road, and Eleanor's hand is in mine as I point out Orion, brilliant in the clarity of the air, knowing, knowing quite surely, that at some hour, some Place, my evolutionary link, Sarband, will stand in a night of such stars, looking upwards, and saying, "I wonder what they thought long ago looking on this same Orion?" Whilst, perchance, as he speaks, the spray will fling up a speck of sand which kisses his cheek, crying, "Greetings, brother. Greetings, and great Pilgrimage."

THE END.

www.ingramcontent.com/pod-product-compliance
Lightning Source LLC
Chambersburg PA
CBHW061516020726
47502CB00006B/2103